PRAISE FOR
SEVEN TEARS AT HIGH TIDE
C.B. LEE

"This magical book puts a new spin on the Scottish mythology of selkies, folk who shift from seal to human. A romantic young adult tale full of beautiful imagery and a blossoming young love that will warm your heart. Debut author C.B. Lee deftly explores issues surrounding race, bisexuality and mixed family dynamics against the sweet summer setting of a Californian sea."

—*MuggleNet*

"★★★★★—This YA novel by a debut writer knocked my socks off, made me get a bit weepy and well, I just loved it."

—*Prism Book Alliance*

"★★★★★—Emotional, in-depth, fun and well written, and the balance between reality and fantasy is a fine line that blended well. This was my first read from C.B. Lee, but it definitely won't be my last."

—*M/M Good Book Reviews*

NOT YOUR SIDEKICK

NOT YOUR
SIDEKICK
C.B. LEE
interlude press • new york

ISBN 13: 978-1-945053-03-0 (trade)
ISBN 13: 978-1-945053-04-7 (ebook)
Published by Duet, an imprint of Interlude Press
www.duetbooks.com

Book Design and Illustrations by CB Messer

10 9 8 7 6 5 4 3 2 1

interlude press • new york

For so-called sidekicks everywhere.

Jess grits her teeth, going for a running start. The gravel on the trail crunches under her feet, the wind rushes through her hair, and she can taste success. This time. This time, she's gonna make it.

The canyon is streaked with color, warm in the afternoon light; golden striations race across the signature rusty reds of the landscape. The sky is a gorgeous, impossible blue, and clouds flutter down the endless horizon, a perfect backdrop for a first flight.

Every step resounds in her body, and her heart races. Blood pounds in her ears.

Flight.

One of the rarest of abilities. Jess' dad can fly, and her older sister inherited the gene. Why not Jess?

Why not me? I could be a hero, Jess thinks as she picks up speed.

Jess is turning seventeen in a week, and then it will be too late for her to register. She hasn't demonstrated any powers at all, not as a child, not as an adolescent, but she's held out hope. After all, there are a few documented outliers: teenagers presenting much later, even as old as sixteen.

No one's presented with any powers after seventeen.

The wind whistles in her ears, and the desert is alive with color, encouraging her on. Where the trail curves and descends, Jess keeps going forward, right for the edge where it peters off into the canyon below. Time and erosion have split the rock formation, leaving a gap of at least seven feet between the edge and the rest of the rock cluster.

Jess doesn't hesitate. She pushes herself forward and leaps into the air.

The desert is silent except for the pebbles that scatter from her movement and tumble into the gap far below. Jess is in the air, and for a few seconds she can taste the sky reaching out to her, welcoming her—

Flomp.

Jess lands hard on the other side of the gap, falls flat on her cheek. She spits dust and cringes at the sting on her face. Her body's going to ache later.

This is the third jump she's made today.

Jess rolls over and stares up at the sky. "All right, so maybe flying's not going to happen," she says reluctantly. She fishes inside her pocket for the list she made of the powers she could inherit from her parents.

flight
~~*magnetic field manipulation*~~
~~*enhanced strength*~~
~~*healing factor*~~
~~*durability/ endurance*~~

She has a longer list too, of all the powers on file with the Meta-Human Registrar, but everyone knows that meta-abilities are genetic. If Jess didn't inherit any of her parents' abilities, the possibility of having *any* abilities drops to near zero.

Jess is covered in dirt and bruised and frustrated, and it's unlikely that she's ever, ever, going to be a superhero.

She runs her finger across the word *flight,* smudging it with red dirt.

The hike back to the car will be beautiful, but for now, she stays put. Jess should accept that she doesn't have powers; maybe she should consider herself lucky that she won't have to go into the Meta-Human Training Program.

But she wants to be a hero, wants to help people.

Jess stands up, winces at the pain, and starts down the trail.

THE MINIVAN IS THE ONLY vehicle in the parking lot—if the small dusty space could be called that. The area had been cleared once; now it's overgrown with creosote bushes and scraggly asters. Jess steps over a sign that reads *Welcome to Red Rock Canyon National Conservation Area,* which is rusting in the path. She gingerly makes her way to the car and fumbles through three attempts to get the lock pad to allow a manual override.

ERROR: SWIPE DATA EXCHANGE DEVICE AGAIN, the tiny screen flashes.

"Đụ," Jess swears. She didn't bother wearing the DED today; she hates the way the data exchange device is heavy on her wrist, especially when she's hiking in the canyons.

Finally her jabs at the manual option succeed. Jess enters her citizen identification number, and the car beeps and unlocks.

"Welcome, Jessica Tran," the cool computer voice says, enunciating every syllable, exactly the way she hates it. It's not a great A.I.; it can't learn anything new, just do basic tasks. Barely.

The car is a Standard Family Vehicle, and they bought it just last year when they turned in their old model, but it's already starting to malfunction. They'll have to buy another one soon. Jess sighs and slumps in the seat, puts her seatbelt on, and waits for the display on the screen to go through the welcome and safety procedures.

"Go home," Jess demands.

The engine comes to life with a low electronic hum, but the display is still loading all the usual standard warnings for operating a vehicle.

"Home," Jess says again and then gives up. The car's voice command system hasn't worked since they bought the damn thing.

Finally it finishes booting up, and Jess flicks quickly through the options and smacks the *home* button. She leaves a dirty handprint on the display.

"Calculating route," the computer says, and on the screen a circular symbol starts twirling, as if to give the illusion that it's working faster.

Jess groans and kicks at the dashboard. The minivan shakes, but the computer keeps processing at the same pace. She wishes she could drive, like in the old times when everyone had self-steering installed in their personal cars.

"Route to residence Tran-Alpha-Two-Five-Nine calculated. Warning. Your route will take you through a Class Three Unmaintained Disaster Area. For your safety, all windows will remained closed, and doors will be locked until the vehicle has entered a Class One—"

"Shut up," Jess grumbles, kicking at the display again, this time hitting the *accept* button with her foot. The engine hums, and the minivan reverses and trundles down the dirt road.

Jess puts on the radio for the hour-long drive. Even though it's a huge hassle taking the minivan anywhere outside Andover, Jess had wanted to be far away from the city so she wouldn't be seen in case she did start exhibiting her powers.

The Nevada region is one of the few areas in the North American Collective where there is still parkland available for recreation. Not too many people in the western half of what was the United States go out on their own anymore. Most of them are still afraid of radiation, even if there weren't any nuclear plant meltdowns there during the X29 solar flare event.

An occasional billboard stands tall against the horizon with fading advertisements for a people long gone. Most road signs from old America still exist; the current government doesn't waste money to take them down or to erect new signs for cities that have sprung up after World War III. Andover is one of them. Like many of its smaller desert neighbors, Andover is mostly made up of immigrants from the East Coast fleeing irradiated areas and, more recently, refugees from what is now the Southeast Asian Alliance.

Jess drives past a sign that reads, "ANDOVER, 12 MILES," and in smaller font, "Proud Home of Smasher and Shockwave."

Jess smiles a little; Smasher and Shockwave are the two resident heroes of Andover. C-list as they may be, they're celebrated here. Jess knows them as Mom and Dad.

Andover is also home to the villains Master Mischief and his partner, Mistress Mischief. Jess has grown up on stories about her parents and their epic rivalry with the Mischiefs. This particular sign is one instance. Although the Collective has come a long way since the war, resources are still scarce, and any new road signs are usually just welded atop the old. Every now and then, the Mischiefs deface the sign; Jess can see how they've tilted it recently.

The mile counts for Andover on one side and Las Vegas on the other are now at an angle, revealing the rusted metal and, still readable, the words "LOS ANGELES, 282 MILES." Jess isn't sure the road still goes there, though Nuevo Los Angeles was certainly rebuilt in the same place. The sign proclaims that it's *only* 282 miles away.

Jess can't fathom that people used to drive that far; she's pushing it taking the minivan all the way out to the canyons. There are countless guidelines about personal vehicle use, all to do with safety and how long the electric engines can hold a charge, and besides, there are always the hovertrains that connect major cities. There's no need for anyone to venture out on their own.

The minivan is the only vehicle coming from the canyons, and Jess nervously eyes the occasional oncoming truck on the two-lane highway until the lights of Andover appear ahead. She loves the bright red hues of the rocks, the colors of the cliffs, the strange silhouettes of the Joshua trees, all of it, but the numbing vastness can be ominous in the dark, and Jess is careful always to get home well before sundown. She's stayed out later than usual today, but made good time on the road, despite the minivan's computer delay. Jess relaxes as she passes through the outskirts of Andover and joins the rest of its citizens, who are using their personal vehicles as intended. Jess will have to wash the minivan later; the telltale red dust sprinkled generously over the windows and exterior of the minivan stands out a little too much against the other clean vehicles on the road.

The sun is setting; the glare bounces off the fields of solar panels surrounding the town. It's a dazzling view, especially with the pink and rosy gold hues of the sky, but Jess has seen it too many times to pay it much mind now. She is still caught up in thinking about the many tests for possible powers she's done these past few weeks.

Disappointment settling heavily inside her, Jess sighs as the car passes through downtown, then Old Town Andover and up the hill toward the suburbs lining the eastern side of town. Andover Heights is quiet, and the uniformity of each home is dully familiar to Jess. She's never left the Nevada region; Jess wants nothing more than to travel to New Bright City, the dazzling metropolis where all the greatest heroes in the nation gather at the League headquarters.

It seems that's never going to happen.

The car pulls into her suburban driveway just as the last jingle of a commercial plays on the radio.

"And the finishing touch to any superhero outfit isn't my cape," Captain Orion's commanding voice says. "It's my smile! I use Eversparkle Teeth Whitening Cream to get the perfect smile, and you can too!"

Jess glances at her reflection in the chrome surface of the dashboard as another cheery voice announces how Eversparkle will make your teeth shine like the stars, just like Captain Orion's. Captain Orion, A-list superhero and Commander of the Heroes' League of Heroes, with her perfect smile and perfect hair, keeping the North American Collective safe every day. Jess tries to copy

Captain Orion's trademark confident grin but, on Jess, the smile is exaggerated and unnatural.

Jess drops the smile and sighs in disappointment at her messy black hair and her plain-looking face smudged with dirt. Her skin is flushed; red undertones are just visible under her brown skin. Her skin throbs, and is painfully hot to the touch. Great, she's sunburnt again.

Her ponytail is a mess. Jess pulls her hair out of the elastic band, tries to comb the tangles out of it, and gives up.

I'm never going to be amazing like Captain Orion.

"You have arrived at your destination," the computer says, cutting off the too-cheerful tune of the Eversparkle advertisement. "Would you like to program another—"

Jess turns off the car, and then readjusts the seat for her mom, who's a few inches shorter and always lectures Jess on leaving the car as she found it.

She slams the door shut and walks to the house. It's a lovely, modern two-story home, courtesy of the North American Collective. Her parents do well for themselves, not because of their cover jobs; their income is mostly compensation from the government. Their house doesn't compare to Captain Orion's elaborate mansion in New Bright City on the East Coast, but her parents are good C-list heroes, constantly working for the greater good of the country, and their home reflects that.

The curvy teal minivan befits their supposedly very normal suburban family and is mostly for show. Their other vehicle, a modest navy blue sedan, isn't in the driveway; her mom must be at her cover job as a realtor. The Trans don't need either of these cars. Her dad flies everywhere, even when he shouldn't, and in the secret garage is a flashier vehicle that her mom drives to solo missions, but Jess hasn't seen it used in a few weeks.

Jess kicks some dying roses by the path, and tries once, twice, three times to get the keypad to let her in. Ugh, going anywhere without a DED is such a hassle. Citizens are advised to always wear the data exchange device when it's not charging or synced to a desktop, but Jess has always found that annoying. She never wears it when she goes out to the canyons; there's no signal out there anyway.

Frustrated, Jess gives the door a good kick, and the keypad beeps and accepts her code at last.

Jess hates the fall; the days are so short. It's still only late afternoon, not even five o'clock.

She stalks into the empty living room and scowls, glad to be alone so no one will ask about her mood. Her brother isn't home from school, and her dad is probably flying around looking for trouble. Jess huffs and stomps upstairs to her room. The way the stairs clunk beneath her feet is satisfying, and Jess continues with more force than necessary. She's not paying attention and nearly trips over their MonRobot.

It cheeps sadly at her as it continues to struggle to climb the stairs. The wheel extensions are out, and it's rolling back and forth on the step, trapped. Another extension should allow it to maneuver household obstacles, but Jess can see the little arm sticking out of the back of the round body, waving about for balance.

"What are you doing, Chả? You know you always get stuck on the stairs." Jess pets the round curve of the robot. "You're supposed to just clean downstairs. You don't have to vacuum up here; it doesn't even have carpet."

Chả meeps at her.

"All right, little guy." She sighs, picks up the poor thing, and carries it to the top of the stairs. Chả cheeps and begins vacuuming the floor, going back and forth slowly. The Trans got the robot about five years ago, and although Chả does a fairly good job of tidying up, it tends to be rather clumsy and forgetful. It'll repeat the same motion, over and over, without moving forward. They really should get a new one, but robots are ridiculously expensive. And Jess can't imagine replacing Chả, even if it doesn't do the household chores very well.

She pats the MonRobot once more, goes to her room, and throws herself on her bed.

Paper crunches beneath her. Jess scowls, grabbing whatever is between her and her soft bed. She squints at her handwriting. Did she start a homework assignment and forget—oh. It's her latest research reports on tests of her possible abilities.

Jess rereads her report on her attempt at calculating enhanced strength—now *that* was a disaster. Her arms still ache from last weekend's bench press incident. Jess scowls at the numbers, crunches the paper into a ball, tosses it aside, then discards another report, and another, until her bed is free of the evidence of all her attempts.

Jess flops on her back and spots the framed photograph of her parents, dressed as Shockwave and Smasher, vibrant and powerful, the pride of their small city. Her stomach curls with the sting of disappointing them.

Jess closes her eyes.

Her older sister Claudia had already been in the Meta-Human Training Program for two years by her seventeenth birthday when she got an offer to join the Heroes' League of Heroes when she graduated. The Trans had thrown a huge party to celebrate.

When Jess turns seventeen, it'll be official. She's not special.

Jess groans. She roots around and finally finds her DED on the floor, half under a sweater. She grabs the slim, square device by the wrist strap and looks at the small screen to see if she has any new messages, but the screen is dark and unresponsive.

Great, she let the battery die again.

It takes her another minute to find the charging dock on her cluttered desk. Jess plops the device onto the dock and it buzzes as it syncs with her desktop projector, which hums to life and throws multiple projections into the air—holopages from the Net, a half-finished homework assignment, pictures of Captain Orion, and a series of text messages from Emma and Bells. As the DED connects to the Net, it updates with new messages, and Jess is bombarded with rapidly scrolling notifications. The buzzing continues until Jess flicks the DED screen.

Jess scowls at the largest open holopage, which is projected above her desk. She'd been reading it and rereading it before she left, checking the fine print to see if there was any way she could qualify as a meta-human.

NORTH AMERICAN COLLECTIVE
META-HUMAN REGISTRATION

Section 4.2 Power Classification *is determined by the total duration the citizen can utilize their meta-ability actively per twenty-four hour period.*

CLASS-A- *More than two hours*
CLASS-B- *One to two hours*
CLASS-C- *Twenty minutes to one hour*
CLASS-D- *Less than twenty minutes*

Section 4.3 Meta-Human Training Requirements
The North American Collective understands that the meta-gene expresses itself in various and numerous forms and appreciates the documentation of all abilities. However, only abilities listed in Section 3.1 are currently accepted for application for Meta-Human Training. If you would like to register with a meta-ability not listed in Section 3.1, read subsection 3.1a and 3.1b on abilities that are not accepted. If your ability does not fall under the Unacceptable category, proceed to fill out the petition under Section 15.2.

Jess brushes aside the holopage, and the text disappears in trails of blue light. Ugh, registration. Jess doesn't even have one of the "unacceptable" abilities, like Emma's cousin, who can make his breath go minty fresh with just a thought, or her neighbor down the street, who can change the color of his fingernails. Well, three of them.

They're still considered meta-humans, though, and are registered, even if they didn't go through the training process to qualify for the League.

The holopage has re-formed after Jess' outburst, and she flicks the correct place to close it. All that's left hovering in the air are her messages from today.

From: Emma 1:22pm
hey are u ok? are u having a down day?

From: Bells 2:40pm
YOU DIDN'T RESPOND TO EMMA SHE THINKS YOU MIGHT BE SICK I HOPE YOU ARE OK I GOT YOUR HOMEWORK ALSO THE PIC PEOPLE CAME THRU AND I PLACED YOUR CUTIE ON THE CLASS PAGE AND HER HAIR LOOKED FIIIINE YOU MISSED OUT AM SENDING YOU HOLO

Warm fondness for her best friends distracts her from her disappointment. She clicks to open the attachment, and the DED projects a hologram. The likeness is indeed, very cute. *How do French braids even work?*

To: Emma 5:23 pm
i'm fine, just didn't feel like school today <3

To: Bells 5:24 pm
thanks Bells it doesn't beat the braids she did in september but this is pretty, i'm sad i didn't get to see it in person

From: Emma 5:25pm
u sure, i can pick up bells and come over later?

Jess chats with her friends until they're reassured and she has caught up on what she missed today and then works on homework until Chå's welcome chirp alerts her that someone is home.

"How was your day at school, honey?"

Jess shovels more rice into her mouth. She chews and points apologetically at her face. Her dad adjusts his glasses as he looks across the table, making Jess roll her eyes. Why does he keep on his "civilian" disguise when he's at home? They all know he's a superhero. Her mom says it's something to do with maintaining appearances and practicing being normal, which is hilarious, considering their family. At least at home Mom doesn't try to pretend that she can't bench-press a car and doesn't wear the dorky fake prescription glasses that match her husband's. It's funny how they approach being just Victor and Li Hua Tran differently.

"All right, we'll get back to you," Victor says, giving Jess a doting smile.

Brendan, Jess' youngest brother and all-around genius, pipes up. "Today I made a lot of progress on my experiment! It turns out that the problem I had with last week's sequence was that I didn't properly isolate—"

Jess has no idea what he's saying, but her parents seem reasonably impressed. Brendan is thirteen and precocious; he attends the local college and has been upstaging Jess ever since he was born. He hasn't demonstrated any meta-abilities, but Jess is sure he wouldn't have wanted to be a superhero even if he had. Brendan's more into... okay, Jess isn't sure exactly what he's studying. Something to do with plants and energy, but she has no doubt that Brendan's going to make a name for himself in the scientific community.

"That's really nice. We're very proud of you," Li Hua says, smiling as she steals a piece of bok choy from her husband's plate. "Jess?"

Jess swallows, the rice sticking in her throat. "Been thinking about getting an internship or something. It's bound to look great for college, right?"

"Oh, that's a great idea!" her mom says, nodding in approval.

Victor perks up. "I know someone in the mayor's office is looking for an assistant, and Mayor Bradley owes me a favor—"

"Dad, I don't want to get my first job because of your favors as Shockwave, okay? I want to do it on my own terms, because of me and my own abilities."

Her parents look at each other, and even Brendan has the audacity to snort. "What abilities, Jess?"

"Shut up." Jess feels her face flush hot with embarrassment.

Of the three children in the Tran household, only one of them was born with the meta-abilities that are commonly known as superpowers. Claudia, the eldest, moved out of town after graduating from college and is now starting a fledgling life in Crystal Springs as a journalist slash superhero. Brendan is going to be a famous scientist and discover new things every day. Jess? Jess doesn't have powers. After today, she's exhausted every possible variable.

The only way she can move forward is to focus on what she *can* do. A job is a good idea, but she doesn't want it to be handed to her just because of who her parents are.

"*My* abilities," Jess says, determined. "I might not know what all of those are, but I'm going to be good at something, you'll see."

She leaves the table before she gets too frustrated to talk. She doesn't want this to turn into a conversation about her lackluster grades or her parents' expectations and then a comparison to either of her siblings. She puts her dishes in the dishwasher and hurries to her room.

As far as her high school career goes, Jess barely keeps a B grade point average as a junior and is fairly forgettable to all the faculty. She doesn't play any sports, never had any more than a passing interest in clubs, and certainly isn't winning science awards left and right like her younger brother or flying around fighting crime like her sister.

Jess groans and flicks the desktop sync on her DED. It flickers, and then her desktop projects a large workspace screen and a keyboard. Jess flicks through her documents. She could get started on a paper for world history, but that's not due till Friday. She can put that off. Besides, there are more pressing things, like following through with finding a job.

It has to be something cool, something she'll enjoy, and something that will look good on her college applications.

Jess pulls up one of the holopages her guidance counselor gave her, one that sorts listings of internships and volunteer opportunities by geographic location. She scowls, scrolling through listing after listing, rejecting one after another.

"Ugh, you need a job to get experience and experience to get a job!"

The Las Vegas Philharmonic needs someone for basic office work and to keep all their sheet music organized. It sounds okay, plus she'd be around creative people, and it looks as if they're okay with a high school student with no experience. It'd be a terrible commute, though; at least an hour if there's traffic. Andover isn't quite big enough to merit its own stop on the hovertrain route, so everyone who drives to Las Vegas is bottlenecked onto one road.

It would be a long drive there and an even longer one back with all the people leaving Las Vegas for the outer cities.

Jess wants to do something *more.* She wants to make a difference somehow, even if her best talent is meticulously organizing things—which her mother says isn't actually a talent—and stubbornness.

Jess blinks when she sees the next company. "No way. Monroe Industries has high school internships?"

Jess clicks the link and glances outside her open bedroom door, where she can hear Chả busily cheeping away, still trying to vacuum. This MonRobot model was revolutionary when it came out, and it still functions today, if albeit a bit slower and quirkier. Any other brand would have been defunct by now.

Monroe Industries has state-of-the-art technology, and their products are everywhere from the home, to the office, to private schools. MonRobots can be programmed to perform any number of everyday tasks, from cleaning and cooking to being a personal assistant, although those advanced A.I. systems are incredibly expensive. Chả is one of the basic models, used primarily for household chores. The robots in the basic line aren't cheap, though. Jess remembers her parents being very excited about the discount they got for being in the Associated League of Heroes.

Jess scans the listing to see if she's qualified, and while a few science and business internships require experience and references, one position catches her eye.

> ***WANTED:*** *Motivated intern for administrative and office support in select experimental research division. Responsibilities include word processing, creating*

spreadsheets and presentations, organizing reports and research data, and filing. Computer experience, Net research abilities, and strong communication skills are preferred. Sensitivity to confidential matters and discretion is required.

Jess taps her fingers on her chin. It's a paid position, as are all the other internships, but this one is surely going to be in high demand because of the entry-level qualifications. The DED listed for inquiry is registered to a person named M.

A quick search of the company's website brings up absolutely nothing about this person or the experimental division, so Jess doesn't have any other information with which to tailor her cover letter, but she's willing to try anyway.

Jess crafts what she hopes is a compelling cover letter and résumé and sends them in.

On Saturday, Jess declines going to Crystal Springs with her parents to visit Claudia. Jess should be babysitting her younger brother, who also was "too busy" for a day trip, working on his project for an upcoming science fair, but Brendan is ridiculously self-sufficient. He hasn't left his room all day.

Jess is in the basement, looking over her collection of antique DVDs, when she hears a car pull into the driveway. Panic races through her. What if her parents' nemeses have found the house?

A door opens and shuts.

"Hey, Jess! We brought you food since you couldn't go out." That could only be Bells' voice, bright and exuberant.

Jess grins and dashes up the stairs. She can see the Robledo's cherry red car pulling forward at an impossibly slow pace. Jess laughs; Emma must be driving. She throws open the door, and Bells is waiting on the porch, holding two delicious-smelling bags and rolling his eyes.

"Princess is still parking the car," Bells says, shaking his head. His hair is a vivid red today, shaved short on one side and long on the other. It was purple the last time Jess saw him, but this is normal; Bells thrives on constantly changing his look. The crimson locks fall in an artful fringe, framing his face; the color is vibrant against his dark skin.

Jess seizes him in a hug, and Bells exhales audibly. "Been working out, have we?" he asks with a grin.

Well, yes, but it's not like Jess has superstrength. She knows; she's got the numbers to prove it.

"Emma! What are you doing?" She calls to where the car is still moving.

"Parking," Emma says, flipping her dark curls over her shoulder as she reverses once more, her hand on the steering wheel. "It's gotta be perfect, you know?"

Jess shakes her head, takes one of the bags from Bells, and gestures inside.

Bells unzips his boots and toes them off, tossing them where the rest of the Trans' shoes are scattered in the entryway. He follows Jess to the kitchen, where they set down the bags and watch Emma park.

Emma rearranges the car three more times before she's satisfied and finally turns off the engine, steps out of the driver's seat, and beams as the car locks behind her. She puts her hands on her hips, and her petite frame stands proudly in the driveway. She grins; her bright lipstick matches the car perfectly.

The sleek and shiny vehicle looks out of place among the dull cars on their modest street, especially because of the steering wheel mounted on the dashboard. The driver-operated car screams of old money and connections; it's incredibly difficult for citizens to be approved for the privilege of driving. Even with Emma's parents both working in prominent government positions, it took the better part of two years for her license application to get approved.

Jess also has a license, but she can't tell anyone about it. The Smashmobile is driver-operated, and she's qualified to drive it, but only in case of emergency. Claudia got her own driver-operated car for her eighteenth birthday, but that was a gift for being accepted into the League. Jess thought the whole thing was ridiculous: Claudia could only drive it secretly. It's not like any of the middle-class Trans would have ever been approved for a license, let alone afford one of the coveted cars.

Still, Jess can't really be jealous of her friend. Emma has to share her car with her older brother, and she always offers to drive all of them.

"You didn't have to come over," Jess says, even though she's incredibly happy to see them. "I thought I told you to go to the movie without me."

Emma takes off her sandals and tucks them neatly into one of the cubbyholes in the entryway shelving. Jess' dad designated it for shoes, but he's the only one of the Trans who remembers to put them away in their proper place. It usually only has his shoes, and Emma's.

"No way," Bells says.

"You ditched school yesterday," Emma points out. "And you've been acting weird all week."

Jess bites her lip. Emma's very intuitive, but Jess can't tell her about her superpower difficulties without revealing her family's secret. She settles for looking at her feet. "Yeah, I know, I'm sorry..." Jess mutters.

Emma shrugs. "It's okay, I mean, you don't have to tell us, you know? But I didn't want you to mope all weekend about whatever it is."

Jess is seized by grateful appreciation and she wants to sweep Emma into a hug, but if she does that, she might burst into tears.

Emma nods, smiles, and steps into the kitchen. Bells pats Jess on the shoulder and follows Emma in. The two of them grab plates and utensils and usher Jess back downstairs. Jess is handed a plate of steaming tamales, and Bells and Emma plop down on the old, battered couches next to her and start eating and talking about the upcoming literary projects in Ms. Rhinehart's class.

Jess can't help but smile as the conversation surrounds her like a familiar and comforting blanket. She unwraps a tamale, inhales the delicious scent of the masa, and takes a bite. Jess nearly drops her fork when she tastes the seasoned beef. "Meat!" she says.

"Yeah! My uncle is visiting from New Bright City, and it was his birthday last weekend, so we went all out. You're lucky I hid the leftovers in the freezer when I did," Emma says brightly.

Jess takes her time, savoring every bite. "Your mom is the best. Tell her thank you when you get home."

"Of course," Emma says, elbowing Jess. "You know that also means next time you come over, she's not going to stop feeding you."

"I don't have a problem with that." Jess grins through her mouthful of tamale.

"Uh-uh," Bells says, waving his fork. "Do you remember when we were like, ten, and I said I liked that rice milk that one time? Now Mrs. Robledo always puts it out whenever I'm over, and I can't *not* drink it, even if horchata is too sweet for me."

Jess laughs and then gets drawn into a conversation about their parents' quirks. The afternoon might seem almost the same as it was before they arrived: no real plan, just hanging out in the basement. But instead of Jess flipping channels alone, she and Emma and Bells eat and make fun of Bells' apt reactions to reruns of his favorite detective show.

Even though they've seen this particular season finale many times, Bells cries out and throws up his arms in frustration when his favorite character dies. His empty plate flips over, and pieces of corn husk and sauce fly all over the holoscreen, distorting the projection.

Emma and Jess groan in unison.

"Really," Emma says, rolling her eyes. "Did you think it would end differently this time?"

"Shut up," Bells says, picking up a husk and tossing it at her. He flops back onto the couch and winks a challenge.

Jess grabs Emma's plate before they start chucking food everywhere. "C'mon, guys, it takes forever to clean this thing." She looks at the holoscreen. There's sauce splattered all over it and pieces of corn husk everywhere. Jess picks up what she can, but the image is still distorted. "I'll go get a rag," she says.

"You have a MonRobot, though," Emma says. "Where is that thing?"

"Chả is charging," Jess says. "I don't think it'll be a good idea, you know how it is with stairs—"

"Chả!" Emma calls loudly. "Please come clean this up!"

"Cancel clean order," Jess says immediately, hoping her voice carries enough, but it's too late; she can already hear metal clanging upstairs.

A few moments later, Chả's oblong silver body comes tumbling down the stairs, bouncing off the steps with heavy thunks. The little lights in Chả's display blink rapidly when it sees Emma and Bells.

Oh no, it's going to try and impress them. No verbal commands will stop it now; nothing short of manually rebooting the MonRobot's system or uninstalling the A.I. will stop it once it has a task in mind.

Jess slumps on the couch and watches helplessly as Emma directs Chả to the mess. The robot shakes eagerly, rolls right to the holoscreen, and starts the cleaning process. Chả's display screen flickers orange to signal a "busy" mode, and it starts sweeping methodically, an inch at a time.

"You do realize this is gonna take an hour," Jess says.

Bells shrugs. "You've got something better to do? Because this is pretty entertaining."

Emma is directing Chả at the holoscreen. The robot is stalled, cheeping at Emma.

"Like this," Emma says, moving in a circular motion, hips swaying.

Chả follows suit, spinning around the screen, whirring as it cleans. Bells is watching Emma; his expression seems wistful. Jess watches and smiles; it's odd how someone who's so animated can get so focused. Bells glances back at Jess and shifts when he notices her watching. Jess lifts an eyebrow and watches with delight as Bells starts to blush.

"You know, I think I have a lot of homework," Jess says. "You two should go watch the movie. I'm cool here."

Emma looks up. "What? No, we came over to hang out with *you.*"

"We'll watch that movie next week," Bells says, running a hand through his hair. No matter what he does, the overall effect is always unmistakably *cool.* The way he's lying on the couch should look ridiculous: upside down, feet dangling over the back of the couch, lanky frame sprawled everywhere. But he looks as if he belongs in a fashion magazine.

"We could just... leave," Emma says, waggling her eyebrows. "I mean, Brendan totally doesn't need someone to babysit him; he hasn't left his room for hours." Brendan had actually come downstairs during an episode of *The Gentleman Detective* to grab a box of circuits, but he'd taken one look at Jess' friends and squeaked, "Hi, Emma and Bells!" before dashing back up the stairs.

He is largely self-sufficient, if a bit socially awkward. Jess can't blame him; Bells' hair does look spectacular today.

"Yeah, but he might try and use the stove again, and last time he almost set the kitchen on fire," Jess says. "You guys should go watch the movie. Chả is gonna take forever."

"You know, we don't have to use the holoscreen to watch a movie," Emma says, glancing over to the shelf where Jess hides her DVD collection.

Bells' eyes widen. "Jess! You still have that vision-tella thing?" He sits up, and his back goes rigid. "You know that we're supposed to surrender any pre-Collective tech so it can be recycled!"

"I know," Jess says. "But, um, my dad, when he was flipping this old house, found this storage locker, and I just really wanted to see if they had a sequel to that movie we watched last week."

Several weeks ago, Shockwave had actually taken one of Master Mischief 's caches in a successful raid and had found boxes of contraband tech and media. Victor hadn't turned it in to the League yet, and Jess—Jess loved the stuff. She'd hidden a television and a box of DVDs a few months ago when they uncovered the first stash, and she and her friends have pored through every movie.

Jess couldn't just turn in this new stash without looking through it. She put together a box of some of the tech—movies she didn't like, electronics that didn't work, random assorted cables, a clunky rectangular player that didn't take the DVDs—and gave all of it to her father to turn in to the League. Jess knows the laws about pre-Collective tech are to conserve resources and she agrees that's incredibly important, but she doesn't see the point of banning most of the media produced before 2035. Why is Shakespeare allowed but *Star Wars* isn't? The Collective banned most of Jess' favorite films.

It was sheer luck that her parents found another cache just a few days ago. Jess hasn't had time to go through the films, and had been hoping to watch them with her friends, but she hadn't counted on Bells being such a stickler for the rules.

"Come on, these films from Old America aren't that cool anyways." Bells crosses his legs, leans back, and scrunches up his face. "Like the picture was all flat, and it's boring, not being able to see it from whatever angle you want."

"Really? I remember you really liking this one." Jess presses the hidden lever under the bottom shelf, and the back panel opens to reveal her hidden compartment. She roots about and pulls out a colorful plastic case that's decorated with Old America's superheroes, before anyone actually had powers. The film was a lot of fun, and Jess liked the story a lot more than what passes for entertainment in the Collective. She waves the case and sees Bells' eyes light up. "Yeah?"

Bells huffs in mock reluctance. "You know me too well." He takes the case and reads the title and summary fondly. "Yeah, we can watch this again."

Jess reaches back inside the compartment. "Didn't I say I found the sequel?"

Bells' mouth falls open, and he's already making grabby hands. "I guess it's all right," he admits. "I mean, you're going to turn all of it in after we watch it, right?"

"Right," Jess says. "Here, help me with this."

The television is a small, unwieldy block made of different types of plastic. The three of them pull it out from the hiding spot, and Jess pulls out the box with the DVD player and all the assorted cables. It's been a while since they last used it, but finally it's all set up, and they flop back on the couch. Jess leans back, and Bells slings his arm around her shoulders as Emma puts her feet up in her lap. Jess pokes at Emma's socks, and they laugh when Bells tries to get the DVD player to accept a voice command.

"It's not my fault this stuff is ancient," Bells says.

Jess laughs, gets up, and, amused at the flimsy plastic, puts the colorful disc in the player. An old-fashioned menu pops up, and Jess has to use the arrows on the primitive machine to start the movie.

"It's not *that* old," Emma says. "My nana still remembers what it was like."

"Really?" It always seemed like ancient history to Jess. *In 2028, the solar flares that would ignite the events known later as the Disasters and throw the population into a time of social and economic peril and great food insecurity...* any student could recite a version of the events that changed the world forever, and it always started with "in 2028." "How old is your great-grandmother?"

"A hundred and seven," Emma says. "She was born during the Disasters. She was old enough to remember when they formed the Collective after the war. She doesn't really like to talk about it, though."

"I bet. Everything must have been so chaotic," Jess muses. "I mean, people springing up with powers for the first time?"

Emma nods. "Can you imagine making something like this today?" Bells asks. He holds up the DVD. On the case, a luridly costumed male superhero holds a swooning woman. "Captain Orion would have a fit."

Jess laughs. "Yeah, if the Collective made movies with superheroes." All the official entertainment is so boring. That's one of the reasons Jess likes twenty-first century movies: people seemed to have free reign to be creative. Still, rules against fictional media about superheroes makes sense; the lives of the actual heroes provide enough interest. "I bet Captain Orion would be the one holding the swooning—"

"Ooh, Starscream?" Emma says with interest. "I heard they were on again."

Jess shakes her head. "Nope, broke up, according to yesterday's *Gazette.*" She never reads the entire newsholo, but Orion's love life always makes headlines.

They gossip about Captain Orion's romantic life and then get into a silly discussion about the most attractive heroes in the League. The movie is playing but they aren't paying much attention. Jess lost track of the plot a few minutes in. She's enjoying her time with her friends as they argue about who is hotter: Starscream or Copycat.

Emma and Bells are waving their DEDs at each other, flicking through their favorite holos. Bells' projection of the official League holo of Copycat and Emma's holo of Starscream keep bumping into each other, causing both holos to flicker.

"It has to be Copycat," Bells says. "She's got those stunning green eyes, you know?"

"Yeah, but Starscream's jaw!" Emma says. "No, this holo isn't a great one, no, I need a better—Jess! Help!"

Jess laughs, throwing up her hands. "I refuse to get in the middle of this. I'm a Captain Orion gal myself, but I will bring my desktop down so you can find all the pictures you want."

Beeping as it wheels back and forth, Chả is still trying to clean the holoscreen. Shaking her head, Jess picks up the robot. She carries it up to the main floor and sets it down in the living room. "You can clean here," Jess says. "I'll do the holoscreen later."

Chả cheeps in affirmation and starts vacuuming. It promptly gets stuck under the coffee table, meeping until Jess picks it up and turns it around. Chả chirps and heads down its new, clear path. Jess trudges upstairs, lingering outside Brendan's room. She hears a few beeping noises, but that's normal.

She grabs her desktop projector and goes downstairs, where Emma grabs it and syncs her own DED to it, to look up photos of Starscream. She gets distracted checking her notifications and then she gasps.

"Oh my God, there's a new superhero over in Devonport."

Jess looks over her shoulder at the projection. Emma waves at the air, closing all her open windows: various messages, homework documents, and photos of Starscream and Lilliputian. She enlarges the newsfeed holo from the official Heroes' League of Heroes. "Oh, wow! He's our age. The bio says sixteen."

Emma pokes Bells in the shoulder, but he just shrugs and gets up to manually turn up the television's volume.

Emma faces the holo toward them, grinning as she waves her hand to play a featured clip from a news segment.

"And what do we call you?" On the holo, Wilton Lysander, the most popular newscaster of all the latest superhero news, stands in downtown Devonport in front of its iconic fountain. With a broad smile, he holds his microphone out to the brightly clad hero next to him.

"I'm Chameleon!" Like most meta-humans in the public eye, Chameleon wears a mask; it matches his brightly colored rainbow-hued bodysuit and sits high on his face. A shock of dark hair spills over the forehead. The tight outfit shows off his broad shoulders and tapered waist, and Emma sighs and reaches out to trace the air around the projection.

Chameleon stands with a hand on his hip and points to the reporter. Then, in the blink of an eye, Chameleon turns into a duplicate copy of Lysander, from his coiffed blonde hair to his navy suit, complete with the matching pocket square.

"Amazing!" Lysander gasps. He turns to the camera and winks, gesturing theatrically. "Welcome, Chameleon, the newest and *youngest* member of the Heroes' League of Heroes!"

Chameleon hands the pocket square to Lysander, who compares it to his own. The camera zooms in on the pocket squares; they match. Lysander is examining them when the second pocket square disappears. The cameras pan back to Chameleon, who is back to his own look. He winks at the camera.

Emma stops the holo. Leaning back on the couch, she grabs a pillow, clutches it to her chest, and squeals, "Isn't he cute?"

"Can't see half his face," Jess says. "No idea." She turns to Bells for his opinion, but Bells is staring at the television. "Bells? What do you think?"

"Like you said, we can't see half his face. I can't tell if he's cute or not," Bells says in a monotone.

"But it's an incredible power," Emma says. "I've never seen anything like that. Do you think he's A-class? I mean, he's working with the League already."

"Well, they do like to introduce their younger members before they start on their own," Jess says. "Remember Powerstorm? She was like, fifteen when she first started."

Jess remembers it well; it was her sister's introduction as a new superhero. For a time, Claudia had tailed along after the League and they had helped get her name out as she handled minor search and rescues and a few reconnaissance missions on the Villain's Guild. Jess is pretty sure she was mostly fetching coffee for the members of the League, but Claudia played it up as a huge educational experience. Claudia was still in her training program when the League started introducing her to the public, but they always hand-pick the most promising to join the League. "He's probably still in Meta-Human Training," Jess says thoughtfully. "And if he's a teenager, he probably hasn't had a lot of time to practice control."

"Well, the League doesn't accept just anybody," Emma says. "Bells, come on, back me up. Isn't Chameleon amazing?"

"Do you seriously like him just because he has powers?" Bells blurts out, his voice sharp with annoyance.

"What?" Emma frowns. "No, I just think he's cute and really cool, you know."

"Like Jess said, you can't see his face," Bells points out. "So all you know about him is what's listed on the League's holo and this video. Kinda soon for a crush, don't you think?"

Emma huffs. "How is this different than what we've talked about with any of the other heroes we find attractive?"

Bells gets up and grabs his backpack. "Whatever. I just realized I have to finish my history essay. I'll see you in school."

"Do you need a ride?" Emma calls, but he's already at the top of the stairs.

The basement door shuts with a thud, and they can hear Bells' footsteps echo through the house and then the front door open and close.

"I guess he's walking." Jess bites her lip; it's not that far to the nearest bus stop.

Emma's mouth is still open, and she's frozen, staring up the stairs. She shakes herself. Her eyebrows knit and she turns to Jess. "What was that about?"

JESS AND EMMA FINISH THE movie, but the mood has changed. Emma keeps biting her lip and looking toward the stairs.

"I'm gonna go see if he's okay," Emma says. "I feel like I should apologize, but I'm not really sure what for. Like how is me finding Chameleon cute different than Starscream or Copycat?"

Jess brushes through her hair as she thinks. She ties her hair in a ponytail as Emma watches her. Great, Emma knows all her tells; she probably thinks Jess knows something.

Jess has suspected for a while that Bells has feelings for Emma, who crushes on a new person almost every week. Her focus is intense but fleeting, and she always wants to talk about them.

It's only lately that Jess has noticed that Bells gets a withdrawn, resigned look whenever Emma talks about a crush, except a crush on celebrities or superheroes. Maybe Bells doesn't care about Starscream and Copycat because they are older and unattainable, but he's upset because Chameleon is their age?

"Maybe you guys should just hang out and talk about it," Jess suggests.

Emma nods. "That's a good idea. See you around, Jess."

Jess cleans up in the living room and heads upstairs to charge her phone. She runs into Brendan at the top of the stairs.

"Mom and Dad are doing hero-stuff with Clauds," Brendan says. A pair of goggles dangles around his neck, and he smells like burnt rubber. Jess isn't sure she wants to know about the scuff marks on his face. "Mom said we can order food."

"Cool, you want pizza?"

"Oooh, can you pick up a mushroom and cheese from Lenny's? And also I need a few more parts from the hardware shop." Brendan hands Jess a list.

Jess scowls. "I'm not running your errands for you, and we can just order delivery from Pizza Joe's. Lenny's doesn't deliver, and I'm not supposed to leave you here alone."

"I'm thirteen, not three. Look, I know they left the Smashmobile at home and I won't tell them you took it out. You know, if you wanted to drive it instead of taking the minivan."

Jess narrows her eyes, but the temptation of driving the sports car is too much. Besides, she can park in an alley across the street from Lenny's. No one would notice her getting in and out of the car.

And she could get Thai tea from the shop next door.

"Fine," Jess says, and strides to her parents' office. When she finds the drawer with the Smashmobile keycard, a thrill of exhilaration runs through her. She grabs her backpack.

The modified sports car drives like a dream. Her mom's logo is painted on the side, and inside there's a complicated dashboard with a communication relay to League headquarters. Grinning, Jess runs her fingers over the console. She takes the car for a spin around the block, and then on a whim zips out of the suburbs. She laughs as the wind catches in her hair as she drives down the highway past the gleaming solar fields.

The desert landscape opens out in front of her; but she doesn't want to risk running the car out of charge or worse, having someone mistake her for her mother and ask for help with hero stuff.

Jess zips around the outskirts of Andover, taking twenty minutes to herself. She imagines she's flying. It's thrilling, and then it's too easy to remember she's just driving a car. There's nothing special about that, even if she's controlling the vehicle instead of the computer.

She turns back into town and drives to the hardware shop to get Brendan his things. At least he knows what he wants, knows what he's doing in his life, and he's only thirteen. He doesn't have any powers and it doesn't bother him.

Then again, he's also a super-genius.

⇄

JESS IS GRATEFUL WHEN MONDAY rolls around; she's impatient to hear back from Monroe Industries, and Bells and Emma were both busy on Sunday. Being around both her parents is exhausting. She always feels like a disappointment, even if they don't say anything about her lack of powers.

And they're around a lot more now ever since the Mischiefs went missing.

The resident villains of Andover, Master and Mistress Mischief, have been her parents' archenemies as long as Jess can remember. They've had countless confrontations over the years, all of them well-documented in the *Andover Gazette,* the local news holo.

The Mischiefs haven't been around the past few weeks—no ridiculous electronic shenanigans, nothing flying through the air, no chaos whatsoever. It's been strange, and while the rumors are that Smasher and Shockwave caught them and sent them to Meta-Human Corrections at last, Jess knows better.

Her parents have no idea where the villains are.

Even the usual sort of hero-work has declined since Chameleon was introduced, and with the lack of pranks from the Mischiefs, there's been woefully little for Jess' parents to do. Her father in particular has been using his extra time at home to focus uncomfortably on Jess' future.

At least there were only a few awkward conversations over the weekend. Jess can't say she's looked forward to a lot of Mondays, but this is definitely one of them. She hopes, whatever the Mischiefs are up to, that things get back to normal soon.

School is routine, as always. In her classes, Jess takes notes idly and drifts off into daydreams. She's fairly forgettable as a student. Freshman year she was known simply as "Claudia's sister." Her teachers were all excited at first, exclaiming different versions of "Claudia was so spectacular; I'm so excited to have you in my class!" But Jess fell short of all their glowing expectations.

Jess hunches down in her usual seat in the back of the classroom. The other kids greet each other as if they haven't seen each other in ages. Elizabeth Phang sweeps her friend Denise Ho into a hug, and more friends swarm the two girls. The group talks eagerly before the bell rings for third period. Jess snorts; Elizabeth and Denise just saw each other during first period. But it's not as though when lunchtime comes around Jess won't be doing the same with her own friends.

Unfortunately, Emma and Bells aren't in most of her classes. Now, they're in AP World History, while Jess is in regular.

The bell rings, and the class comes to order; Mr. Liu starts by asking questions from the reading last night. Even though she knows the answers, Jess doesn't bother raising her hand.

She's given up trying to stand out. People tend to forget her and remember the Elizabeths and Denises of the world, that combination of confident, smart and pretty that always draws people in.

Jess is certain she's none of these things. She could probably pass for cute if she tried hard enough, and smart, well, she works hard for her grades. She's working on developing confidence, but it's a constant effort. The only time she's come close to being "known" was when she accidentally came out as bisexual during sophomore English class while talking about her favorite poem.

That's old news now. No one really cares, but it was exciting at the time. Jess had a few overwhelming weeks of curious looks and some intrusive questions from over-curious students until Emma and Bells put an end to it.

The bell rings, and Jess shuffles off to her next class, only to be accosted by Darryl Flemings, Andover Heights' most out-and-proud student. He smiles with teeth dazzling white enough to rival an Eversparkle holo. Darryl's brown hair is slicked back with a copious amount of gel. He waves at her in greeting; his DED display is on, projecting distorted images and messages everywhere, and Jess can read a half-finished AHHS Club Event proposal flickering in the air. She doesn't say anything, even though it's incredibly impolite to leave your personal display on when you're not using it.

Darryl's nice enough, but he's also incredibly intense, especially about the Rainbow Allies club. It's not a terrible idea for an organization; the twenty-second century isn't perfect, after all. Jess attended a few meetings freshman year but found, like most of the clubs on campus, it's more a social organization than a service one. She doesn't feel too bad about it; a lot of students identify but don't participate in the club.

"Heyyy, Jess," Darryl says, smiling at her.

Jess looks at the floor. "Hey, I'm on my way to class."

"So, did you hear we're raising money for—"

Jess pushes past him. "I'm not in Rainbow Allies."

"I know, I know! It's just that, you know, you're always welcome, you know, and I know you're part of the community—"

"Get to the point."

Jess makes a quick turn around a corner. Darryl, to his credit, manages to keep up with her.

"We just need more volunteers to help us meet our fundraising goal for the quarter—"

"You're fundraising for *new T-shirts,*" Jess says. "You guys don't really do anything other than hang out together at lunch and occasionally wear the matching T-shirts."

"Oh, c'mon, we totally petitioned the school board about—"

"It's a 'no,' Darryl; I'll see you around." Jess steps into her English class. She frowns, hearing Darryl curse to himself before the door shuts.

The room is peaceful; lining the wall are familiar colorful posters about books she'd loved discussing or projects she had fun working on. This is an AP class, and it's her only one. She loves Ms. Rhinehart, an eccentric woman who favors circular seating patterns and has no problem when students curse in class or even eat snacks. Ms. Rhinehart makes up for leniency with frequent written quizzes, challenging projects, and interesting reading assignments.

The door opens again, and Darryl follows her into the room. Ms. Rhinehart is the advisor for Rainbow Allies, but she's got a laid-back attitude in contrast to Darryl's gung-ho persistence, and raises her eyebrow as Darryl keeps talking about the fundraiser.

"Darryl, you're not in this period," Ms. Rhinehart says.

"I know, I just wanted to see if Jess wanted to help with—"

She places a firm hand on Darryl's shoulder and points him toward the door. "Bell's about to ring."

Darryl casts Jess a frustrated look before he leaves, not before saying something sharply under his breath that Jess hears with a cold pang of hurt.

"Sorry about that," Ms. Rhinehart says. "He gets a little carried away with his president duties; for some reason he thinks trying to raise money is the same thing as annoying people into helping him, even if they might not be interested."

"I'm *not* a traitor to the cause," Jess says softly.

"Did he call you that?" Ms. Rhinehart clicks her tongue. "I'm going to have words with him after school."

Jess sits down and, with a sigh, pulls up the holobooks for class on her DED. The class starts with ten minutes of quick writing in their journals, and then moves on to a discussion of *The Wasteland*. Jess eagerly starts planning the visual project for their current assignment.

Lunchtime is much more fun, and she waves brightly to her friends in the cafeteria as they join the throngs of students lining up for food. MonRobots are distributing the lunches in an efficient fashion, ladling out government-issue vegetable chili with sides of tater tots and wilted salad greens. Andover Heights isn't a particularly rich neighborhood, but a few students scattered throughout the cafeteria have brought their own lunch. Jess can smell the rich aroma of roasted chicken wafting from a nearby table.

She thinks about one of the twenty-first century movies she saw last week, where hamburgers were served at a typical high school lunch, and wonders what that must have been like. Not just the availability of meat, either, but the abundance and diversity of fresh fruits and vegetables. Ever since the Disasters, it's been a struggle to grow enough food to feed everyone. Now everyone makes do with what can be grown from the little fertile land left.

The Nevada region is fairly lucky; they're close enough to a huge swath of unaffected farmland from the California region, but most of the best quality produce is still sold to the highest bidder.

It's always guesswork, which line has the most palatable food. Most of the produce sold to AHHS is just about to spoil, and the food usually borders on inedible. But it's hard to ruin a simple potato, and Jess is fond of all its forms, particularly tater tots. They're consistently good here, and by good Jess means not terrible.

Emma makes a beeline for the shortest line, but Jess redirects them to a slightly longer line to the right and is pleased when this particular line yields a fresh batch of tater tots.

They grab their lunches and find their usual spot outside. Students mill about, talking and laughing, and the orange-red of the landscape shimmers in the desert heat beyond the city. Jess steals Bells' portion of tater tots and leaves her chili on his tray. She picks at her food as Emma talks about her morning.

Emma's crushing on a different guy this week, having abandoned her previous idea that Carter on the basketball team is the most adorable person to ever exist. Today she thinks Jimmy from chemistry is the one for her. Bells listens while sketching a picture of a dragon and tosses his hair casually out of his face. It's blue today, with dark purple streaks.

"The red not work out for you?" Jess asks.

"Too loud," Bells says.

Emma laughs. "I didn't know you understood what that meant."

"Just liked the idea of two colors and wanted to try it," Bells says. "Jimmy has streaks in his hair."

"Yeah, so?" Emma says.

Jess shakes a container at them. "Who wants the rest of my tater tots?"

By the time school ends, a light drizzle is falling wearily. Bells and Emma get on the bus to their neighborhood; Jess boards her bus. It's crowded, and Jess has to sit on a "seat" that already has two students on it; she's mostly hovering in the aisle. The bus smells of damp hair and wet clothing, and a rhythmic *rat a tat tat* pings on the metal roof of the bus.

The route goes through Old Town Andover, a colorful area with signs in many languages. Even in the rain, a bunch of people mill around on the sidewalk. Jess catches sight of her favorite sandwich shop, and her stomach makes the decision for her; she follows the students getting off. She can always take the city bus home later.

Old Town is dominated by businesses run by immigrants. *Nha Trang Bánh Mì* is no exception. Jess has heard plenty of stories about the scenic coastal city in Vietnam for which it was named. Her dad was born there and has many fond memories of it. It's far from idyllic nowadays, especially with the recent conflict over joining the Southeast Asian Alliance. And this little sandwich shop isn't the only nostalgic business; plenty of stores in the area are named for cities in countries to which there's no way back, countries that are wasteland now.

Clutching the strap of her backpack, Jess waits in line. The bánh mì shop is crowded, and she can pick out snippets of Vietnamese here and there, phrases that she can recognize, mostly, and conversational bits and ends about people picking out snacks and chatting about their days. It's a familiar cacophony of women behind the counter shouting out order numbers and menu items, scanning receipts quickly, handing out fragrant bags full of food.

Behind her, the in-restaurant patrons read newsholos and sip slow-brewed coffee; elderly men argue vehemently in Vietnamese. Amused, Jess watches as one man her grandfather's age exclaims loudly while the other sighs in exasperation.

A woman steps in front of her and orders in Chinese—two specials, pickled vegetables on the side.

Jess gives the woman a cross look; she was here first, but to argue would be pointless.

"Also how much is this?" the woman asks, holding up a wrapped container of roast chicken and broken rice.

"Thirty credits," the cashier responds in Chinese.

The woman scowls, cursing softly. Jess winces; didn't she see the same entree last week priced at twenty?

The cashier shrugs and jerks a shoulder to the sign behind her that reads: ALL MEAT ITEMS ARE SUBJECT TO MARKET PRICE. "Do you want it?"

The woman makes a remark under her breath about the freshness of the entree and sets it down.

Finally it's Jess' turn. She smiles at the woman behind the cash register and gets an inpatient look and a jerk of the head.

"Hai nam đặc biệt," Jess says.

"What?" the woman says in English.

Jess flushes, then says, "Two number ones, please."

"You want everything inside?" The woman frowns, pointing at the picture of the sandwich on the menu behind them.

Jess knows the cashier is about to explain that the sandwich comes with pickled vegetables and raw jalapeños. "Yes, I know. All the extra vegetables and the peppers, please."

The woman nods; the explanation is complete. Jess noticed she hadn't asked anyone else to confirm their order.

The cash register dings, and then at the last moment Jess adds, "And a Thai iced tea."

The cashier sighs but restarts the order, adding her tea and then ringing it up. "Five credits."

Jess waves her DED at the scanner and then flops down at an empty table to wait for her order. She tugs self-consciously at her sweater, stares at the table, and listens to the other customers order their food. It's a mix of Chinese and Vietnamese, and Jess can also pick out a few words of Malay and Thai. Everyone is ordering in their own language. Jess mouths her order to herself, taking note of how noticeably different the words sound when she says them.

It's not that her pronunciation is terrible; it just that she should have known it was easier not to try in the first place. It's as if they just look at her and know. Or assume that she *doesn't* know, because of her age, which is mostly right, because Jess can count how many Vietnamese words she can say that aren't food items.

But it's her favorite sandwich, and her favorite tea drink, and it's cheap and filling and the perfect afternoon snack.

Jess loves this area of Andover; the old neighborhood is a bit run down, but it's part of what makes Andover wonderful and not just another a medium-sized town in the region that was once known as Nevada. Andover is a haven amidst this vast desert, far enough inland that tidal waves and earthquakes aren't an issue. The city attracted many people fleeing first the uninhabitable nuclear meltdown sites immediately after the Disasters and then the epic third world war—the grand battle over resources.

It's been about a hundred years since the war ended, but the world is still recovering, slowly. New countries and alliances were formed, and people are stronger than before. In the face of dwindling resources and lost farmland, innovative minds and new technology made survival possible.

Unlike Emma, Jess doesn't have surviving relatives who lived through World War III, but her grandparents on both sides grew up while the Southeast Asian Alliance was still being formed. Unlike the original United States, Mexico, and Canada, which took only a few years to come together as a single Collective, the many small countries in Southeast Asia, still smarting from WWIII, didn't reach a united front until 2108.

The conflict was long and bloody, and Jess' parents were among many refugees. Although Vietnam and China no longer exist as they remember them, Jess' parents try their best to pass on the language and customs of their forebears. Jess tries her best, but she wasn't raised speaking the language; her parents only spoke English with her because they didn't want her to have an accent.

The solar flares started a horrific chain of events—a number of disasters and the ensuing war—but it also awoke something strange and new, a latent gene that catalyzed a number of fantastic abilities in some people. The heroes who came after the flare and helped people survive became idols.

Jess opens her backpack and thumbs lovingly through her newest comic book, grinning at the unbroken spine, the glossy cover. She had splurged last week and ordered the newest edition of *Captain Orion,* and it just arrived in the mail. She's been saving it to open and read this week, one page at a time so she can digest the newest story slowly.

Her friends always tease her for buying the print comics and not just the holos. Emma says that it's just art celebrating the most recent and epic battles of the greatest superhero in the North American Collective, but Jess loves the comics even if she already knows all the stories. It's completely different from seeing the events unfold on the news.

Jess takes out her journal, decorated with a blue sky and a few fluffy clouds; "Dream big," in script in an inspirational font floats across the dream sky.

It's old-school to write by hand, but Jess likes the way the words blossom under her fingertips. It's not as if she's ever going to type it up and send it anywhere. These scribblings and imaginings are for no one else.

Jess opens the journal to the last blank page and scrunches her nose. She left her character Xyra in a rather unfortunate predicament. An idea comes to mind, and Jess grabs a pen from the backpack pocket and starts to write, lost in the scene.

"Take that, and that," Jess mutters to herself as her main character fights off a herd of bad guys.

"Number twenty-four!"

The crowded little sandwich shop has disappeared. Jess is in a forbidding forest filled with looming trees—and a little bit of sunlight, Jess decides, because it would make for dramatic lighting. Xyra does a spinning kick, sending another guy into unconsciousness, and Jess makes a note that she will probably have to name all these evil henchmen later. *Some sort of army. Does the villain have a name yet?*

The forest is foreboding, and then there are reinforcements, and all is lost except when a new warrior joins the fray, a stunning beauty with red curls and—

"You. Number twenty-four," says a curt voice, and Jess is startled right out of the story.

Her sandwiches and tea are set on her table, and the worker mutters "Con nhỏ này," before she goes back to the counter where responsible customers pick up their orders from the correct place.

Jess bites her lip. She does know that phrase; she's heard it enough. *That girl.* It's not really derogatory, but the only times she's heard it was when her parents were talking to each other in annoyed, hushed whispers. They didn't use her name, but she knew they were talking about her anyway.

She glances at the other people in the restaurant. Are they looking down on her, too? Looking down on her for not being fluent, not following procedure, not living up to her heritage, any of it. Jess often feels as if she's not Chinese enough in certain situations and not Vietnamese enough in others. It's awkward when you're not quite one but not quite the other.

Jess sighs. She takes one sandwich out to eat now and stuffs the other in her backpack. She unwraps the sandwich and takes a bite. The juxtaposition of the crisp baguette and the thin slices of chả lụa chay is perfect with the pickled vegetables and jalapeños. There are few soy proteins that Jess genuinely enjoys, and the way the imitation chả lụa is seasoned, Jess really can't tell it from the meat version. The Thai tea is sweet and refreshing, and she enjoys her meal for a bit before going back to writing.

Jess only looks up when she has to stop and un-smudge some of the ink on her left palm and hears a familiar voice.

"Oh gosh, why did you pick this place? It's so fobby! My mom eats here!"

Elizabeth Phang and what looks like the rest of the AHHS volleyball team come into the shop, and no, no, please no—

A flash of reddish-gold hair.

Yup, it's the entire volleyball team, which means Abby Jones, captain of said team, is also with this group, and they're all going to see Jess sitting in the corner eating her sandwich with crumbs all over her face like an absolute nerd. Jess shrinks into herself and pulls her hood over her head.

Why are they here? Didn't Elizabeth declare this place incredibly uncool ever since Jess tried to bring up the idea of selling the Vietnamese sandwiches as the AHHS Honor Society fundraiser at the fall harvest festival? (Elizabeth's idea to sell cheesecake from the Pie Factory downtown was voted into the plan.)

Denise Ho, who Jess doesn't quite mind so much, walks in after Elizabeth and laughs at her comment. "Well, yeah, but that's the point! Team dinner means we try something new! And you know you wanna give them something authentic and awesome."

Elizabeth grumbles, and Jess tries to finish her bite. Jess would leave, but it's raining a lot harder now, and even though the bus stop is right outside, the next one won't be here for another forty minutes.

Jess just hopes that her sweatshirt is inconspicuous enough. She doesn't care if Elizabeth or Denise see her; she's used to teasing from them.

The three of them actually used to be pretty good friends. The Asian community in Andover is close-knit, and their parents had sent them all to the same Chinese school. Although Jess could speak Cantonese well enough, she'd struggled with Mandarin and Vietnamese, especially the written forms. As there wasn't a

Vietnamese language school in Andover, her parents had settled on sending her off to Sacred Heart Chinese Language Academy every Saturday.

The school, with students of all ages, from grade school kids still learning their *buh-pu-muh-fuhs* to older students taking more advanced classes, was not without its cliques.

Jess, Elizabeth, and Denise were the only three girls in her grade level. The other students, mostly children of more-recent immigrants, had formed close friendships already at their Chinese language pre-school. Jess felt an immediate bond with Elizabeth and Denise. The trio goofed off during classes. After all, they weren't being graded; they went every Saturday to stay out of their parents' hair and learn a bit about the language and the culture.

Jess only went to the language school until seventh grade. She struggled at remembering the hundreds of different characters. It wasn't as if her parents knew the written forms either, and as long as she could talk to them, she felt okay. She'd only kept going as long as she did because she liked hanging out with Elizabeth and Denise. Elizabeth liked making fun of the other students' accents in English, at their fashion choices, at how they were clearly "fresh off the boat." And that criticism didn't stop with the other students, or fobs, as Elizabeth was quick to call them, but Elizabeth was critical of Jess' everything, from her hair to the clothes she was wearing.

Jess was uncomfortable with that, and then one time her mom had been picking her up from the Chinese school with a younger Brendan in the back seat. Brendan was quite precocious but he didn't care much for fashion; he was wearing three different hats from the colleges that were courting him. Elizabeth was waiting with Jess in the parking lot, and as soon as she spotted Brendan, she started laughing her ass off.

"Look at that kid. Gosh, he looks like such a nerd. What's up with all those hats?"

"He *is* a nerd," Jess said hotly, "But he's also my little brother. And he's amazingly smart and applying to colleges already."

"Oh, I didn't know. Sorry." Elizabeth's tone signified that she wasn't really sorry that she'd insulted Jess' little brother, and she went on to criticize someone else.

Jess didn't want to go back to the school after that, and then middle school had started, and it seemed Elizabeth and, by default, Denise hadn't wanted to spend time with her anyway. She spent a few lonely lunches by herself, but then she met Bells and Emma and never missed Elizabeth and Denise. Those two went on to join the volleyball team and tried to make the best of their high school career, and Jess, living in Claudia's shadow, gave up participating in anything.

The varsity volleyball team is rowdy, still in their uniforms, and, yup, there's Mrs. Delgado bringing up the rear. They must have just won a game and gone out to celebrate.

Jess chances a peek and sighs.

Abby is wearing her hair in a high ponytail, and a few errant curls are escaping from it, gently wafting on the nape of her neck. She smiles at one of her teammates and nods at what the other girl is saying, and then gets distracted by the menu on the wall. While the other girls are wrapped up in conversation, Abby looks around the restaurant, and her eyes light up when she sees the colorful stacked display of pastries and the Vietnamese desserts. She scans the room, and then locks gazes with Jess.

Jess freezes. She's not invisible, but she should just be a faceless maroon lump in a school sweater. It's the sweater; Abby is smiling—*smiling!*—at her because she recognized the dancing horse, the Mustang's mascot on the sweater, and it's because Abby is *nice* and school spirit or solidarity—

Oh good, she's not looking anymore.

It's not as if she would have recognized Jess anyway.

Jess hastily wraps the rest of her sandwich, stuffs it in her bag, takes another slurp of tea, and dashes out to wait for the bus in the rain.

The next day, Jess ignores the entrees for the school lunch and gets a plate full of tater tots. Emma eyes Jess' lunch and rolls her eyes, and then gives Jess a fresh apple from her bag lunch. Bells gives her half of his peanut butter jelly sandwich from home, too.

It's not that the food is completely inedible at school—but the government isn't spending tons of money on the public high school lunch program. There are a lot of important things, like, running the country and making sure that there's going to be enough food and power for everyone. And stuff like defense isn't cheap either; having a strong military is important in case something like the Disasters ever happens again.

Idly scrolling through her messages on her DED display, Jess munches on the crispy potato bites. There are a few funny holos from Bells of cats wearing cute sweaters that she saw already and a whole bunch of notifications from the Captain Orion Fan Club. She's set up for an alert for anything new about her hero, but usually what she gets is either something she's already seen or the group discussing stuff.

Jess deletes one message after another, and then she blinks, startled. "Hey, I got an interview!"

Bells looks up from his sketchpad. "For what?"

"This paid internship I applied for at Monroe Industries!"

"Whoa, really? I didn't even know they took high school interns. Is it like, super-competitive? Did you have to write like, five essays?" Emma asks. "Are you going to be working with the robots?"

A MonRobot flies by and picks up some trash. The school's able to afford some of last year's models. This one is sleek and efficient, chirping a greeting at the three of them as it passes by.

Jess laughs. "No, I applied for this office position that was pretty vague, but I don't think they'll let me anywhere near the technical stuff. Probably just boring work, like filing or getting coffee, but a job's a job, and I bet any college will look at Monroe Industries and be impressed, right? That's *if* I get it, though."

"I bet you will," Bells says.

"Thanks."

Jess types a response, fingers flying through the projected mini-keyboard, to let them know when she's available after school this week for an interview. By the end of lunch, she has an official message from M that says they want to fill the position as soon as possible and suggesting that, if she can't come into the office today, they can do a video interview.

Jess high-fives Emma and Bells and confirms for five o'clock.

JESS GETS HOME FROM SCHOOL just as her mother returns from picking up Brendan from the college campus downtown.

"Dad home today?" Jess asks. "I wanna use his office for a backdrop. I have a job interview via holo, and I need it to look really professional."

"Yeah, he's out doing—" Mom casts a furtive look to see if any neighbors are listening in. "—the work, you know."

"Right," Jess says as she goes inside. "I'm sure helping old ladies cross the street is a great purpose. Maybe one day the Mischiefs will show up again. I hope they do. Dad has been so weird about finding hero stuff to do."

They're lucky they live in Andover, where the biggest thing to worry about is Master Mischief stealing all the oranges again or Mistress Mischief turning all the street signs upside down. The Mischiefs aren't A-class villains; they have C-class powers, just like her parents. They've never harmed anyone, not like Dynamite, the cruel and heinous villain in New Bright City. Dynamite was responsible for that awful explosion in that shopping center. If Captain Orion hadn't been there, the bomb could have destroyed half the region.

But without the Mischiefs to stir up trouble, there isn't much for a superhero to do: no switcheroos at the art museum, no thefts from local factories, no industrial supplies gone missing, not even strange robots playing pranks on people.

The Mischiefs are just gone, without warning, or notice, and that's strange for a couple known for their loud and dramatic stunts. Since they've disappeared, Smasher and Shockwave have no hero work to do, and Li Hua and Victor Tran have had to adapt.

Jess' dad has been acting really weird. He goes out of his way to do good deeds, until the mayor asked him to stop helping people cross the street. Jess' mom, on the other hand, really happy about having extra time to work on her novel, has adapted very well to the lack of hero work. She's even put in actual hours at her real estate "job."

It's not Jess' problem. But she does wish Dad would listen to Mom about maybe doing more at his "job," or picking up a hobby.

Jess, heart hammering, bounds up the stairs, two at a time. She drops her backpack and rushes back downstairs to the study. With a desk on one wall and a whole shelf of trophies, it's a trophy room as much as an office, and Jess loves it, loves her parents' personalities reflected on the walls and the knickknacks on the shelves, how it's a mix of her mother's love of bright colors and her father's fastidious organization. She chuckles at all the static projections from the *Gazette,* holos of her parents as Smasher and Shockwave saving the day, and repositions the one of her mother lifting a car. That accidentally activates the news-holo clip. Jess takes a moment to watch her mother set the car aside and retrieve an injured cat. Wilton Lysander steps into the frame; his image flickers on the edge of the projection. "And Smasher once again shows that big muscles also come with a big heart—"

Jess switches it off, and the holo freezes again on her mother's determined face and on her biceps bulging in the sleeves of her Smasher outfit. As Jess tidies the room she looks at all the memorabilia and the special desktop with the League logo on it.

Jess taps a numeric pattern on a hidden keypad on the shelf. The bookshelf beeps and revolves, hiding all the superhero memorabilia. The new bookshelf displays holos of the Trans on various vacations. There's one holo of a young Claudia carrying a five-year-old Jess on her back, and the projection is frozen on the two of them laughing. Jess flicks it; the image comes to life: Claudia racing forward, holding Jess by the knees. "C'mon, Jessie Bessie, let's fly!" the miniature Claudia giggles.

A bitter pang sweeps through Jess, but she takes a deep breath. No time for feeling sorry about her powers now; she's got a job interview.

Jess syncs her DED to the desktop projector and brings up the video application. She checks to make sure everything looks good: the background, the lighting, and fiddles with the camera to get the best angle and distance. Jess looks at the T-shirt she threw on this morning, a hilarious graphic tee that reads "Master Mischief Was Right About the Cheese." The shirt references an incident a few years ago when the villain drove her parents round the bend by stealing all the cheese products from every single Andover grocery store. A video of her dad ranting about what an awful crime this was went viral, but it turned out the cheese had been infected by a strain of mold that was deadly. Mischief had done something kind of heroic.

Jess shakes off the thoughts of the weirdness of hero-villain dynamics when the *boopbeepboopbeep* sound announces her video call from Monroe Industries.

Jess waves at *accept call* on the display and stands in front of the bookshelf, smiling. "Hello?"

The screen is dark.

A distorted electronic voice speaks. "Applicant number eighty-seven, Jessica Tran. High school junior, no listed talents or extracurricular activities."

"*Excuse* me," Jess says.

She can make out a blurry distortion, like someone moving in front of the camera; possibly a silhouette of a person sitting, but she can't be sure.

The electronic voice warbles. *What's with this company? They're supposed to be a leader in the technology and they can't seem to get their holocam to work. Well, the noise does sound like laughter. Maybe it's a good sign?*

"I like your shirt," the figure says.

"Um, thank you." Jess pulls on her shirt. She should have changed, but she wasted too much time messing with the camera and the background. It seems to be okay, though, if the interviewer likes the slogan.

"All right, I decided, I'm hiring you," the figure says.

"Wait, what?"

"Yes, good."

The questions spill out of Jess' mouth. "What's your name? What division will I be working for? Will I get to see the robots? I should tell you, the job description was super-vague and that I am probably not at all qualified to do any technical stuff. I made something explode in chemistry last year."

There's some electronic whizzing in the background, and Jess thinks she sees a spark or two as the person—robot? Person controlling a robot? An android with a new type of artificial intelligence? "You can call me M, for a start."

"Only if I get to be Bond," Jess says with a snort, and then realizes she's not supposed to know who Bond is. Referring to contraband vintage media is definitely not the way to look professional. Fortunately, the figure doesn't respond or react, and Jess exhales in relief. "M it is," she says quickly.

"Regarding the other questions, the division you'll be working for is going to require the utmost discretion. I will tell you more, but you need to sign a non-disclosure agreement first," M says.

"You may have heard that Monroe Industries has had some financial setbacks recently."

Jess knows some trade weirdness is going on in New Bright City, but mostly the news has been about Captain Orion's recent battle with Dynamite. Her mom and dad couldn't stop watching the newsholos for a week, keeping an eye on the ongoing conflict. It was the talk of the town. There was even a running commentary on Captain Orion's outfit and hairstyle and how every day she'd come to the battle with a new look.

"That why you're hiring high school students?"

"Maybe. But you are very qualified! You didn't have any typos in your resume," M says. "And you didn't freak out with the..."

There's a blurry gesture that Jess takes to mean the Darth Vader thing they've got going on.

She interrupts. "... totally weird interview setup? You know it's odd, considering you're a multi-billion credit industry."

"Yeah, well, it was at your convenience! So you didn't have to come into the office. We're downtown; it can be difficult for a high school student. We don't discriminate based on whether or not you have reliable transportation," M says. "Okay, well, if you want to think about it, or if you want to visit me at the office, I'll answer any questions you want." M gives a downtown address and Jess makes a show of dutifully writing it down.

Something electronic sparks behind M, and M topples over with a metallic clank. Jess can hear some cursing and then the call ends.

Jess snorts and then turns off the desktop projector, unsyncing her DED. She goes back to her room, shaking her head. A job would have been cool, but this seems like a joke.

Maybe she should just apply to that sandwich shop downtown. At least she'll get discounted sandwiches. And it wouldn't really be that impressive on her college resume, but maybe if she got to be like a manager. If she worked steady hours, wouldn't that show she was responsible?

Jess starts works on an outline for her history paper on the causes of the third world war. She opens a new browser to look up more information about the nuclear meltdown sites and possibly some images, and then mooches around on the Net and reads up on the latest comic book news. Her bedroom wall is covered in projections—Jess' outline, her history notes from class, articles about the Disasters—but most of the holos are images of Captain Orion and Jess' favorite excerpts from the latest comic.

Her DED chimes with a new message notification.

To: Jessica Tran
From: M, Monroe Industries

Please disregard the interruption during our video interview; we had an electronic malfunction. Our company would be pleased to hire you for our office intern position. We are located at 3529 Seventh Street. Pay starts at twenty-five credits an hour, starting Monday.

-M

Attached is a short list of office duties, not much more detailed than in the job listing: filing, sorting, answering phone calls, organizing. There's also an "as needed" clause for "various office duties."

Jess rereads the email. Her heart skips a beat when she sees the pay rate. That's way more than double minimum wage. And Jess thought getting nine credits an hour at the sandwich shop would have been great.

Looking up Monroe Industries again, she searches "experimental divisions" and then blinks. She finds many holopages; apparently there's a whole bunch of archiving for old projects that needs to be done, and there's a list of other mundane duties that anyone can do.

"Strange," Jess mutters. She swears they didn't have this section of the site yesterday. Maybe she just didn't see it before.

Still, the job is worth checking out, and M did say they would answer any questions. Showing up for the first day isn't committing to anything if she hasn't signed any paperwork. Jess just wants to see what this is about.

Jess sets down her stylus, shuts the textbook browser, and closes the outline for her paper. She yawns, and then notices a new message blinking.

From: Emma 8:42pm
hey how'd the interview go?

To: Emma 8:43pm
got the job! it's kinda weird tho? the interviewer didn't show their face

From Emma 8:45pm
bad hair day

Jess laughs; that's not really a reasonable explanation. But they are a tech company. Maybe they were testing something. She chats with Emma and her worry lifts as Emma makes a joke out of the entire thing. She's doesn't think it's that weird that the interviewer wasn't visible on the video call. Emma has a good idea about asking Jess' mom to investigate Monroe Industries.

Li Hua Chen, now Tran, had been a journalist before she took on real estate as her "official cover." Apparently when the Heroes' League of Heroes signed her on as Smasher there were already enough people using "journalist" as a cover. Jess thinks it was a waste; her mother is a great writer and definitely still has the investigative chops to figure out if M is using Monroe Industries as a front.

"Hey, Mom?" Jess finds her mom in the study, where she's got a communication link set up on her DED, and is apparently talking to Victor while he's out on patrol.

"All right, see you soon," Li Hua says into her wrist with a note of exasperation in her voice.

"Dad find something to do?" Jess asks.

Her mother shakes her head. "Apparently he tried to stop a robbery, but it was actually the owners of the house who had locked themselves out."

Jess can picture it: her dad, in full Shockwave gear, giving the supposed robbers a speech on honesty and integrity.

"Is he really embarrassed?"

"He's having a moment. Flying over to the other side of town, buying your favorite sponge cake. I think he feels bad for being too hard on you at dinner the other day, too." Li Hua's eyes soften a bit, and she stands up to pat Jess on the shoulder. They don't touch much; her family isn't big on physical affection. Li Hua's voice is sincere and even, as if she's thought about how to say this for a while. "We don't mean to come off that way, and we just want the best for you. And your brother doesn't mean—"

"It's fine, Mom." Jess pats her hand, wondering if her mother would be weirded out by a hug. She settles for an appreciative nod.

Her mother nods back, and Jess impulsively goes for the hug.

Li Hua strokes Jess' hair. "You know, if you don't get—"

"I applied for a job, and I actually got hired, but I wanted to see if you knew anything about the experimental divisions of Monroe Industries. It seemed kind of odd." Jess explains about the video interview and how strange the interview had been.

"Oh! That could have been the electronic firewall we have around the house. To prevent villains from hacking into our servers, you know. It's such a nice thing that the Associated League does for us, to protect our secret identities..."

Jess nods and listens for a while about the heroic agency and how amazing it is, and finally is able to duck free and head back to her room. Flashing lights shine from under Brendan's bedroom door, and Jess considers asking about them, but keeps walking.

An hour later into homework, her mom knocks on her door and pokes her head in before Jess can say anything. "Hey, Mei-Mei."

Jess bristles at the nickname. Her parents use it a lot, and she's the only one of their children that actually gets called the childhood nickname. She's not even the youngest—they didn't stop using it when Brendan was born, but he got to be Bren-Bren, so it's not *that* bad.

"I'm so proud of you for getting this internship, and with Monroe Industries too! The company does so well, nationally and overseas. It's a great start to be around all those amazing and talented people. The experimental division checks out, definitely. They've had a few projects in Crystal Springs and apparently now they're here." Li Hua smiles, her eyes alight.

"Thanks, Mom. I really appreciate it."

"Do you want me to take you shopping for work clothes?"

"Ah, they want me to start on Monday? And I have some clothes from debate team last year that still fit. I'll just wear one of those outfits." Jess smiles at her mother, who nods back and ducks out of her room, closing the door behind her.

THE WEEKEND IS SLOW; HER parents are called away to Las Vegas for an Associated League of Heroes meeting Saturday, and they expect it will run late. Jess is supposed to be watching Brendan; she wastes time flicking through the Net and idling through her homework, listening for any explosions from his room.

It's not until Jess looks up and notices that the sky outside her window is dark that everything seems to catch up to her, especially that sharp, aching hunger that comes from forgetting to eat. *Brendan must hungry too; lunch was so long ago. Ugh, it's almost eight o'clock.*

She sighs and goes to Brendan's room. "Hey, what do you want to do for food? There's some frozen dumplings I can make. Or some leftover rice from lunch that I can fry with eggs."

Wearing a pair of safety goggles on his head, Brendan opens the door. He scrunches his face. "Mom and Dad leave you any credits?"

"For an emergency," Jess says, rolling her eyes. There's plenty of food in the house.

Brendan raises his eyebrows. "What about Bells' restaurant? I like the food there."

Jess' stomach grumbles; Creole food does sound amazing right now. She hasn't eaten since lunch and was too focused on her research to snack. It's a great idea, and wouldn't cost too much. Bells *is* on shift today, and the Broussards love her. And seeing Brendan flail over Bells is always entertaining.

Jess conjures up that image and snickers. "Okay. Do you need like, an hour to change?"

Two spots of color appear high on Brendan's cheeks. "What? No. I'm ready, just—"

Grumbling, he closes the door, and Jess laughs to herself. She flicks through her notifications on her DED until the door opens again. Brendan has changed into a clean T-shirt and jeans, and there's some gunk in his hair. It takes a moment for Jess to realize it's a temporary hair product, and there are clunky red streaks in his hair.

She grins but doesn't say anything.

The minivan takes forever to boot up as usual, and it also tells them, "You have arrived at your destination," when they're still two blocks away from the Broussard family restaurant. Jess and Brendan get out of the car and walk; it's not as bad as the time the car almost took them to Las Vegas when they just wanted to go to the Andover Mall.

The Broussard's restaurant, Home Away from Home, is in an historical building, Art Deco reminiscent of twenty-first century roadside-diner architecture. The inside, however, is a riot of warm, friendly color, lush oranges and reds, a nod to the Broussard family's roots in Louisiana before they moved west after the Disasters.

Jess' stomach grumbles as a waitress passes by carrying a steaming plate of jambalaya; the rich aroma of the spices wafts decadently.

Brendan pulls her to a table in Bells' section, and it isn't long before Bells appears, with his bright hair—blue and orange today—tied neatly in a little ponytail at the back, and wearing an apron over his tank top and jeans.

"Hey," Jess says. "Little bro was hungry. Thought we'd come by and say hi."

"Of course," Bells says with a wink.

Brendan makes a high-pitched noise that could be a greeting.

"Like your hair, dude." Bells smiles at Brendan and then flicks off the holo projected on the table. "The usual?"

"Yes, please," Jess says in the wake of Brendan's stunned stupor. She and Bells share amused looks and Bells heads off, chuckling to himself.

"Shut up," Brendan mutters.

"Didn't say anything."

Their food arrives quickly: the jambalaya special for Jess and red beans and rice topped with a heap of green onions for Brendan. Bells comes back with a generous chunk of cornbread for them to share and sits down, knocking Jess' shoulder companionably before he has to get up and fetch things for other tables.

Jess savors the way the textures and flavors come together on her tongue: the crunch of the green peppers and the vibrant flavor of the soft rice contrasting with the eggplant and zucchini. She drinks a sip of water and dives back in for more of the delicious spicy dish. The Broussards have their own way of spicing the protein that makes their "sausage," and it tastes good, almost passes for meat.

The vegetables are fresh and delicious, and Jess settles back in her seat with a happy sigh. She waves at the open window to the kitchen where she can see Bells' older brother Simon working at the grill, and he gives her a jaunty wave.

"How's everything tasting?" Simon calls.

"Delicious, as always," Jess says back.

"Home grown and organic, can't go wrong with that," Simon says, waving a pair of tongs at her. The Broussards have their own greenhouse where they grow all their produce despite the Collective guarantee that crops are stable and will continue to be stable. Bells' great-grandparents survived the Disasters because a combination of paranoia and self-sufficiency led them to stockpile supplies. They're still quite suspicious about the government. Bells and his siblings think that their dad's rants about privacy and government meddling in farm management are silly, but they work the greenhouse and the restaurant anyway.

"I like having fresh vegetables," Bells said the first time Jess asked about it. "I don't believe in all the theories my dad has about the government, but everybody's got to have a hobby, right?"

And all of Andover adores the Broussards' "hobby." Home Away from Home has been a beloved restaurant for years and was even featured in a newsholo feature in New Bright City.

Brendan polishes off his dish with a happy sigh, stuffs a chunk of cornbread in his mouth, and mumbles something about winning prizes before he ambles over to the crane game machine in the corner.

Jess watches him as he keeps swiping his DED for attempt after attempt at winning a stuffed animal.

The dinner rush is over; they're the only ones left in the restaurant. Bells sits down next to her, chuckling. "You wanna tell him that machine hasn't given up a prize for anyone in ten years?"

Jess leans back. "Nah." She pokes Bells' shoulders playfully, surprised at the firmness of the muscle. "You've been working out?"

"Huh? Yeah, my brother was complaining that he didn't have anyone to do weights with." Bells shrugs.

Something else is different, too, something that Jess can't quite place. His tank top is well-fitted, stretched over his chest—

"Oh, dude," Jess says, nudging him with her hip. "It's really late. You've been wearing your binder all day. Feeling okay?"

Bells blinks. "Oh. Yeah, I'm good. Took a break after school." He steals a bite of cornbread, talking as he chews. "Hey, first day of your new job is tomorrow, right? Downtown?"

"Mmm."

"Not really a nice area. Are you driving?"

"Bus from school, and then walking," Jess says. "Monroe Industries is in the industrial part. It's not that bad, really."

Bells furrows his eyebrows.

"Don't worry," Jess says. "It'll be fine."

MONDAY AFTER SCHOOL, JESS TAKES the school bus to Old Andover and transfers to a city bus. Bells gives her a new canister of pepper spray, just in case. It might be overkill, especially with her dad flying around looking for any excuse to help anyone, but she takes it.

The bus is crowded, but Jess manages to get a seat next to a window. The glass pane vibrates as she leans against it and the bus rumbles as it moves through the colorful streets of Andover. From an advertisement on a wall for Eversparkle Teeth Whitening, Captain Orion's gleaming smile beams at the bus riders. A video projection at the front of the bus shows a news-holo from New Bright City. Apparently the Heroes' League has had another success: They found a Villain's Guild base and destroyed it.

When Jess transfers to go downtown, the new bus is so crowded with people on their way home from work, she has to stand. Everyone is in business attire and looking pointedly at their DEDS or talking to each other about things like stocks and portfolios and quarterly returns. Jess is painfully aware of how young she is. Her shirtsleeves don't quite extend to her wrists; after a growth spurt last summer, her debate clothes don't fit as well as she thought. She feels as if she's playing dress-up.

Jess sways as the bus turns and almost misses her stop. She jerks to attention when she sees the Monroe building at the end of the block.

She holds the straps of her backpack so it doesn't bounce as she strides quickly—she's going to need to reschedule with M in the future if taking the bus from school is going to take this long.

A bunch of people loiter about the street; some of them look unsavory. It's not that this area is bad, but downtown is where a lot of people end up. Even though World War III was long ago, there are always conflicts abroad that involve the Collective. Jess doesn't know too much except that there are always veterans on the streets without many resources. There are a lot of drugs moving in this area, too, but no one ever talks about that.

Jess is almost there when she's taken aback by a headful of long, flowing red-gold curls next to her, almost the color of Abby's hair, but too bright to be realistic.

The woman walking alongside her is incredibly tall, with a long aquiline nose and wearing a sleek green dress. She smiles at Jess and slows her pace to match Jess' own, and Jess nods, somewhat reassured by the kindness.

"There is a man following you," the woman says, and Jess starts.

"Oh."

"I can walk with you. Where are you going?"

"Just to the end of the block," Jess says.

They fall into stride. The woman is imposing, and familiar, but she can't place how. Jess is struck by her blue, blue eyes; a crystal color that she didn't think was possible.

At the Monroe building, Jess nods at the woman. "Thank you." The woman nods back, smiles, and strides down the street, her striking copper curls bouncing.

Jess watches her and then kicks herself for not asking whether her hair was natural or dyed. That was the kind of thing Bells would appreciate.

She shakes herself and straightens her shirt collar and turns to face the towering height of the office building. It stretches to the sky, large and imposing, shining in the afternoon sun. On the top floor, Jess can make out the huge letters spelling out MONROE. Shadows bustle about, and she can see the whizzing of elevators through the glass walls as people go about their business.

Jess squares her shoulders and pushes open the door. The air conditioning is cool against her skin. The reception area is bare, except for a potted bird of paradise plant in the corner and some leather chairs. An empty desk bars the way to a long hallway. Beyond that, a few employees walk around in a central lobby, presumably heading for elevators and their own workspaces.

"Hello?" Jess asks. She brushes down her now slightly wrinkled slacks and the prim button up that's a little too tight around the shoulders. Looking nervously at her reflection in the sleek surface of the wall, she fiddles with the collar a bit more. At least she didn't attempt to wear heels; that would have been a nightmare. Jess has no sense of balance whatsoever.

"Welcome to Monroe Industries. How can I help you?" A gleaming silver orb hovers in front of Jess. Its front panel scans Jess' face. "Tours are over for the day. If you like, I can provide you a list of times they will be available this week."

The smooth, electronic voice is the same one installed in all vehicle computers. Jess rolls her eyes. She likes the old-school MonRobots, from before they started talking. This one seems to have an attitude.

"Actually, I'm here for an internship—"

A sharp clack of heels echoes from down the hall, and then Abby Jones skids across the tiled floor and stumbles over her feet as she dashes into the entryway. "It's all right, I'll take it from here," she says, and presses something into the robot's back panel.

The orb cheeps and goes back to the desk, hovering in standby.

Unlike Jess, who is more than a bit rumpled after that bus ride, Abby looks impeccable in a black blazer, blouse, and pencil skirt combo. She's even wearing a bit of makeup; her pink lips stand out against her skin, and her bright red hair is swept up in a glamorous French roll.

"Jess Tran!" Abby says. She smiles, holding her hand out. "Hi, I'm Abigail, but call me Abby, everyone does. We go to the same high school, but I don't think we've met."

"Hi, yeah, um, yeah, I know you," Jess says. "You work here too?" She cringes at the question, but at least her self-preservation kicked in before she asked *you know my name?* Then again, if Abby works here, she must have been expecting Jess, so that look of recognition wasn't about knowing Jess from school; it was work.

Jess has never so much as talked to Abby before, but Emma, who is on the junior varsity volleyball team, hardly ever stops talking about the varsity members she admires and, of course, their team captain. Abby led the volleyball team on a winning streak last year and so far is continuing that this year. In AP English, the one class Jess shares with her, Abby has no problem mouthing off to Ms. Rhinehart, and she earns nothing more than an amused laugh.

She was on student council last year, and was supposedly a shoo-in for president this year, but apparently she quit the student council for some reason.

"Yup, I'm in the same experimental division as you," Abby says, tucking an errant strand of red hair behind her ear. "They told me to see if you were here this afternoon. Weren't sure if you'd be here or not."

"*Ah.* Well, I wasn't sure if the department was an actual part of the company, because the internship seemed made up, but apparently my mo—the Net seems to think you guys are a real thing."

"Definitely real," Abby says with a smile. She hands Jess a folder. "Here's all the paperwork you'll need for tax purposes and to make it official. I'll show you to the lab where we'll be working and then I'll go get M for you."

She leads Jess down the hallway; her pencil skirt rustles, and Jess blushes and tries to ignore how well it fits her. Jess tries to remember if she saw Abby wearing that outfit at school today. She must have changed into it before she started work. She probably hadn't taken the bus, either. Jess has seen Abby's sleek driver-operated Mercedes, which Abby used to give Emma and the other girls rides home after volleyball practice. Emma did mention at lunch today that Abby quit the team; Jess wonders if she quit to make more time for her internship.

Abby's stylish black button-up and skirt combination makes Jess' work outfit look dull, and she hopes that M or whoever else works here isn't going to judge her on her lack of style.

They pass by a few other employees, but the lobby is mostly populated by MonRobots flying or whizzing around the floor. They're variations that Jess hasn't seen, models that probably aren't out yet.

Abby waves her hand at a clear glass elevator and the doors open. Jess stares at the numerous buttons for all thirty-eight floors and an official looking keypad at the top; it must be motion activated because Abby just waves her hand and a small button labeled "B7" lights up.

The elevator doors close, and Jess tries not to be nervous, being in a small, enclosed space with her crush. *Oh gosh, her hair looks especially nice. Are we going to work together?* Jess isn't sure she can handle it.

Abby smells nice too, like warm cinnamon and sugar on a cold winter's day. *That's not even a smell. Abby smells like a cookie fresh out of the oven, made with a dash of nutmeg. Or maybe like gingerbread.*

Great, now she's hungry.

Jess notices they're dropping floors at an alarmingly fast pace. She wants to ask about the experimental division and what's expected of her, but she's too tongue-tied.

Finally the elevator comes to a stop, and Abby presses a combination onto the keypad before the doors open again.

"Okay, here we are!"

The floor is well lit, but it lacks the hustle and bustle of people and robots moving everywhere as on the floors they passed. Jess' first impression is that the place is a *mess.* A single white reception desk is emblazoned with the luminous text: *EXPERIMENTAL DIVISION.* The desk and the chair behind it are the same sleek, modern furniture as in the lobby, but everything else is haphazardly thrown together: tables and benches and pieces of scrap metal.

Behind the reception area, Jess can see a huge open space filled with boxes and electronic paraphernalia. There's a dedicated area for computer consoles and a raised table covered in tools. In the distance is the sound of drilling, and desktop projectors are scattered everywhere, projecting different holos intermittently.

Abby leads her down a hallway to the right, and Jess peers at the line of doors, wondering who else works here. They stop at an open door at the end, and Abby gestures inside with a hopeful smile. The office also has modern furniture, which contrasts with the heaps of dusty boxes overflowing with paper files.

"Sorry about the mess," Abby says. "We just relocated from New Bright City. Here, sit down. M will be with you in a minute." Abby's heels tap out a quick beat as she dashes down the hallway.

What's the rush, Jess wonders, as she gazes around the office. It's not decorated, and everything appears to have been placed in a hurry, as if they haven't had time to move in properly.

A new desktop projector hums on the glass desk. A few DED chips are laid out, but other than that, everything seems to be dated. Paper files were almost obsolete even in the twenty-first century. Is it a security thing? *Paper isn't hackable,* Jess muses.

Jess can't hear any other people on the floor. Maybe this room is soundproofed. No, she definitely heard Abby walk down the hallway.

The boxes are labeled in an untidy scrawl with various—codes? One is labeled "January attempts and failures"; there are more of those for each month, and also a very slim file labeled "successes" and it's just for the year.

Jess flips open one of the files from the "successes" folder.

What?

This doesn't look like a financial report or like anything she would expect from a robotics manufacturer. There aren't designs or anything MonRobot-related. This looks like headlines reporting a string of robberies, all for—

Jess gasps. "Master Mischief."

"I hope that won't be a problem," comes the electronic voice, and why, *why* hadn't Jess put it together earlier?

His eyes glowing, he stands in the doorway. Master Mischief's mechanical armor clanks as he steps into the room. The faded "M M" logo is blistered in purple paint on his chest.

Jess' brain stutters. *Has he figured out her parents' secret identity? Is this is a kidnapping? A ruse to draw her parents out?* She steps back and grabs for the pepper spray in her backpack, but that'll be little help. Mischief is blocking the only exit.

He's not an A-class villain, but Jess has never met any villain in the flesh. Despite all the funny T-shirts and silly videos of Mischief, and despite Jess' arguments that some of what he does isn't villainous at all, it's hard to shake off years and years of seeing villains do terrible and destructive things in the news.

And now a villain stands in front of her; his electronic suit crackles with power.

Mischief can manipulate tech, but what is he's doing here, in the heart of Monroe Industries? He's certainly in his element. Anything electronic that isn't too complicated, he can manipulate and control for a limited time. Jess has seen him direct cars to rebel against their owners and reprogram traffic lights and signs and computers.

Jess swallows and stands her ground. *He's silly. He mostly does harmless pranks. He's ridiculous, not scary.*

But it's one thing to casually joke about villains and another to see one in person.

"I know we were deliberately vague in the job listing and interview, but I hope you understand why we needed the utmost discretion," Mischief says. The voice is a little different than what she remembers, but that could be her imagination. It's more electronic—is that a thing?

"Master Mischief?" Jess asks.

Mischief tilts his head; he almost fills the doorframe. But Mischief is quite a few inches shorter than Mistress Mischief, and the difference is always exaggerated in the comics.

He looks taller than Jess, and the suit—she can see black fabric at the knees under the metal armor, as if it doesn't quite fit. And the logo is *old,* too; this version of the suit hasn't been seen for at least a year. "What's going on here?" Jess asks. "Why do you have Master Mischief's mecha-suit?"

"Ah, I see you figured that out. I'm M, by the way. Nice to meet you."

"Who are you?" Jess demands. "Do you actually work for Monroe Industries?"

"I'm not Master Mischief, that's for sure. But yes, he works for Monroe Industries, and I do too. I was his assistant—am his assistant. He's busy at the moment, and I'm running his lab in the interim." M folds his arms and tilts his head and lights flicker without a discernible pattern on his helmet's front panel. "You can laugh now. Villains need jobs too."

Jess doesn't laugh. It makes sense, actually. Mischief's power of technological manipulation would be incredibly handy here; if his meta-powers weren't low-level he'd be a formidable and almost unstoppable villain. As it is, he can't use his powers very long before he has to recharge, just like her parents. "If you're his assistant, why don't you have your own suit? What do you do exactly? And is this internship with Monroe Industries or with you and Master Mischief?"

M shakes his head, and makes a noise that almost sounds like a laugh before it is garbled into electronic static.

"I'm wearing an old prototype of his suit because we've been incredibly busy working on other projects. New mecha-suits aren't a priority right now. And yes, you will be working for Monroe Industries, in a subsidiary with special interests. If that's something you're still interested in?" M asks.

"This isn't a kidnapping, is it?"

The panel on M's helmet blinks various shades of orange, and he throws up his hands. "No, no, absolutely not," M says. "We wouldn't kidnap you, do you—do you want to leave?"

"Why are you here? What's going on?"

"Why would we kidnap you? Monroe Industries isn't about hurting anyone. Neither is Master Mischief. We just like to cause a little mayhem, rob the rich, and generally mess with Shockwave and Smasher."

"Yeah, that much is true," Jess says. She knows the title "villain" is a slightly inaccurate moniker for someone who is just a glorified criminal in a mechanical suit, who for the most part just keeps her parents and their superpowers occupied. And, just as her parents, as C-class heroes, are only in the Associated League of Heroes but not in the Heroes' League of Heroes, the Mischiefs, as class C villains, are not in the United Villains Guild.

"You're here because you applied for the job. And I—I think I could trust you, you know. We just need a lot of help in this—secret experimental department."

M stands still, the lights on his face panel blinking at her. The rapid pattern almost looks... hopeful.

Jess steps forward. Her shoulders relax and her heart rate slows to normal as she unclenches her fists. She hadn't realized she'd been in a "ready" position to fight, even though her skills are poor and unpracticed. Li Hua had tried to train her in the Nán quán style she'd learned as a child from her own mother, but nothing beyond the basics stuck with Jess.

Her initial fear quickly gives way to curiosity; the so-called rivalry has always been a source of entertainment for Jess, and, she's sure, for many citizens of Andover.

With M standing there in front of her, Jess finds his suit garish, but not frightening. M is standing, shoulders hunched slightly, looking to Jess for a response—it seems as if he's nervous.

Working for Master Mischief? This would be an act of sheer rebellion. Her parents would be livid if they ever found out.

And it would be hilarious.

And so much more interesting than working at the sandwich shop.

"I'm in," Jess says.

M's suit makes a gleeful whirring noise.

THE FIRST AFTERNOON IS SPENT working out a schedule with M. Jess plans to work three days a week after school for two hours, and then five hours on Saturday. She doesn't have any clubs or sports to interfere with that schedule and finds herself looking forward to work.

On paper, Jess doesn't seem to be the brightest of students, but that doesn't mean she isn't intelligent. She just gets nervous when taking tests, what with all those bubbles and the whole thing being timed, and she's left-handed, so essay questions make her smudge graphite all over her fingers.

Unfortunately, Andover Heights High School is all about standardized tests: pass this test to get into this class; take all the approved tracks for your career of interest; finish all these prerequisites to apply to this college. The Collective provides many career options; it's just that she wants to be a hero. A proper one, like Captain Orion.

So maybe Jess can't get into the training program because she has no superpowers. She just needs a different goal. But she's working with Master Mischief's company now, and she can learn more about their tech and have access to their resources. If she's good at her job, she can get into a great college, and maybe she can be CEO of a company like Monroe Industries one day. Or have a job here, one that doesn't have to do with robots.

Jess knows she's good at learning. When she finds something interesting, she throws herself wholeheartedly into it. She's really good at research papers.

It's going to be great.

Afterward, Jess takes the bus home. Out the window the streetlights flicker. Excitement flutters in her heart.

A COLD PLATE OF SPAGHETTI waits for her when she gets home. She can hear her mom in her office, writing away and cursing loudly at her characters, and from upstairs come the noises of Brendan's video games, or experiments. She can never tell. "How was your first day at your job, Mei-Mei?" Li Hua asks as she passes by the office door.

"Great. I worked out a schedule so I'll be there after school and Saturdays. Where's Dad?"

"Still patrolling downtown." Li Hua sighs. She yawns and stretches, and then puts the notes on her desk aside.

"How's your new novel coming along?" Her mother has been trying to break out of writing the backstory for the Smasher and Shockwave comics and to tell her own stories for a while. She's extremely interested in detective noir fiction, set in Old America.

"It's going pretty well. I just added a character whose husband lost his job."

Jess laughs. "You tell Dad that?"

"Maybe I will. I'm hoping he'll throw his focus onto something else. Actually focus on real estate, I don't know."

Jess can't help a grin that spreads from ear to ear. "I don't think Master Mischief or Mistress Mischief is really gone. Who knows? Maybe they're taking a break. Building up to something big. Biding their time. They're still around."

"Don't you guys have any organization at all?" Jess curses as she trips over a box, toppling forward. She winces, trying to catch her balance.

There's a heavy *flop* as something is dropped behind her and she hears the whir of a mechanical suit.

M catches Jess before she hits the floor. Jess expects the metal to be cold, but the suit is pleasantly warm, with a thrum of electronics. They're both suspended in the air for a few seconds before M lands neatly on the ground and the thrusters turn off.

"Are you okay?" M asks, the electronic voice sounding a lot less electronic than any time Jess has heard it.

"I'm good, it's kind of a walking hazard, all these boxes."

"I'm not good with paperwork," M says, and the voice is back to the even electronic cadence Jess remembers. She imagines M flying around the office in the mecha-suit, dropping paperwork everywhere, trying to hold files in the clunky hands of the suit.

Jess laughs, and M's panel flickers in pink and yellow. *Do the colors these correspond to mood?* She should start keeping a log of what the colors might mean.

After a moment of studying M's helmet, Jess realizes she's still being held. "You can put me down now." she says.

The panel lights blink white, and then M sets her down gently and waits for her to stand upright before moving back.

"Thank you. I did mean to say thanks first," Jess says. "Could have brained my head on that other box, but you saved me. My hero."

M laughs. "I don't think I'm anything of the sort, not here at least."

Jess grins. She doesn't try to be funny often; it's better to leave that to Bells and sometimes Emma. "You're not exactly a villain, are you? I mean, you work for Master Mischief, and you're… sorry, my friend Bells would probably get me for not asking sooner, but um, what are your pronouns?"

"Oh! Sorry, I—I forget that I look like a robot."

"No, not really. I mean, the suit's really cool—and it *is* Master Mischief's suit, right, but I want to make sure I don't misgender you or anything."

"She and hers are fine, thanks for asking," M says. "We should probably keep that between us, though, because some of the other employees here—um, well, I'm trying to take care of some stuff for Master Mischief in the interim, and so he… asked me to work some things out in his place. So it's important that some people think I'm him."

The secret sends a thrill through Jess at being trusted with this information. "Ah, so you're pretending to be your boss—"

"At his request!" M sounds indignant, and the electronic voice skips and suddenly it sounds much younger.

"Wait, are you my age? Oh my God, I thought you were a senior employee, wearing the mecha-suit and everything! Please tell me you're not an intern."

"I'm a *senior* intern. And I wear the suit because I need to make sure it stays functional. I have a job to do. You just… Yeah, I'm gonna get more boxes."

M flies off in a hurry, leaving Jess standing there puzzled. She's just getting back to work on the file system she's created when M starts bringing in box after box. The room smells strongly of dust and rocket fuel.

Jess recalls that Master Mischief used his powers to operate the mecha-suit—was this one modified so a person without abilities could use it? It does seem a bit unwieldy to walk in. But really, is it necessary to fly *inside* the building?

The mechanical suit clanks stiffly as she sets down another box.

"Why are you wearing that thing anyway?" Jess asks. "It's not like you're gonna be doing battle with anyone in here."

"Upkeep. And it's helpful. For protection, you know, in case—"

"Right, because I'm super-powerful and dangerous." Jess waves her hands in a mock imitation of her father manipulating magnetic fields. It's his standard pose for all his press stuff.

M must not get the reference because she just stands there with one green light blinking, watching Jess flail about, until Jess realizes how absurd she must look and stops.

M's visor panel is all green now. The lights keep blinking.

"Are you laughing at me?" Jess asks.

M shakes her head, and the panel lights are still green.

Jess snorts. "Fine, you can just say it; I know I look ridiculous. You're the one who didn't stop me."

"Maybe I found it entertaining," M says.

"Well, we're both interns and on the same level. I think it's perfectly reasonable to tell me why you have to wear the suit.

It can't just be a pretending-to-be-the-boss thing because this whole experimental lab is just you, me, and Abby." Jess is talking to herself more than to the robot, but she follows the idea until she finds the next most logical reason. "It's a secret identity thing, isn't it?"

"You could say that."

"But you already told me you're pretending to be Master Mischief. And for Abby too, I'm guessing, since she's not freaking out that you're not the actual Master Mischief. Where is Abby, anyway? She could be helping me with this."

A few lights on M's panel blink blue, and then yellow. "She's busy. In her own office. Doing some important letter-writing."

Jess laughs. Abby, who she knows is in all AP classes, who writes essays on the wrong topic in English class and still gets an A because of her "impeccable style" and being "irreverent," *that* Abby is doing secretarial work? While Jess is being trusted to handle all these old files and secrets?

She sets down an old box, sending dust through the air, and laughs until the laugh turns into a cough.

"What's so funny about that?" M demands.

"I dunno. It's *Abby Jones*!"

M's suit is silent, and Jess realizes unless she also goes to AHHS, she has no idea what this means.

Trying to find the words describe Abby, Jess waves her hands. "We go to school together. That girl, I swear, would never be satisfied with just letter-writing. Unless it's like, epic scale change-the-world letter-writing. I dunno. She's like..." Jess sighs, unable to explain the amazing combination of idealism and determination that is Abby. "Why don't you have me do the letter-writing and

Abby do all this important stuff? I mean, you hired her, you know what she's good at, right?"

Green, pink, and white lights flicker across the entire visor panel. Jess isn't sure what that means. Every time she's seen M, the panel has been blank, just a sleek black metal casing, mirroring the surroundings. It's blinked a few colored lights before, but today's the first time she's seen the whole panel light up. *What does it mean?*

"That's an interestingly take on Miss Jones," M says finally.

Jess shrugs. "I don't know her that well; we just have the one class together." She looks at the box, grateful that Emma and Bells aren't here to tease her about her crush. It had been a thing freshman year when Emma first got onto the JV volleyball team and she and Bells would go watch all of the games.

Jess didn't understand the sport, and she would clap and cheer whenever Bells did, but her attention had always wandered to the other side of the gym, where the varsity team was playing. Abby was captivating. She was demanding, angry, so vibrant and full of life. The one freshman on a team full of juniors and seniors, she somehow bypassed all of them in energy. She took toss after toss, spiking and standing tall at the net, yelling at the other team. Abby was formidable and beautiful and Jess could not look away.

It was a thing. And it kind of still is. Jess never planned on acting on it; she's not the kind of person who would just go right up to someone and ask them out. Plus, she doesn't know if Abby is into girls, and asking just seems rude.

Jess deftly changes the subject. "Anyway, where's Master Mischief? Or Mistress Mischief? I'd love to meet them. I like how both their outfits don't really match but they're complimentary, you know? But my—I mean, you know Shocker and Shockwave, they have the whole coordinated colors and everything. Everyone knows they're a couple so it's not really necessary and it's super-cheesy. But yeah, the Mischiefs are really cool. Are they around?"

"It's not of import," M snaps. She walks to the other side of the room, opens a box, and starts sorting.

Jess guesses even though she's working in the secret lab, she's still probably not important enough to meet the Mischiefs themselves. Mistress Mischief is telekinetic and, with Master Mischief's technology manipulation, they could be quite a formidable team if their power class wasn't so low.

It takes ages for Jess to sort through the files, but her diligent perseverance and tendency to obsession pays off; she creates a cohesive file of robbery successes, and even starts an electronic log of all the valuable items Mischief wants to steal.

In the background, M clinks and clanks, bringing more and more boxes, and sometimes taking things away.

"I don't know what's the point of stealing this trophy," Jess says, holding a fat file filled with details on all the times Mischief has stolen the large silver cup and her parents have retrieved it and put it back in the museum. She stares at the picture; what is it for? The photograph of it doesn't say what it is. It took an entire group of those men—a sports team—to lift it into the air. Jess has no idea why it looks as if knives are strapped to the men's feet. She flips through the current plan to steal it and the protection details once it is stolen. "Whenever the Mischiefs steal this thing, either Shockwave or Smasher is just gonna steal it back."

"I know, right? It's the stupidest thing to fight over," M says, giggling.

The visor on M's mechanical suit is dark, but green and blue lights flash and then the electronic voice is back, noticeably deeper. "I mean, yeah, I tell Master Mischief that all the time."

"Okay, I made a search system where you can just look up the plan by date or location or object focus. And I'm gonna update everything that's in this room."

"Perfect," M says.

Jess yawns. "Hey, can I take a quick break?"

"Sure."

"Just gonna ask Abby if she remembers how many chapters of *The Awakening* we're supposed to read for English." Jess gets to her feet.

"Oh, okay," M says, "You do that. I'm just… off to the bathroom."

Jess snorts. "Must be difficult with the suit."

"You have no idea."

Jess takes her time as she walks down the hallway, checking the rest of the offices. They're empty aside from one office with two strange-looking robots cheeping at each other. When Jess opened the door, they both made high-pitched noises, so she just closed it. She couldn't tell what they were doing, hovering over a metal frame—possibly building another mecha-suit?

There aren't many employees, but because this is Master Mischief's secret lab within Monroe Industries, that does makes sense. The criminal mastermind could have a whole crew working away to help plan his elaborate pranks.

But using just robots makes sense, too. The two robots down the hall didn't look like any MonRobots Jess has ever seen.

Experimental division, Jess reminds herself.

She walks through the main lab to the elevator, but the receptionist's desk is empty. "Abby?" Jess calls out.

Abby's desktop projector scrolls a line of text, which reads: "Running an errand on the seventh floor, be right back!"

"Hm."

She plops down in Abby's swivel chair, spins about playfully and hums. She sits upright, curling a loose strand of hair behind her ear. What it's like to be Abby Jones, beautiful and put together all the time?

Footfalls echo down the hallway, and Jess jumps. Abby appears, sprinting.

Did she take the stairs?

She's not dressed in the stylish skirt-suit combo Jess has come to associate with her at work, but in what looks like a black fitted shirt and yoga pants with a funny-looking dot pattern running down the sides; her stockinged feet make soft noises against the tiled floor. Her hair isn't in a French braid or any other complicated style, but is pulled into a messy ponytail with strands of red curls escaping in a frizzy red cloud. Abby blushes and grabs a sweatshirt from her desk drawer.

"Hey," Abby says, her face flushed with exertion.

"Hi," Jess says. "Um." She's never seen Abby look anything other than picture-perfect; even at volleyball games her hair has always been done and her makeup simple but elegant.

It's strangely intimate that Abby is okay like this in front of Jess.

"I uh, I was working on a mechanical project for M, and my clothes got singed," Abby explains as she struggles to put her arm through her sweatshirt.

"Oh okay, neat. Mechanical project?"

Tendrils of smoke waft from Abby's hair in delicate spirals.

"Yeah, I'm, er, working on an experimental robotics project for the company," Abby says. "I used to work on the seventh floor in the main research department, but I've got my own projects I can focus on down here. I like it; it's quiet and being around the Mischiefs' business is great. I was just up there helping the team with a quick thing."

"Cool, I didn't know you were into robotics. I was kinda telling M you were wasted as the receptionist. Not that you couldn't be a receptionist if you wanted to, I mean, you're really talented and… ahhh…"

The bodysuit is skintight. Jess blushes, looking away from how fitted the workout clothes are on Abby and…

She's just gonna stop speaking now.

Abby pats her hair until all of the sparks are out. "Did you need me for something?"

Jess tries to get up and Abby's chair continues to spin until Jess grabs an armrest to stop it.

"Yeah, I, uh, I was super-daydreaming during English today and totally spaced out. Didn't pay attention at all. Did you take notes on Rhinehart's assignment for next week? And how many chapters we're reading tonight?"

"Sure. Ah, it's just chapter five. And I don't have the notes for next week with me, but I can message them to you later, if you want."

Jess grins. "Awesome."

She trudges back to her office, continues with the never-ending process of filing, and congratulates herself for a successful interaction with her crush. She whistles to herself.

M comes back twenty minutes later, suit clanging, with another box.

"Hey, M, are you like super-strict on the dress code here? Obviously, you're wearing a hunk of metal, and Abby's running around getting her suit caught on fire and now is wearing yoga gear," Jess says. "I mean, it would be super-simple if I just came to work in the clothes I was already wearing for school."

"Sure, you can wear whatever you want." M waves to the empty lab around them. "No one will care."

They work in silence for until Jess' curiosity gets the better of her. *How old is M, anyway? Is she another high school student, like her and Abby? Has she worked for the Mischiefs for a long time? Does she know them personally?*

"You know, I won't tell anyone who you are," Jess says slowly, smiling. She looks up at M, at her face panel, hoping she looks sincere. "I mean, you already had me sign a nondisclosure agreement about the company and all the supervillain stuff. And I'm sure Mischief would find a way of keeping me quiet anyway."

M stands up. "That's not really the issue. I'll leave you to your work." She scoots backward, exits abruptly, and clanks down the hallway.

"Okay then," Jess says, eyebrows raised. She thought that she and M were getting along pretty well. She guesses the question is too personal.

At lunch the next day, Jess takes a bite of her peanut-butter-and-jelly sandwich and promptly spits the thing back out. "Ugh, it's still frozen inside!"

Bells nudges his container of carrots and celery sticks toward Jess. "You can have half my sandwich if you want." Today his hair is bright pink and looks soft despite the product in it to get it to stand so high. Jess loves seeing Bell's looks. He enjoys bright colors in both his hair and outfits, and changes his hair about every week.

Jess has only tried to dye her hair once, with Bells' help, but her thick black hair refused to hold the color longer than a week.

Jess smiles, accepting the egg salad sandwich as Emma sits down next to them. She holds a lunch tray with a dismal offering—sad-looking protein nuggets and cold tater tots.

"So how has work been? Monroe Industries treating you well? Have you destroyed any robots yet?" Emma asks. She picks at her lunch until Bells pulls out another sandwich from his backpack and hands it to her.

"Oh yeah, no, it was great. It's just, boring office work. Like I said, I don't do any of the robotics stuff, I'm mostly in a file room, and their files are a mess because they moved, but yeah, it's cool. Abby Jones works there too."

Emma's eyebrows nearly reach her hair. "Abby? Wow. I wondered what happened. I mean, out of nowhere last week she just drops out of the volleyball team and Coach is like *Hey Robledo! Here's a new uniform!* I mean, I'm happy to be on varsity but I can't really replace her, you know. They just picked me because I was the best JV player, but the volleyball team still sucks without her."

"Aw, you're great, though, you have that awesome spike," Bells says.

Emma shakes her head. "Spiking is useless unless you have someone to set up the shot. And Abby was the best setter."

"Yeah." Jess takes a thoughtful bite out of Bells' sandwich.

Emma nudges Jess, then catches Bells' eye and both of them giggle.

"So..." Bells starts.

"So... what?"

"You still like her, right?" Emma teases.

"You guys are never letting that go, are you?" Jess tries to fight the hot blush rising on her cheeks, but she can't. It only gets worse when Bells and Emma start laughing. "Oh, come on, I never made fun of you for liking—what's-his-face all last year!"

Emma looks at Bells, and they both burst into giggles.

"Okay, maybe I lovingly joked about it with you, but that's different! The two of you crush on people all the time! I don't know how you do it. You just... like someone? Or you ask them out? Or then it goes away? Or you like someone else? But like..."

Jess sets down the sandwich. "You both have dated people. I've never... I don't even..."

"It's okay; it's all out of love," Emma says, drawing Jess into a hug. "So, what's it like? Do you have intense sessions of eye contact? Do you work together?"

"No, not at all, like I barely even see her. We're on the same floor, but she does this complicated robotic stuff for the company, and I'm in the back sorting files for this side project." Jess stares at the sandwich and nudges a stray piece of egg back in.

"Aw. Well, you get to hang out with her, at least?" Bells says.

Jess shrugs. "Maybe. There's another girl, M, that works there too, she wears a mecha-suit. I've been hanging out with her mostly; she's pretty cool." The words are already out of her mouth before Jess remembers the NDA she signed, and then she runs through the clauses. It was mostly about Master Mischief, and secret patents, and stuff like that. Mecha-suits aren't extremely common, but Jess knows lots of hi-tech factories use them, so it's probably okay to talk about them.

"A person in a mecha-suit? Like Master Mischief used to clunk around in?"

"Kind of. Monroe Industries is a tech company, so it makes sense."

Bells laughs. "Oh gosh, remember when Mischief did that thing where he like, put soap all over the golf courses and then activated the sprinklers?"

Emma nods, then laughs. "I totally haven't seen that video in a while, it's great. Here, let me pull it up."

Emma pokes about on her DED until she finds the video: a grainy holo of the golf course, its perfectly manicured grass startling green against the red-gold landscape of the desert. Jess and Bells lean close to see the projection, and Jess can't help chuckling before she even sees it happen. Then there's movement, sprinklers going, bubbles floating everywhere, and in the midst of the chaos, Master Mischief strikes a dramatic pose. Then, he attempts to fly out of the bubbles, but the suit freezes up. He gets a foot high in the air before the suit clanks to the ground, when Smasher and Shockwave arrive on the scene, apprehend him, and hand him to the authorities.

"This is your favorite part, here," Emma says, rewinding the holovid with her fingers and pausing on the exact moment Master Mischief strikes his pose. Bells dissolves into peals of laughter, shaking as he slumps onto Emma's shoulders, and she props him up. "Look, I think there's one of this bit on a loop."

Jess grins as she scoots back, watching her friends.

A stray curl falls in front of Emma's face, and Bells tucks it behind her ear. Emma scrunches her nose and looks up at Bells, who looks away quickly.

Jess bursts into giggles.

"What?" Emma asks.

Bells' eyes widen.

"Ah, did you see this holo of this cat Bells sent last night?" Jess says, deftly changing the topic.

THE IMAGE OF MASTER MISCHIEF's suit malfunctioning sticks with Jess, and the next time she's at work, she eyes M's mecha-suit until finally she can't bear not knowing. "Is your suit waterproof?" she blurts out.

"Oh God, yes, my—er, Master Mischief discovered that not having a waterproof suit was incredibly debilitating. Especially after the soap bubble incident."

"I thought the soap idea was pretty funny."

"Yeah, good, it should teach the country club not to waste water. Those fairways are ridiculous. We live in a desert!"

Jess pauses. She always just thought the Andover Heights Country club paid for the water. Images from her history holobooks flick through her mind, of people desperate for clean water during the time of the Disasters. There are always public service announcements from the Collective about using only the water you need, but Jess never really thought about where the water had to come from. Those desalination plants and reservoirs always just seemed like a distant certainty, but it must take a lot of time and resources to get that water to where it's needed. "I didn't think about it like that. Everyone just said it was to be funny, you know, like how Mischief's always doing these pranks—"

"Yeah, because the press is too busy following Smasher's newest hairstyle or like, I dunno, whatever they want to focus on. I guess our town isn't so bad, but my dad says even if the Mischiefs spelled out exactly what they were trying to do, the media would probably still mess it up." M's face panel lights blink colorfully.

"I knew about the cheese! It was spoiled," Jess says.

"Yeah, thank God for Net conspiracy theorists. I loved your T-shirt, I think it's great that you have one."

Jess grins. "My parents hate it."

"Ahahaha, most people think the shirts are dumb. Or that the Mischiefs are dumb. I know better—well, *we* know better. Like, don't you think it's weird that we don't know much about historical heroes?"

"What historical heroes? We know that Captain Orion's grandfather was the first one who researched the meta-gene and the different ways it was expressed after the X29 incident."

"Yeah, but there must have been more meta-powered people who found out about their abilities right after the flare," M says. "Why is Lieutenant Orion one of the few heroes mentioned in the history books?"

Jess shrugs. "He's not the only one," she says. "I mean, there were a bunch of people, Gravitus, Photon—"

She really doesn't know much about Gravitus or Photon or any of the early meta-humans other than Lieutenant Orion. "There probably weren't a lot of people documented until after Lieutenant Orion because well, people were just figuring out about meta-humans back then. And it wasn't until Lieutenant Orion was established as a hero that the vigilantes started stepping forward."

"I've never thought about it like that. What about..."

Talking to M is easy. Jess enjoys the electronic cadence of her voice. Emma and Bells have been encouraging her to use this time to get to know Abby, but the minute she gets in the same room as her crush, she gets distracted by the color of her lips or the way she scrunches her nose as she types, and freezes up.

Jess' seventeenth birthday is a relatively quiet affair; her parents take her and her friends out for dinner and cake. Emma gives her a set of collector's edition Captain Orion comics and Bells hand-painted the covers of three new journals for her to write in.

Jess sits back, full of food. Bells and Brendan play with the light-up display that reads "JESS" in colorful blue lights, a gift from Brendan. It's a thoughtful present, and Jess is thankful for the dinner at her favorite restaurant.

Her parents haven't said anything to her about not presenting with any powers, but they're probably waiting until Emma and Bells go home.

"Oh, isn't that Elizabeth Phang?" Jess' mom asks.

Sure enough, a few tables away, Elizabeth looks as if she's out with her parents.

"Why didn't you invite her to your party? You two used to be such good friends," Li Hua says.

"Not really. Uh, we were gonna go see a movie, right?"

"Yes, the movie starts in twenty minutes; thank you for dinner, Mrs. Tran," Bells says as he gets up.

They make their escape before it gets awkward.

"Happy birthday to youuu," Emma singsongs at her.

"Thanks, you guys."

THEY'VE BOUGHT TICKETS, AND JESS and Emma are waiting for Bells to come back with the popcorn. He does, but he's also staring at his DED and frowning. "Sorry, guys, there's an emergency at the restaurant; my parents need me to come back." He hands them the bucket of popcorn and gives them each a quick hug before running off.

"Bells! Do you need a ride?" Jess calls.

"Ah, my brother is picking me up, thanks!" Bells calls back, running toward the parking lot.

"That sucks," Jess says as they sit. "He was really looking forward to this one, too."

"Isn't his older brother away at college?" Emma asks, narrowing her eyes.

Jess munches on popcorn. "Simon works weekends sometimes."

"Do you think Bells is mad at me?"

"No, why would you think that?"

Emma shrugs. "I haven't seen him around much. We used to hang out all the time after school, and I know he works at his family's restaurant, but not that much, you know? And since you started working too, it's like… I think he doesn't want to hang out with just me, you know? These past few weeks it's just been him coming up with these lame excuses, like… I'm doing homework or I'm dyeing my hair tonight; we used to do that together, and I…" she trails off, a forgotten piece of popcorn in her hand.

"That does sound weird. I'm sorry, I've been super-busy at work after school and …"

"I know, I know, you're hanging with your girl. And I miss all three of us spending time together, and for some reason… I dunno. Bells is just being weird, you know? Do you think he's dating someone secretly, and why would he hide it from us?"

"No idea."

⇄

FRIDAY NIGHTS, THEY USUALLY PLAN to hang at Emma's house; they always rewatch a few episodes of *The Gentleman Detective* before watching the newest episode. Bells is late. Jess and Emma have already seen three episodes when they hear the doorbell ring. Emma beats the Robledo's MonRobot to the door and flings it open.

After a few hours of "Hey, where's Bells?" and "What is that supposed to be anyway? Ugh, Bells would know," and "Jess, Bells said today that he was coming, right?" Jess thought Emma would be pleased to see their friend. But instead of giving the expected hug, Emma stands in the entryway and gives him a flat stare.

"Hey, where've you been?" she asks.

"Oh, I had family stuff. Ran late," Bells says.

"Like what? My mom ran into your mom at the grocery store. Apparently everything is chill?"

"I like your new hair," Jess says, trying to diffuse the tension. She doesn't want her two best friends fighting. "Did you get extensions? It looks great longer; I like it a lot."

Bells blinks. "Ah, no, it must be the way I've styled it."

"Oh, so you had time to go do your hair, but you don't have time to message me and say you're gonna be late? What's going on with you, Bells? You know you can tell us anything, I just—feel like you don't trust us anymore."

"I can't tell you everything!" Bells snaps. "You know what, I came here to relax and hang out, not get interrogated."

Jess' mouth falls open; she's never heard Bells raise his voice, ever.

Bells turns to Jess. "Are you just gonna stand there and let her accuse me of this?"

"Emma's feelings were just hurt because you kept blowing her off," Jess says. "Us, I mean."

"Yeah, I don't see her getting all high and mighty with you and your big new job, busy every day after school now!" Bells says. "You know what, I don't need this."

He whirls around, leaves, and slams the door behind him. He hadn't even stepped past the entryway.

Emma and Jess stare at the closed door, and then Mrs. Robledo calls out, "Was that Bells? I made horchata; he likes it better than hot cocoa!"

Emma sniffs, grabs Jess by the elbow and leads her back into her bedroom. "We don't have to marathon this anymore; Bells is the only one who likes this dumb show anyway."

Jess sinks onto Emma's bed, deflated.

"I don't think those extensions looked that great," Emma says. "Who gets extensions like, for two inches of hair?"

"Bells is very serious about his hair." It wouldn't seem like a stretch for him to ask for a specific thing, like only two inches or so, but it's not as if Jess is an expert on hair extensions.

"Yeah, but it's not possible to just get your hair just a *bit* longer. It's usually at least six inches. My cousin, for her quinceañera, had the whole nine yards: hair, makeup, everything. Isn't just a little bit longer *weird*?"

"I guess," Jess says.

Emma changes the channel; the characters from *The Gentleman Detective* dissolve and reform into Lilliputian and Starscream. Wilton Lysander stands in front of the camera, gesturing frantically. "I'm here in Orange Port where Lilliputian and Starscream are taking on Coldfront."

Lysander nearly gets shot with an ice blast, but ducks just in time. The narration is interesting, despite the somewhat routine fight. Lilliputian and Starscream apprehend the villain easily, and soon Emma is rewinding the clip to play it again.

Something occurs to Jess during the rewatch. "I wonder how the cameraperson knew they were there," she says.

"They probably just showed up."

"But look at all the angles. Like how we can see Starscream's face perfectly here, and then Lilliputian here when he gets small, and then here when they fight again on this ledge. This fight only takes about five minutes total, and there's no way there was a photographer at each of these spots with a holocam. It's put together like a movie."

Emma blinks. "I guess? But look how you can see Starscream's face here. Aren't his eyes dreamy? And that jawline. And the stubble."

"Yes, he's hot, but I'm saying that … actual news footage wouldn't look like this. It would be super-zoomed in, unless they were fighting where people were already set up for the angles."

"Maybe the reporters are just really good at their job," Emma says. She props her face in her elbows, eyebrows furrowed. "I'm not in the mood to figure out what's going on here. I just want to veg out and watch Starscream's butt in his tights."

"All right." Jess says. "Hey, come here." She pulls Emma into a hug and Emma sniffs, as if she's been holding back tears. Jess rubs her back; Bells is better at this than she is, but Bells is the reason Emma's upset.

They settle back and watch the fight again. Starscream and Lilliputian work together effortlessly, and Coldfront goes down, shuddering when the two heroes slap the tantalum cuffs on him and lead him away.

With a neat, packaged finish, it's not unlike any of the other battles Jess has seen on television, but now she remembers how other battles were similar, from the confrontation to the one-two punch and right down to the final arrest. It varies depending on the hero and the powers, but the pattern is totally familiar.

Emma seems as though she's doing better after a few video compilations of Starscream's greatest battles. Jess looks at the pile of snacks and vintage board games Emma had pulled out in preparation for the night. There's even a brand-new sketchpad and a set of expensive markers Bells would never have bought for himself. With a sad smile, Jess touches the gifts and hopes that things work out soon.

Emma suggests that Jess sleep over, but Jess doesn't think it's a good idea. Mrs. Robledo likes sleepover guests to have a big breakfast with the family, but Jess wants to avoid the awkward questions about why Bells isn't there.

After Emma drops her off at home, she looks for footage of previously aired battles, starting with the major heroes in New Bright City.

Jess compares. Same too obvious camera angles. Same finish with the tantalum cuffs. No one ever gets injured, no one is actually in danger, and nothing is really at stake. Jess hadn't realized that what she's been seeing play out in her own small city—the Mischiefs causing a minor disturbance, her parents chasing them away or recovering the item they stole—was happening all over the country. Jess thought the harmless pranks were just because they were C-class heroes and villains, but it's the same everywhere, though at grander scales.

There's a cheeping outside Jess' door, and Jess opens it to find Chả blinking up at her. "Hey dude." Jess says. "Come on in."

The MonRobot rolls inside, knocks into the foot of Jess' bed and continues vacuuming haphazardly. It's only halfway through with the room before it runs out of battery and cheeps sadly until Jess picks it up and carries it to its charging station. "Poor baby, I just charged you yesterday. Hey, I wonder if I get some sort of employee discount and can get you an upgrade?"

Chả cheeps.

⇄

SATURDAY AFTERNOON, JESS TAKES THE bus downtown. She straightens her best pair of jeans. M said to wear whatever she wants, but she can't help but worry that jeans are unprofessional. Still, they are a lot more comfortable than her dress slacks from freshman year.

The Monroe building is fairly empty, and the robot at the front desk bobs at her in greeting and says, "Hello, Jessica," in an even tone.

Jess swipes her own keycard to access the special floor on the elevator, and it whirs to life, heading downstairs.

Abby is already at the reception desk, typing away at something at the computer. "Hey," she says with a disarming smile. It's blinding, that's what it is, and Jess doesn't assume that it's meant for her; Abby's just nice to everyone.

Say hello. Say something. Anything. How's the weather? You look great. Your skirt is amazing. Why do you smell so good?

Finally Jess just nods, and congratulates herself for not saying anything awkward.

"M will join you in your office in a bit," Abby says. She stands up and brushes off imaginary dust.

"Are you—are you going to be doing more robotics work today?" Jess asks.

"Yeah. And M liked your idea about the casual attire—as long as you're comfortable, you know."

"You're still wearing a dress."

Abby lifts an eyebrow, and a smile tickles the corners of her lips. "I'm wearing a dress because I like it. I'll see you later."

Jess mutters to herself and walks right into the wall. She winces and rubs her shoulder. Ugh, at least she was out of sight. She can't believe she said that. It sounded awful, as if she was judging Abby for her fashion choices. She cringes. *You're still wearing a dress?* There's nothing wrong with dresses, in fact Abby looks great wearing them.

Abby looks great in her volleyball uniform. Abby looks great in her workout clothes. Jess probably has no chance of interacting with her like a normal person because she always is gorgeous, no matter what she wears.

Jess slumps face first onto the desk until she gets motivated to pick herself up and read today's to-do list.

The first item is to go up to the fourteenth floor and pick up parts for M. Jess pulls the instructions onto a DED chip and loads it into her own, and then adds the three more orders of magnesium and aluminum alloys M mentioned she needed yesterday. The elevator is empty all the way up to the first floor, and then dings for the lobby. The doors open, but no one enters.

"Close doors," Jess says.

"Wait, wait, hold the elevator!"

Jess sticks her arm out so the doors don't shut, and a breathless teenage boy dashes in.

He's wearing what seems to be a flashy blue designer suit; it looks exactly like the one Wilton Lysander wears on the news. The boy grins at Jess and runs his hands through his blond hair; there's a matching blue streak running down the left side. "Hi! Thanks so much," he says.

He looks familiar somehow, but Jess doesn't think she's seen him at AHHS.

"No problem," Jess says. "Are you an intern too? I haven't met any of the ones in the other departments."

"Yes! I'm an intern," he says. "I'm Barry." Oddly formal, he holds out his hand for Jess to shake.

"Jess." She shakes his hand. It's going to be one of those things, she can tell, like figuring out who is that one extra in that one movie. "Sorry, you just look really familiar. Do you go to AHHS?"

"Ah, no! I live in Devonport. I must have one of those faces, you know."

"Do you know what floor you're going to?" Jess asks. They've already passed the fifth through eighth floors, where most of the research and development takes place. Jess was pretty sure all the other internships were for that area, but she could be wrong.

"Oh, ah, fourteen."

They stand in silence for a bit until the boy blurts out, "So, how are you liking the job, Jess?"

"It's great. I mean, I don't have any other internships to compare it to, but I like the people I work with, and the projects are interesting."

Barry keeps smiling and nodding as she talks. Jess goes on a bit about the tedium of filing, and finds his active interest in her pleasant. She's not one to make friends quickly. It reminds her of the first time Bells sat down with her at lunch and just started talking to her.

"How's things in research and development? I would have applied there, but I don't really know much about robotics."

Barry shrugs. "Ah, it's great. I love it. Lots of explosions. Just kidding!" He leans in and lowers his voice, even though they're the only two in the elevator. "Hey, have you seen anything weird around here lately?"

"Weird? Like what?" Jess folds her arms.

"Anything. You know... I heard that Master Mischief was seen a few times going in and out of this building. Maybe he's hiding out here." Barry lifts his eyebrows.

"I have no idea," Jess says, more fiercely than she intends. The Mischief's lab is supposed to be a secret. "That sounds like something the conspiracy theorists on the Net would come up with."

Barry leans back against the elevator wall. He opens his mouth, but the elevator door opens and a few more employees join them. Two women are complaining to each other about project deadlines, but the conversation ends when they get in the elevator and they glare at the display. One man is flicking furiously at the messages on his DED. He's wearing jeans and a polo shirt. All the employees look pretty casual, much to Jess' relief. It must be a Saturday thing, and now Barry looks overdressed.

The other intern keeps eyeing her as if he wants to talk more about his Mischief theories. The women get off on the tenth floor, and, on the eleventh, the man still on his DED walks right into a MonRobot hovering at the elevator doors. It spins about in confusion even as it's scanning him, and the man just walks right past. "Bill Neighton, Thermodynamics Specialist," the MonRobot mutters.

"Hey, watch it," Jess calls after the rude man, reaching out to steady the MonRobot.

"Thank you," it says in a steady monotone. It scans Jess' face briefly and makes an affirmative noise. "Jessica Tran, Experimental Division Intern." The MonRobot turns to Barry, scans him quickly, and then makes a series of panicked beeps. "No employee or registered guest facial match. Intruder! Intruder!"

Lights flash from the MonRobot, and Jess flattens herself against the wall in a panic.

Barry gives her a small salute. "Later, Jess. Have a great day at work!"

He ducks out of reach of the MonRobot's emerging arms and shrugs out of his suit jacket. Barry tosses the jacket over the robot. The MonRobot spins about in confusion, chirping "Apprehend the intruder!" over and over.

People join the chase, and the MonRobot finally shakes off the jacket and flies after Barry. Jess sees the MonRobot chase him down the hallway and around the corner while startled employees leap aside.

"Hey, where'd he go?" a woman calls out.

The elevator door starts to close, and the eleventh floor hallway is empty despite the noisy chaos around the corner. On the floor, Barry's jacket shimmers and... disappears.

Jess rides to the fourteenth floor. Barry hadn't seemed dangerous, just another kid. *What was he doing here?* He was asking questions about Master Mischief.

Maybe Barry was looking for Master Mischief?

And what was up with that jacket? Maybe it was some advanced tech from a rival company. Barry was probably a spy, Jess decides.

Too bad. He seemed nice.

THE FOURTEENTH FLOOR IS FILLED with row after row of shelved tech, working and not. A MonRobot takes the datachip from Jess' DED and hums to itself as it whirrs about the shelves and fills a box.

Jess thanks the robot and carries the box back down to the lab. No one joins her in the elevator this time; the ride is short and silent. She leaves the materials outside M's office; strange noises are coming from behind the closed door, which is marked *NO ENTRY WITHOUT PERMISSION.*

She goes back to her office and works until noon; M joins her after about an hour, and they make good progress, organizing all golf-course-related pranks into one folder. M excuses herself to lunch in private, and Jess goes to the small break room down the hall.

She sits on a hard metal chair, pulls out the sandwich she brought, and nibbles on it. A few moments later, Abby appears and pulls a box of Orion's Favorite™ chicken pot pie from the freezer and heats it up in the microwave. Jess has seen those in the grocery store, but they're expensive and her mother thinks they're a waste of money, putting real meat into frozen dinners.

Abby grabs a chair and sits. "So do you take the bus here?"

"Yeah." Jess puts down her sandwich and wipes the crumbs off her face.

"How long does it take?"

"'Bout an hour."

The microwave beeps, and Abby pulls out the steaming pot pie. She jabs a fork into it, breaking the flaky pie crust. The scent of herbed broth and chicken fills the air, and Jess' plain peanut butter and jelly suddenly seems incredibly unappetizing.

"Here, have some, I can't finish this whole thing by myself." Abby pulls out another fork and hands it to Jess. She pushes the pie toward Jess and smiles.

"Thanks," Jess says, and takes a bite. The pie is salty but delicious, in that wonderfully guilty way of frozen dinners. The meat is savory and tender, and Jess doesn't think it's a waste at all.

They share the pie as Jess tries to think of conversation. It's really difficult because Abby is sitting so close, eating with vigor; flakes of pie crust stick to her lips.

Finally Abby breaks the silence. "You know, since we are both coming from school on the weekdays, I could drive you; it's not a big deal."

"Really? That would be great," Jess says. "Are you sure? Don't you usually—" Jess falters. Should she admit she knows Abby quit the volleyball team? "—take your friends home?"

"Not since I started working here. I'm not on the volleyball team anymore. And my friends have cars too; it's not like I was the only one who has a car."

"Oh. That's really nice of you, thank you."

They eat in silence, and then Jess surprises herself by asking when Abby got her driver's license, and they actually make small talk about the terrible bureaucracy that is the Collective's system for keeping track of the limited number of drivers in the country.

Jess mentions the incident in the elevator, and Abby just laughs. "Yeah, probably a spy. We get a lot of those. Lots of patents and secrets here that our rivals would love to get ahold of. I'm surprised they got a teenager involved, though. That's new."

Abby throws her whole head back when she laughs; the mirth travels through her entire body, and she shakes with joy. "I have no idea why I thought you were shy. Guess it takes you a while to warm to people, huh?"

"Maybe," Jess says, with a smile. Or maybe it takes her a while to get over the awkwardness of interacting with someone she's liked for a long time.

Either way, she's kind of proud of herself right now.

ON MONDAY JESS SAYS GOODBYE to Bells and Emma and walks past the crowds of students and the line of cars waiting to pick people up. Abby's car stands out among the dusty old vehicles in the parking lot; the shiny Mercedes gleams in the afternoon sunlight.

Abby waves her DED at it, and the car beeps and turns on automatically.

The dashboard has a unique electronic interface. Jess can't see the touch display for commands. All cars have them, even the driver-operated ones.

"Oh, um, it's a custom model, I just use the steering wheel," Abby says when she notices Jess' confusion. "Did you want to listen to the radio?"

Jess nods, and Abby waves a hand at the dash; Jess doesn't see any buttons, but it must have some advanced motion-tech because soon a jaunty pop song is playing over the speakers.

They pull out of the parking lot and are about to pull onto the road that heads downtown when Jess remembers. "Hey, do you mind if we stop by my house to get my MonRobot before heading to work?"

"Oh?"

"Yeah, it's just super-old and I wanted to see if I could get an employee discount on an upgrade."

"I could fix your robot," Abby says.

"Really? Are you going to be doing it at work?"

"Sure, no problem. I was testing this new A.I. software anyway and I could try it out at no cost to you." Abby grins.

Jess' house is empty but she finds Chả still sleeping in the charging station. She picks it up and holds it out to Abby. "This is Chả."

Abby runs her hand along Chả's silver case. "Hi there." She peers into the little display of lights. "I named mine too," Abby says. "What does Cha—um, am I saying it right? What's it mean?"

"You're saying it almost right." Jess chuckles. "It's short for chả trứng hấp, a Vietnamese meatloaf. The first night we had the robot we were having dinner, and some fell the floor, and this little guy tried to vacuum it up and got stuck. Even after we fixed it, the next day it got stuck on some chả lụa and my mother got mad because it was a waste of good food, but I thought it was really silly. Thought it made a great name."

Abby laughs. "All right, let's look at you." She turns Chả over and examines it carefully.

"Wow, this is one of the first models," Abby says. "I'm surprised to see it's still running."

The robot cheeps as Jess pats it.

"See, it recognizes you. A.I. is still good, just needs a tune-up," Abby says.

On the way to the lab, Jess is just filled with questions. "So how long have you been interested in robots? What are you working on in the lab? I'm so glad for you that M is letting you do more things; that receptionist position was totally wasted on you."

Abby laughs. "Oh, yeah, um, I didn't mind doing that. But there used to be tour groups or the board of directors would come to see what the Mischiefs were working on, so there was more of a need. But now it's just me and you."

"And M."

"And M." Abby nods. "She does all the high-tech research stuff. She's like the second in command under the Mischiefs, so now she's in charge of everything."

"Everything is great so far. I hope she liked my organization system. Those files were ridiculous and all over the place," Jess says.

"No, we really appreciate the help in organization."

Abby carries Chả into the building. In the elevator is a man, tall with oily gray hair and wearing an expensive suit.

"Miss Jones." He sniffs. "And you must be the new hire."

"This is Jessica Tran."

"I give you one hire and this is who you get? Another teenager," the man says. "How are we going to get anything done at all?"

Jess bites back a retort about how teenagers do so much, and the man gets off at the next floor.

"Who was that?" Jess says.

"That's Gregory Stone," Abby says and sighs. "He's the chair of the board of directors. Pretty much runs everything, from the sales to the patents to the new designs."

"Is he always a jerk?"

"Pretty much. He relies very heavily on my—bosses to make certain things and needs results right away, and right now that they're gone, it's all—it's all on M, and it's very stressful." Abby shakes her head and then the elevators doors open on their floor.

"Oh, here already!" Jess exclaims. She didn't see Abby key in her code.

Chả makes a happy-sounding beeping noise.

They get to the lab and find an empty workspace in the back. Abby pats the MonRobot and flips a switch to put it to sleep while she works on it. Jess hovers, waiting.

Abby blushes. "Um, it's hard for me to concentrate with someone watching. Do you mind? And I think M left you a list of tasks in your office, too."

Jess blinks. "Sure. Okay. Good luck!"

She goes to her office and gets to work. The tasks are routine by now. Jess creates a new electronic file for each of the different projects, entering them in the database she created the first week.

Jess finally she looks up from her desktop to take a break. Usually M would have come in by now to say hello or to take away completed projects or to give her new ones, but she hasn't even heard the familiar whirr of her suit.

Jess wanders to Abby's workspace. "Abby?"

She hears a clatter.

Jess rushes forward and sees Abby with Chả at the table and a bunch of various circuit boards and metal electronic pieces on the floor. Abby winces. "I, uh, I dropped a wrench on my foot."

"Oh no! I'll get you some ice," Jess says. "How's my buddy?"

"Doing well, I'm almost done, thanks." Abby smiles.

There's no ice in the kitchen on this floor, so Jess runs to the elevator and goes up a floor to get ice from the kitchen in the lab upstairs. A few other employees are on their break; Jess ignores them as she roots around in the freezer for something frozen.

"Ugh, I can't wait until the day when they activate the thing, then it'll be nothing but smooth sailing for all of us," one of the other employees says.

"Hear, hear," someone else says, and coffee cups clink.

Jess finds the ice pack and heads back downstairs.

As she approaches Abby's workspace, for a second Jess thinks she sees a circuit board float in the air with a wire moving in and out of it. But when she looks again, it's on the table in Abby's hand.

"I'm done!" Abby says.

Chả cheeps and Abby sets it on the floor, where it wheels in a proud circle, moving faster than Jess has ever seen it.

"For your foot," Jess says, offering her the ice pack.

"Oh, thank you." Abby sinks into her chair and toes out of her shoes. She props her foot on the table and puts the ice pack on her foot. "I get startled easily."

"Hey, do you know if Monroe Industries is launching some sort of thing that will result in lots of money for all the workers?"

Abby scrunches her face. "No idea. Where'd you hear that?'

"In the break room upstairs. Seems like a bunch of people are excited about something happening soon."

"Weird, I didn't hear anything about it. And I hear everything."

The sound of the elevator startles them.

Abby frowns. "That's strange. I'm not expecting anyone else today."

"It could be M; I haven't seen her come in yet," Jess says.

"No, M is in the back." She blinks. "Oh no, the code. It's Stone's code. He's coming to inspect. He must have remembered he had an upcoming inspection and decided to do it today! I gotta—" She looks around. "I gotta go tell M."

"The lab looks fine," Jess says, but she hurries to pick up the pieces of discarded circuitry around Abby's workspace and makes a passably neat pile. She picks up Chả and stashes it in her office, and then goes to the main room.

The elevator door opens and Stone walks out. He sneers at Jess' T-shirt and jeans. "Monroe Industries has a dress code standard."

"M said I could wear whatever I wanted. It's just a few of us down here, it doesn't matter. It's not like I'm presenting to your clients or anything."

"M?" Stone asks, raising his eyebrow. He glances behind her and nods in recognition. "Ah, there you are! Master Mischief, how are the plans for the new line of MonRobots coming along?"

Jess turns around, curious to see the villain she's been working for, but only sees M, walking forward in the suit.

"Gregory," M says, but it's in a different voice, electronically pitched lower. "I thought inspection wasn't until next week."

"Ah, well, I ran into two of your interns and was reminded of all your little projects here," Gregory says, frowning. "I keep telling you that Abby Jones is a right smart girl; we should have her back up in Research. You shouldn't be keeping her for yourself."

"She can be more creative here and she likes it here."

"Maybe you should ask Abby instead of just talking about her like she isn't here," Jess says. "I just saw her. I can get her for you." Jess checks in all the offices, even the bathroom, but can't find Abby.

When Jess returns to the central workspace, Stone looks unsettled, but M hands him a few datachips and folders and he seems appeased. He takes the files and gets in the elevator.

"M?" Jess asks.

"Yeah, it's me," M says once Stone is gone.

"You know, I remember you saying something about pretending to be Master Mischief. Why do you need to?"

"Stone can't know that Master Mischief isn't here. He'll run the company into the ground. As long as he thinks that Mischief is still coming up with ideas and plans, we have some semblance of control."

Jess narrows her eyes. She'd asked M a few times if Master Mischief was ever going to make an appearance in the lab, but he always seemed to be either busy or their work was "not of import" yet. In fact, yesterday M had told her the Mischiefs were travelling. "I thought you said he was out of town with Mistress Mischief."

"They are, it's just, well they're trying to solve a problem right now, and it's taking much longer than expected."

"Where have *you* been? I haven't seen you all day," Jess says. "I missed you."

"Oh. Yeah, thanks, I had something pressing keeping me in the back."

"Oh, I did have a question about this project. Is it true that Plasmaman and Miss Mischief are related?"

"Oh yeah, they most definitely are. I mean, a number of meta-humans are related to each other; the genetic expression is inherited, of course. Not always, but sometimes." M turns her head a little. "You really missed me?"

"I don't know how I got anything done without the sound of your suit in the background." Jess smiles, and M's face panel lights go bright pink.

CLAUDIA IS VISITING FOR THE weekend. She has a new haircut and blonde and brown highlights that make her look incredibly glamorous. She keeps tossing it, ever so casually, to keep it fluffy and voluminous. It's also Captain Orion's newest haircut, as seen on the holocover of *Fashion Today*. It's almost as if Orion is sitting at their dinner table, albeit shorter and Asian and well... Claudia.

Jess pushes the vegetables around on her plate as Claudia prattles on about her newest exploits in Crystal Springs. She got a key to the city, blah blah, new hero award, blah blah blah, is doing exciting missions with the League.

Victor listens, spellbound; it's been a dream of Victor Tran's to get a key to the city, even to Andover, but at most he's gotten a certificate and a sandwich named after Shockwave.

But Claudia is a star.

Despite their seven-year age difference, Jess and Claudia were inseparable before Brendan was born. Jess adored her older sister, hero-worshipped her, and was constantly in awe as Claudia grew into her powers.

Flying was the first thing Claudia learned how to do. By age eleven she was already outracing their dad, following behind on him on missions. She was able to use her powers for much longer than their dad, and it was clear that she was going to be A-class.

"And then there will be three of us," Claudia said. "We'll be the best crime-fighting team ever, once you get your powers and then the baby, too."

Claudia took Jess on a secret flight once, right when their mom was pregnant with Brendan. Jess was scared, but held on tight as Claudia flew over the vast desert, all golden hues, where cactuses were standing tall.

The warm afternoon light stretched out to the horizon, and Claudia giggled as she flew them over a broad canyon to marvel at the green-blue river below, at the water calmly traveling to its final destination. Jess marveled at the feeling of the wind running through her hair. Her superstrong sister held her aloft as if she weighed nothing, and they soared through the air until the city was nothing but a glittering streak in the vast desert.

The blue, blue sky was laced with light, the sun was starting to make its way toward the earth's edge, and they soared past fluffy clouds, whirling around and around them until Jess laughed hysterically. Claudia threw her up in the air, and, for a few breathless moments, Jess was flying on her own, hearing nothing but her own blood racing through her body and her heart pounding furiously as she started to—fall—

Claudia caught her. "Not yet, Jessie Bessie," she said, chuckling. "Soon, soon! You'll be able to fly too."

Jess never learned to fly.

After that night, Claudia got caught up in training with her parents, and then a few years later, while still in high school, she started the Meta-Human Training program early.

When, at puberty, Jess didn't show any signs of having powers, Claudia ignored her to hang out with all her new friends in Meta-Human Training.

Now Jess hardly recognizes her sister. They have the same flat nose, the same brown eyes, the same black hair. Claudia blossomed in adolescence. Now she's full figured, with model-worthy hair and designer clothes. She finished college with honors and graduated Meta-Human Training with an offer to join the League. She's a larger-than-life hero.

Even their parents seem in awe of her.

"And then Captain Orion said—"

"Wait, you got to meet her?" Jess perks up. "What was she like?"

Claudia pauses and takes a drink of water. "Absolutely down to earth, you know? Like the pressure of being the country's greatest superhero hasn't fazed her at all. And she's got so much on her shoulders, with the League and the never-ending fight against crime."

"Okay, what happened at the Battle of New Miranda? I heard Coldfront *died*."

Claudia looks scandalized with her brows drawn tightly together and her mouth slightly open. "He's being held in a high-security cell at Meta-Human Corrections. He couldn't have died; the League doesn't kill anyone. That's for villains."

"What villains have killed anyone? Not since the War."

"They've killed," Claudia says, waving her hand vaguely. "Oh, before I forget. I got you a present."

"Oh, thanks, I got the gift card you gave to Mom and Dad, you didn't need to get me anything else."

Claudia shrugs. "This was just a present from my last trip to New Bright City. I got something for everyone." She pulls a glossy photograph out of her purse. It's bent in a few places, and in the corner in silver ink is a hastily scrawled "For Tess," and Captain Orion's signature.

"Thanks." Jess holds the photograph gingerly between her thumb and forefinger. It's the same photo she got in the mail last week as part of the Captain Orion Fan Club's monthly newsletter, except that one spelled her name correctly.

"What about me?" Brendan asks. He's practically bouncing in his seat.

Claudia digs into her bag and pulls out action figures of Captain Orion, Starscream, and Copycat and hands them over. Brendan looks disappointed, but he just says thanks and accepts the figures. The thirteen-year-old hasn't played with toys since he was a kid.

"I want to hear all about your super-secret lab," Brendan says. The conversation turns to science, and Jess tunes out.

After dinner, Jess expects Claudia to hang out with her parents, or maybe reconnect with some of her friends in the area, but instead she pulls Jess aside.

"So, I heard from Mom and Dad, that like—oh, happy birthday, by the way—" Claudia says, like an afterthought. There's a holo of them as children behind them: Claudia, a happy teenager, standing next to a young Jess holding baby Brendan. "—that you're not gonna present with any powers. And that's okay, you know, there's nothing wrong with that. But I know you really wanna do the hero thing, and I came up with a great idea."

"What?"

"You could be my sidekick! Okay, usually hero support requires that the sidekick presents with at least a D-class power, but I think if you wanna hang back in the lab, you can totally help with the tech side of things, maybe monitor the holofeeds and work with the communications team? I had to pull a lot of strings. And you can totally meet Captain Orion too! In person! Isn't that great? You could start with us as soon as your spring quarter—it could be like an internship! Mom mentioned you were looking for a job, right, some time ago?"

A few weeks ago this idea might be interesting, but now to be asked to be in her sister's shadow yet again, it's just… patronizing.

She has a job now where she's important and needed. M needs her. Master Mischief and Mistress Mischief need her.

"Thanks," Jess says. "But I'm gonna have to pass. I have a job already."

⇄

Working for Monroe Industries—or M's secret lab—is challenging, but also entertaining at times. Jess finds answers to a lot of questions about how the Mischiefs planned their pranks, but ends up with even more questions about the more elaborate cons.

More often than not, M's suit is clanking away alongside her. Jess wonders: Because this suit was Master Mischief's, can it do similar things? She knows it can fly, but is that a modification or does M have similar powers? Jess doesn't know a lot about the specifics of Master Mischief's powers, but his suit *was* tailored to his technopath abilities. Maybe it's been modified so someone who isn't a meta-human can use it.

Maybe M does just wear the suit to pretend to the rest of Monroe Industries that she's Master Mischief. But the lab is empty, and there isn't anyone working on the many electronic experiments in the main room, despite the large number of workspaces and the unfinished projects scattered all over the room. The receptionist's desk is empty, and there's a light at the far end of the hall where Jess assumes Abby's working on something for M.

"How long has Abby been working here?" Jess asks.

M's suit beeps, and then responds with a stiffly electronic, "Three months."

"Funny, I've never seen her wear those work clothes at school. I mean, not that I notice. But it would be kind of hard to miss, if she was wearing that skirt?" Jess sighs. "She looks great in that skirt. Her butt is so cute."

The suit chirps.

"You okay?"

"Yes, fine. So you're friends with Abby at school?" M asks.

"Um, not really. She's kind of like, super-intimidating."

"I see," M says. The tone of her voice is flat.

"I mean, I think I tried talking to her once, but then I got super-distracted. She has really nice hair. It looks so fluffy and soft."

M makes a strangled electronic noise.

"You okay there, M?"

"Yeah. Uh, I need to get you all the files pertaining to the museums, but I don't know where they are in the warehouse."

Jess shrugs and points.

M's suit chirps at her. "What are you doing?"

"I dunno. Have you tried looking in that corner?"

M pauses, her visor blank and regarding Jess for a moment before she says, "Sure, why not?" Despite the sarcastic tone, M does walk out of the office, and Jess continues with her work. A few moments later M returns with a box and starts unpacking it.

"Thanks."

"Mmhmm," Jess says. "Going with a random direction is useful sometimes."

"Random," M repeats, but she doesn't bring it up again.

Jess has heard many various complaints from other kids at school about their jobs, like annoying customers and difficult tasks. Emma volunteers at the fancy animal hospital downtown, and Bells works at his family's restaurant, so she hears about the difficulties pretty often. But she's come to enjoy working at Monroe Industries much more than she expected.

Jess likes organizing things; everything in her room has a system—books are alphabetized and organized by genre, even all the files on her DED are in intricately labeled folders, one after another. And, it's interesting keeping up with what the Mischiefs have been up to over the years and seeing their side of all those squabbles with her parents. She likes talking to M—it's easy, M's got this dry wit that's really funny, and she's nice and shares Jess' taste in movies. They spend one afternoon filing and debating the triumphs of the recent *Vindicated* movie—an action series whose plot points dried up in the first sequel (there are many) but that still remains Jess' guilty pleasure.

One afternoon Jess finds a dusty box of plastic balls in various sizes and colors. She pulls out a purple one the size of a volleyball and drops it on the office floor; it bounces. Jess laughs, entertaining herself by bouncing it for a bit.

M walks into the office.

"Heads up," Jess says, tossing the ball at her.

"What—" M brings her arms together, hitting it back.

Jess shrieks and ducks and barely gets out of the way before the ball crashes into the wall and a pile of unopened boxes. She grabs the thing before it can do any more damage and puts it back in the box. "What was that?"

"Oh, the balls were for a prank. You know that hill up by the country club? We were going to toss them down—"

"No, I mean the skills!" Jess laughs. "You play volleyball or something?"

"I—I, ah, yeah. Once or twice," M says. "Did you think—"

"What?"

"Never mind," M says hastily and steps forward to take the box. "I'll go put these away."

Twenty minutes later, when she comes back from the warehouse level, she lingers in the doorway. Jess looks up to see the blank visor of M's helmet staring right back at her.

"So... How are things going with your... crush?" M asks.

"What?" Jess fights the blush rising on her cheeks. "I'm not—I don't have a crush."

The blank metal face of M's suit stares back at her.

"Okay, fine," Jess admits. "But like, don't tell her, okay? Please? I'm trying to get better at hanging out with her and not making a fool out of myself."

M makes a noise that could be a snort. "I think you're doing fine. Just be yourself and all that, you know."

Jess huffs. "Well, I guess things are going well? I guess? We carpool from school to here, so I guess we're hanging out more."

Riding together has become a normal thing. When Jess has work, she meets Abby at the tree by the parking lot, and they drive downtown together. Jess was trying to figure out how to hang out with Abby outside of work when Abby initiated it.

Jess tells M, "I had lunch with Abby yesterday at school. It was interesting? Not sure. It was… really random."

And it was. Abby just sat in the grass right next to Bells, said, "Hey," and started eating her school lunch.

Bells stared openly at Abby in her designer blouse and jeans.

"What are you doing?" Bells said.

"Eating lunch, hanging out," Abby said. "Here, you like tater tots, right?" She handed Jess the tray. The tater tots were fresh out of the fryer.

"Uh, thanks?" Jess took the tray and shared confused looks with Emma and Bells. Her friends adjusted quickly and started a conversation with Abby; they shared a few AP classes with her. Abby spent the entire lunch period with them and even helped Emma on an assignment she was finishing for fifth period.

Bells pulled Jess aside, his eyes alight with amusement. "Dude, when did you start dating Abby?"

"What? We're not dating," Jess insisted. "We uh, just work together. That's all. I guess we're friends now? That's why she felt like hanging out?"

Jess relates the story to M, whose lights go green, which Jess now knows means she's amused.

"It's not funny," Jess says.

"I didn't laugh," M replies as the green lights continue to dance about the panel. "It's cute. Your friends think you're dating the girl you like, that's all."

Jess snorts. "I wish. I just... I dunno, both of them have dated people before, I just... it's really daunting, okay! I can't just *ask* Abby if she likes girls or not! What if she doesn't know? What if... I... Yeah. It's too much risk."

M is silent.

Jess chews on her lip and tugs her hair out of her ponytail. She fiddles with the elastic and reties her hair, looking at the floor. Why did she have to share so much? "Sorry, it's a lot; I mean, it's not very professional, is it? Talking about your crushes at work. But technically you started it, so."

You started *it? Way to be professional, Jess.*

M's visor panel blinks short bursts of blue light. "It's fine. I just... well, if you like her so much, why don't you ask her out?"

Jess blushes. "I can't do that! I mean... It's scary."

"But what if she likes you back?" M suggests. The lights in her panel flash blue and purple.

"That is highly unlikely. We never hung out before I started working here. I mean, I'm surprised she even knew my name. How would she know she liked me?"

"Maybe she's just as nervous as you are."

"Nervous? Abby?" Jess laughs weakly. "She's the epitome of the word 'badass,' okay? Like Emma once told me she scared off the opposing volleyball team with just a look."

A computer console on the other side of the room sparks, and M makes a muffled noise that is bitten off by her electronic voice modulator. "I'll go get the fire extinguisher," she says in a slow, flat tone and sets down her box. She leaves the room; her suit whirrs as she flies out.

M *does* have powers.

Ms. Rhinehart is passing back essays when Abby sits in the seat next to Jess. There isn't an everyday seating chart, but everyone likes to sit at the same table, at least.

"Hey." Abby puts her book bag on the table and smiles at Jess.

"Hi." Jess looks at the table where Abby usually sits with Carla and Kylie, who are on the volleyball team. Carla's boyfriend is sitting with them in Abby's place and flipping through *The Awakening* with a dull expression on his face.

"Oh man, that quiz in Cornwell's class was so hard."

"I'm not in AP Bio," Jess says, although she already heard about the killer quiz from Emma.

"Oh, I thought you were in the other period. Sorry."

"All right, quiet down," Ms. Rhinehart says to the class. "This month, we're going to be working on your collaborative writing efforts. Partner up, you have a short story due in two weeks."

"What do you say, partner?" Abby says.

"I—ah—okay."

On the outskirts of town, Abby's house is practically a mansion. It's modern and airy, all sleek steel and floor-to-ceiling glass windows. Jess holds her denim backpack tightly to her chest as she steps out of the car.

She doesn't know where to look: the stunning home with its own solar panels glinting with the afternoon sun, the view of the canyons in the distance, the immaculate rock garden with its artfully arranged succulents.

A garage door opens, and Jess turns around. Abby is waving at her as her Mercedes-Benz parks itself in the garage. The front door is open already; Jess hadn't seen her swipe her DED. *No lock pad.*

Jess wants to look at the doorknob to see if there's an old-fashioned lock, but that would look absolutely ridiculous, especially for her first time at Abby's house.

"C'mon in. You want a snack or anything?"

The living room is large and homey, with chairs, couches, and low tables in scale with the room. Holos of a younger Abby and her parents decorate the walls; a round MonRobot rolls into the room cheeping.

Abby pets the MonRobot. "Hey, Jacks."

Jess giggles. It's great to see her with her MonRobot.

Abby quirks an eyebrow.

"I just love the name; it's so cute."

"Ah, well, I was really into nursery rhymes when I was a kid," Abby says, shrugging. "And I built Jacks' circuit board when I was four or five, and at the time, I had this phase where I just made everything plural, and it stuck. It won't respond to anything else."

"I know they aren't pets, like the animals people kept before, but they're just so cute and they have an A.I., so they think and... I dunno, some people think it's weird."

"Nah. Anything with an A.I. thinks for itself, and even if it's a different level of consciousness, that doesn't mean it doesn't appreciate that you care about it. Right, Jacks?"

Jacks chirps, rolling around in a circle.

"Jacks, can you get me a lemon soda?" Abby asks, then turns to Jess. "Do you want anything?"

"Sure, I'll have the same." Jess has never seen a personal MonRobot do anything other than clean, although she knows fancy ones cook and do other tasks. But they have to be specifically programmed with the order. Maybe Jacks' A.I. is really advanced?

"Hungry?" Abby asks.

Jess nods.

"The school lunch is awful. Jacks, start two grilled cheeses." Abby roots around in the pantry and pulls out a can of tomato soup.

"Oh, thanks." Jess says, watching Jacks work. It's fascinating to see the robot open the fridge, extend its little arms to take out the pitcher of lemonade, and pour two cups.

She pats Jacks as it sets down two glasses of lemonade, and it toots a bit in response before going back to the fridge for a package of cheese. "Jacks... is the newest MonRobot model?" Jess asks.

A panel in Jacks' side opens to reveal another arm with a sharp blade, which slices the cheese.

"Um, he's a special one. My dad made him for me. He's the head of MonRobot design at Monroe Industries. And yes, that's how I got the job."

"I don't—that's not what I thought. I mean, you totally could have gotten any of those robotics internships. That's what you like to do, right? I mean, you're in robotics shop at school and all the AP classes."

Abby shrugs. "I think my dad didn't want me in that area, and eventually just made me, I mean, recommended me to work in the secret lab."

"So he didn't want you in the general robotics lab with the other employees, but felt comfortable with you working in Master Mischief's secret lab?"

"They're friends. It's cool. I've... I've known Mischief since I was a kid. It was the safest option."

Jacks turns the sandwiches; the bread is a perfect golden brown.

Abby heats the tomato soup. She dices fresh tomatoes and tosses them in the soup and then shakes in spices.

"Here you go." Abby ladles the soup into bowls as Jacks plates the sandwiches.

"So, your parents are still at work?" Jess asks as they walk into the living room. There's a huge portrait of the three Joneses in the style of a classic oil painting. Abby is about twelve and absolutely adorable; her frizzy hair is gathered in a high ponytail that poofs out behind her head. She and her mother have the same vibrant red hair; her mother's is styled in an elegant updo, not a hair out of place.

Abby is wearing her hair today in the same updo.

"Ah, yeah, they're at a robotics conference in New Bright City." Abby pushes a plate toward Jess and settles on the couch, picks up her sandwich, and dunks it in the tomato soup.

"So you're here all by yourself?"

"I have Jacks," Abby says. She waves at the robot.

Jacks cheeps, extends a little arm, and waves back.

"I think having the house to myself—no parents, no little brother—for a little while would be awesome. I'd probably have my friends over for endless sleepovers, and we'd probably try to have a party."

Abby laughs. "Nah, not my scene. But that sounds fun. You mean Emma and Bells, right? Emma's great; she's got this great spike, and she's always cheering on everyone when we're doing conditioning. I'm glad Coach bumped her up to varsity; they've been doing great so far. I kinda miss the team, though."

"I think they miss you too. Why'd you drop out?"

Abby looks at her food. "Stress, I think. Just stuff at home, you know how it is. And being team captain, all those girls looking up to me, I just couldn't handle it." She sighs. "Bells is great, though. I love their hair, they always do those bright colors, and so often—"

"He," Jess corrects. "Bells uses he/his pronouns."

"Oh. I didn't know." Abby takes a bite of her sandwich.

"It's okay. I think it's pretty cool you thought of using 'they' when you didn't know for sure."

Abby nods. "No problem. Darryl always does the same workshop at the beginning of the year for everyone in Rainbow Allies."

"Oh. Cool. Do you participate in a lot of their events?" Jess isn't really sure what to say to that; it's interesting that Abby is in that club, but it doesn't necessarily mean she knows for sure Abby is attracted to girls.

But she *might* be.

"Nah, I've always been busy with student council and volleyball, plus there's never too much going on. And it's kind of weird, you know? Darryl and his friends in the club; it's a bunch of gay guys hanging out. Sometimes there will be more people, but that core group hasn't changed much." Abby shrugs and then gives Jess a thoughtful look. "I think I remember seeing you at a few meetings, freshman year I think?"

"Yeah, Bells and I went a few times, I mean, I think the ideas are good..." Jess isn't really sure how to explain it, but the way Abby described it as "Darryl and his friends" makes sense. It's another clique, in a way. "We didn't... I didn't feel like I belonged there."

"Yeah," Abby says. "They're working on it, though. Janelle, the treasurer for student council, also just got the treasurer position there so I think things are getting better."

Jess leans on the edge of the kitchen counter, bobbing her head in understanding. It seems that particular thread of conversation is over, and she isn't sure what to say next. They stare at each other awkwardly; Jess doesn't know any of Abby's friends so she can't ask about them, and they've already talked about volleyball. They should just start the assignment.

"Do you want to watch a movie?" Abby asks.

"Shouldn't we do the writing assignment?"

Abby tosses her hair over her shoulder in cascading curls of brilliant red. "We could, but we've got two weeks. That's plenty of time. We can brainstorm after watching the movie; maybe we'll get some fun ideas."

"Okay."

The couch is comfortable; the food is delicious. Abby picks one of Jess' favorite movies.

Jess is hyper-aware of Abby's arm on the back of the couch, of how casually she's sitting.

"Where'd your robot go?" Jess whispers.

"Docking station, probably," Abby says. "You okay? You said you liked this series, right?"

Jess can't remember if she's talked about *Vindicated* to Abby, but maybe Emma told her. When the fifth movie came out, Jess was really vocal about how much she loved the series and dragged her friends to see it with her three times in the theater. It's only just come out on holoscreen. Jess knows if she starts watching the movie, she'll get into that mindset and not want to work at all afterward.

"Will it help you relax if we got some work done before goofing off?"

Jess nods.

Abby laughs and pauses the movie. "Okay, cool. What should we write about? Ms. Rhinehart said anything goes as long as we collaborate and there's a clear narrative with rising action and all that."

"What kinda story do you want to write? We've done fantasy in class before, and historical, and—"

"Romance," Abby says with a smile. "That's pretty easy, what, the story is like ten pages, right? Girl meets—"

"Girl," Jess blurts out.

"Okay, cool. What are their names?" Abby pulls out a notebook and pen out of her bag, then looks at Jess.

Wow. Okay, so Abby likes the story idea. Jess still has no clue if Abby is attracted to girls.

Why is this so difficult? She could ask, but then it would be too obvious. Jess might as well hold up a neon sign that reads *I've had a crush on you since freshman year* and wave it around hopefully.

"Um. Rebecca. And she's a superhero," Jess says.

"'Kay, she's powered… and she's in love with this other girl?"

"Yes! And when she's in her secret identity, the other girl doesn't know she exists—"

"Michelle, she can be Michelle! I like that name a lot. Okay, what about they… work together? At some boring office job. And Michelle is in love with Rebecca's superhero identity, never knowing that her coworker has been her all along."

Jess giggles. "Ah, that's awesome."

They plot out the story, and Abby writes a paragraph of introduction while Jess plays with a scene of dialogue and makes a brief outline, and then they switch papers.

Abby's handwriting is loopy and messy, and Jess likes the way all her lowercase letters flow into one another. She especially likes the way she writes the letter "y" with the curl arching around the entire word. It's too cute. Jess adds a few lines, and they switch papers again, and Jess finds Abby's added a line of dialogue where she was stuck.

In all of Jess' daydreams, when she finally worked up the courage to talk to Abby, it's played out like a spectacular movie: Jess saving the day with her super-strength; or flying with Abby; or taking her on an elaborate date after presenting her with flowers. It always seemed so far-fetched, an impossible dream, a fun crush to think about.

Maybe Jess was caught up with these ridiculous, impossible ideas because it meant she never had to try for something real.

"Hey," Jess says, tapping her pencil to her lips. "This is fun. I've never written with anyone before."

"Me neither," Abby says, nudging her. "Hey, plot twist."

"Huh?"

"Here, I just thought of something." Abby takes Jess' outline, where Jess enclosed major events in neat little boxes and connected them in sequence. "We can't have a superhero story without a villain, right? So what if..."

It becomes routine over the next two weeks: Mondays, Wednesdays, and Fridays after school, Abby drives Jess to Monroe

Industries and they go to work, Jess in her office with M and Abby in her own office, doing robotics projects. Jess doesn't see her often at work, but she's getting more and more comfortable hanging out and not tripping over her words. Tuesdays and Thursdays, Abby invites her to her house and they work on the project together. They write side-by-side or watch movies.

Today they're at Abby's house, and Jess sits on the edge of Abby's bed, staring up at her ceiling, where Abby's stuck glow-in-the-dark stars. It's too bright to see them in the afternoon, but she wonders how they'd look at night, whether Abby lies here in the dark looking at her own constellations.

"I'll be there in a minute!" Abby calls from downstairs.

"Okay!" Jess calls back, wanting to stay on the bed but also to get up and look around. Jess settles for trying to take in as many details as possible: the navy bedspread, the array of broken computer circuits in the corner, the bookshelf filled with novels and printed comic books. There are many issues Jess recognizes, like the series about Lieutenant Orion and the origin of the Heroes' League of Heroes, but quite a few that she doesn't. Jess almost pulls out a battered copy with the title *Gravitus and the Amazing Rescue!* but stops. She's quite proud of herself; if she gets sucked into the story, she won't pay any attention to work.

Abby said to use her desktop projector. Jess syncs her DED and opens a word processing program. She starts to type up the handwritten bits she and Abby have written so far. She's only a few sentences in when she hears footsteps in the hallway.

"Hey," Abby says, coming through the doorway with two glasses of orange juice. "All right, where're we at with the story?"

"Oh, I've just started typing this part up," Jess says.

"Do you mind music while we work?"

"Not at all."

A radio starts playing in the background, an upbeat pop song with a quick beat. It's a popular song about falling in love and crushes, and Abby hums along to it. Jess bites her lip. *Is Abby humming along to this song about secret crushes because she likes the music or because she relates to it?*

She tries to ignore the butterflies in her stomach and finishes typing up the next section. After Michelle and Rebecca defeat the villain, Jess takes a break and stretches her fingers.

"Oh, I worked on the ending during my math class." Abby pulls a thick sheaf of paper from her backpack and hands it to Jess. "I can type, if you want."

"No, it's okay, I've got a rhythm going."

Jess smiles and takes the papers, glad that Abby started writing this section of the story. They'd agreed a first kiss would go in this part, but Jess was unsure she could write that bit so Abby volunteered. She starts typing, reading the scene for the first time as she goes.

Jess stares at the words and blushes. "Um, do you think this is..."

"What? Is it okay? Too much? Do you like it?" Abby asks with a hesitant smile, curling a finger into her hair and twisting it.

Jess glances back to the page, where the characters are engaged in a furious kiss; clothes are coming off and... "Ah, I don't know if this will be okay for our assignment."

"Ms. Rhinehart didn't say there were any rules against writing sex into the story," Abby says. "Besides, it makes sense. I mean, our characters are two adults in love, and it's fun and silly. Did you like the bit where they take their masks off? I used the same dialogue from your reveal earlier. I thought it worked really well."

Jess' face is hot. "I… can I take this home and tell you later? I just realized I have to do chores. My, um, my MonRobot is really old and has trouble getting up the stairs, so I usually vacuum—"

"But I fixed Chả: Is it malfunctioning again?"

Jess totally forgot about that. "Um. No, Chả is great, I um, I have to babysit my brother this afternoon so—okay! Bye!" Jess is halfway down the hallway before she realizes that Abby drove her here and would have to drive her home.

"Jess, I'm sorry. I should have asked if you'd be okay with it. We don't have to put it in the story; it's just something I worked on in my own time. We were having such a good time working on the separate parts and seeing what the other came up with that I thought putting this piece in was okay. But if it makes you uncomfortable, we can take it out."

Jess takes a deep breath and turns around. Abby stands there, radiant in the soft afternoon light. She changed out of her trendy outfit earlier; in a simple T-shirt and shorts, she seems smaller, vulnerable, and questioning.

"Do you still want to go home?" Abby asks quietly. "I can take you; it's okay."

"I just… I don't think I could sit in your bedroom and write a sex scene, that's all." Jess bites her lip. *What's the best way to say because it's too embarrassing to talk to a crush about sex and read an explicit thing they wrote while they're right there?*

"Okay. Did you want to take it out? We can work on something else. Or not work on it at all. Movie?"

"I have to get home for dinner," Jess says. "I really haven't been spending a lot of time there because I'm either here or at work and... Yeah."

Abby drives Jess home in silence.

JESS ISN'T SURE WHERE SHE stands with Abby.

She tells Bells as much, chatting away on the comm link that night while she's working on her biology homework. She was a little worried that things might be weird after her reaction to the sex scene, but the series of messages between her and Abby afterward suggests that everything is okay. Jess thumbs over the series of happy faces Abby sent her, tracing her fingers over the projections as she talks to Bells.

"It's great hanging out with Abby. You know, we've gone from strangers to what, study buddies? Assignment partners?"

Bells chuckles, his voice light and teasing. "How about friends? Or maybe soon-to-be-more-than friends?"

"Shut up," Jess says, laughing.

Something on Bells' end crackles and hisses.

"Is something on fire?" she asks. "Bells?"

"Ah— I'm fine, I'm fine!"

"I thought you didn't have work today. I can't believe Simon let you in the kitchen."

"Uh, he didn't come back this weekend. I'm... yeah. I'm in charge of cooking today. Gotta go, bye!"

The call disconnects, and Jess shakes her head.

She lies back on her bed, closes the comm link, and thinks about the next time she'll get to hang out with Abby.

BEING WITH ABBY IS SOMETHING to look forward to every day, even if it's just the twenty-minute ride from school to work. Jess is daydreaming about it during class today, fading in and out of consciousness, practically falling asleep. History is right after lunch, and she can barely concentrate. Mr. Liu's voice is such a soothing monotone. Jess' head bobs forward, and when she jerks upright, a few people turn around.

"Ah, Jessica. Can you tell me who was the first meta-human recognized as a superhero in the North American Collective after the X29 solar flare in 2028?" Mr. Liu looks at Jess expectantly, and she's grateful that they're learning a contemporary module on recent history.

And Jess is nothing if not an expert on heroes and villains.

"Gravitus, real name Vance Stackson revealed after his death in 2038," Jess says. "A-class powers of gravity manipulation and was an incredibly formidable hero in the first wave of meta-humans. He was one of the founding members of the Heroes' League of Heroes."

A few of her classmates look bored. Elizabeth is sending a message on her DED and Darryl is nodding, but most people look either confused or ambivalent. Denise is holding back a smirk, as if she knows Jess is wrong.

"I'm sorry," Mr. Liu says. "You must have gotten confused. Gravitus was one of the greatest supervillains of his time. Which actually wasn't that long ago, I mean, my grandfather still remembers that battle between him and—who can tell me the correct answer?"

Denise raises her hand. "Lieutenant Orion," she says. "Also known as the famed astronaut James Oliphaous. A-class powers of superstrength and speed, flight, and manipulation of heat. Defeated the *villain* Gravitus in 2038. Lieutenant Orion is still alive today and attends social functions every now and then. Of his three children, only one was a meta-human and exhibited C-class powers, but his granddaughter, Captain Orion, continues his legacy of hero-work at the A-class level.

Jess frowns, because she distinctly remembers Gravitus as a hero. Sure, he and Lieutenant Orion had a huge falling out, leading to that eventual battle in 2038 and Gravitus' death, but Gravitus surely had never been a villain.

She looks at the holobook she'd been falling asleep in and ignores the trace of drool on the desk, though it shines through the projected text. She scans the summary of the chapter on meta-humans.

> *In 2028 an unusually intense solar flare, measured at X29 intensity, swathed the Earth in cosmic radiation, which awakened the latent meta-abilities of humans with the then-unknown meta-gene. The meta-gene is still under scientific investigation but apparently expresses itself naturally in about 0.0001% of the population. Meta-humans who discovered their abilities went through an extreme period of hyper-vigilante acts until Lieutenant James Oliphaous, more commonly known by the name Lieutenant Orion, established the Heroes' League of Heroes to create a coalition for do-gooders everywhere.*

There's nothing about Gravitus until she flicks through a few pages and finds a colorful module that details the Battle of 2038. Jess reads the section and then reads it again.

The bell rings, but Jess moves slowly. She could have sworn she read about Gravitus' hero work in a textbook. The students pick up their last homework assignments and then pore over their grades as they file out of the classroom.

"What'd you get on number seventeen?" Darryl asks. "I mean, I know I didn't completely explain why Australia didn't join the Global Federation, but I didn't think you'd need to. It's common knowledge where they stood on resources after the war."

"Uh, I got ten points," Jess says, looking over Darryl's shoulder at the holopage still up on his DED, where a big "3" is marked in red over his answer. "Part of the assignment is to explain why; you can't just regurgitate what the book says."

She shows him her own assignment and shrugs before closing the window.

Darryl frowns. "But you just rephrased it."

Jess chuckles. "Yeah, I mean, not what I would do if I'm writing a paper, but in a pinch it'll do. Plus, Mr. Liu has a ton of these things to grade. I'm pretty sure he just scans it and makes sure you don't have what the book says and then he'll give you full points."

"Ah." Darryl nods. "Are you headed to the B building?"

"Yeah, chemistry."

"Ooh! I have math over there. I'll go with you." Darryl falls into step with her. "So what are you doing Thursday afternoon? Some of us are going bowling. It's a combination party and fundraiser."

Jess sighs and turns to look Darryl in the eye. "Look, I like the idea of the thing, but I just… I don't really fit in, you know? And it is pretty much you and your group of friends, Darryl, it's all of you, hanging out together, and I don't—"

"What do you mean, you don't fit in?" Darryl says. "You like girls! You're totally one of us."

"Yeah, but that's not the only— " Jess sighs. She thought Darryl knew this, but apparently not. "I'm bisexual."

"Oh. I thought for some reason—I—you—never mind. But you still totally can come hang out with us!"

"I'd feel weird," Jess says, remembering how she'd gone to a meeting before and felt on edge the whole time, as if she wasn't *enough*. "Thanks, but sorry, I can't."

"What about your friend Bells? He's trans, right?"

"You can ask him if he wants to go, but he usually helps at his family's restaurant after school."

Darryl seems to deflate a little, and Jess remembers what Abby said about the club trying harder; this is Darryl trying. "Thank you for the invite, though, I mean, I do appreciate the reaching out. Maybe next time? I'm kind of swamped with Rhinehart's assignment and everything."

Darryl grins and waves goodbye at her. "Sure! See you later!"

THE GRAVITUS THING STILL BUGS her when the last bell rings. Jess meets Abby in the parking lot as usual. "Hey, we're almost done, right?"

"Yeah," Abby says. "I figured we could finish today and watch the rest of *Vindicated 6*. You in?"

"I actually really wanted to check something at home; it's gonna bother me all afternoon if I don't. I can catch the bus, it's no big deal."

Abby shrugs. "Nah, you're on my way. I can drop you off."

Jess nods and gets into the car. Her house isn't really on the way at all; it's in the opposite direction from Abby's house, but she appreciates the air-conditioned comfort of Abby's car and the company of Abby herself, especially in contrast to the crowded bus and the multiple stops before Jess' neighborhood.

When Abby pulls into Jess' driveway, she says, "I'll talk to you later, okay? And we're still on for carpooling to work, and then Tuesday next week, we'll be finishing the project, right?"

"Definitely," Jess says, and thanks Abby with a smile.

Apparently having finished with her cover job for the day, her mother is at home already. Jess puts her stuff in her room and goes to Claudia's old bedroom. A thick sheen of dust covers everything. Jess ignores the wall of accolades, ribbons, and trophies from Claudia's illustrious high school career and heads right for the bookshelf.

She digs out the old textbook; this must have been the last print edition before the schools switched to all-digital. Jess brings up her holobook on her DED; the contents look identical, aside from the bright colors and new photo on the holobook cover. Jess compares the table of contents, which is exactly the same. She flips to the module on early meta-humans and reads from Claudia's textbook:

Lieutenant Orion and Gravitus were both astronauts on the SS Intrepid during the X29 incident. Longtime stalwart friends who learned the extent of their own meta-abilities together, the partnership of Orion and Gravitus was the precursor organization of the Heroes' League of Heroes

> *after the formation of the North American Collective. They disagreed on the extent of cooperation with the United States Department of Defense, which ended with them coming to blows and eventually Gravitus' death at Orion's hands in 2038.*

Jess frowns. The new book never mentions "hero" or "villain" when describing Gravitus, only briefly mentions his death, and does not say why he disagreed with Orion.

"Mom!" Jess yells.

She can hear her mom respond, but she's too far away to make out what she's saying.

Jess goes downstairs and finds her mom in the office, typing away at her desk.

"I'm in the middle of a really good flow here, Mei-Mei," Li Hua says, but does not look up from the projected display. There are two different word processing documents open; one is filled with notes and the other is her current project. "Is everything all right?"

"Do you remember Gravitus?"

"Oh, he was the one with incredible strength, right?" Li Hua nods, tilting her head. "I didn't arrive in the country until after his death, but I remember hearing a lot about it."

"My history textbook says that he was a villain." Jess shows her the module.

"Hmm. I remember hearing that he did almost destroy all of Main Street in New Bright City once. And that was before Lieutenant Orion showed up."

"What was their disagreement, do you remember?"

Mom shrugs. "It's all so long ago, sweetie. Is it important to you? We did cover it in our meta-human history section of training, but I was busy practicing control of my powers and learning—"

"I know you and dad were in Meta-Human Training together, right after you got to the NAC. But you were in school in China, right? What did you learn about meta-humans? It still must have been pretty new."

Li Hua sighs. "China had its own share of meta-humans, and because of the war with Constavia and the conflict over the Kravian Islands, meta-humans were considered a resource. Even when my abilities manifested as a teenager, it took a few years for me to get my strength. And I had to keep it secret. Soldiers were on the lookout for anything strange, expecting us to fight for one side or another: the nationalists who wanted China independent of the Global Federation; the factions that wanted to unify with other countries and the conflicts over which ones. Too many sides. The fighting went on for decades. And my sisters and I just wanted to get to safety."

"The refugee camps were crowded. I just... I did what I could, but it wasn't until I heard on the radio that the Global Federation was discussing meta-human activities, and it was so novel. I mean, we knew about how Lieutenant Orion came back from space with all these powers, but it still seemed so far away. Unreal. And meta-humans in the NAC, the way they talked about them, it was as though they were celebrated. Given jobs, spoken of openly. Not at all like what we were used to, where our abilities had to be kept secret. There was another one of us, at the camp, but he was taken away."

There are traces of old fear in her eyes now, and Jess thinks she sees tears welling up. She doesn't know what to do, has never seen her mother so vulnerable. Li Hua looks at her feet. "I don't know what happened to him, but I knew that keeping it secret was important. Your father, on the other hand, wanted nothing more than to be useful. He disclosed his new powers to the NAC authorities the first chance he got. I didn't want him to be alone, so I went with him."

"We ended up here, and started working with the Heroes' League, training as best we could. Our power level was never high enough for the government to want us on big missions, but we did want to help. And using our powers, letting them test us, it was helpful. And finally we got the green light to go live our lives, got a little direction on being Shockwave and Smasher, and we settled here and had you kids. It's been great. The government is good to us. Don't ask about Gravitus, not outside this house, okay?"

Jess wasn't expecting the long story, but nods, grateful for the information. She carries her books back to her room and throws everything on the floor.

She turns on her desktop projector and syncs her DED. Her fingers dance over the light-up keys projected on her desk as she searches for "Gravitus" and scans the search results. She finds just a few different accounts, some eyewitness perspectives, and clips from an old documentary in which Lieutenant Orion talks about defeating him.

Jess opens the video, taking in the bright blue mask, the sagging features of the hero of the North American Collective. He still wears the gaudy blue and silver outfit, and the way the camera is softly lit, like a tell-all on a reality show, makes him look smaller than he does in the old holos.

"Gravitus was a danger to all of us in the North American Collective and the Global Federation," Lieutenant Orion says on the video, nodding, still handsome with his graying hair and wrinkled face, the effects of years just starting to take root despite his advanced age. He looks away from the camera. His voice is gritty and rough. "My only regret is that I didn't stop him sooner."

Jess finishes the video and looks at the date. This was aired last year.

In her search results, she can't find anything news-related published from that time. There's one article from 2038, but it's very brief and vague, only speaks about Gravitus' death.

Jess ignores her pile of homework and calls out that she's going to the public library. She takes the minivan. The main room of the library is crowded, filled with students doing homework or using the desktop projectors and elderly people reading newspapers in Chinese or Vietnamese.

"Do you have any news reports from the 2030s?"

The librarian says, "We'd have to request it from the Central NAC Database; we don't have that here. You're welcome to browse our online catalog, to see what was converted into holos, but you'll need special permission and an archival DVD player to view anything before 2041."

Jess thanks him and uses a library console to see if there are any original reports of the fight between Orion and Gravitus. She finds the same article she found online; a short article that doesn't make sense and calls Gravitus a mastermind of nefarious plots. It doesn't have a publication date.

She sighs, logs off, and then drives home.

Jess has messages from Abby. Her spirits lighten as she flicks through them. Abby is looking forward to finishing their project together. Jess takes a bit too long to look at the series of happy faces Abby sends her; she watches them float above her wrist as she tries to decipher the emoticons. *This winky face isn't flirty. Abby's just enthusiastic.*

Jess messages her back that she is looking forward to finishing, too, and then bites her lip and goes out on a limb.

To: Abby Jones 6:34 pm
hey, do you know who gravitus was?

From: Abby Jones 6:35 pm
yeah, why

To: Abby Jones 6:37 pm
he wasn't a villain, right? or am i remembering things wrong?

The DED chimes with a new comm link. Jess picks up. "Hey."

"Gravitus, huh?" Abby says.

Jess explains what happened at school and what she found in Claudia's old textbook.

"So you figured out that the history books change all the time. I'm surprised you had an old one to refer to; usually the feds are really good about getting rid of whatever narrative they're trying to change. I guess it's easier now that they stopped using print textbooks."

"What? No way, they wouldn't do that. Why would they cover up that Gravitus used to be a hero?"

"No idea. Do you want me to come over? I've got something to show you if you're interested in this stuff."

Jess looks at the time. It's almost dinnertime, and she usually tries to shoo Emma and Bells out the door before her parents get all awkward with them, but her curiosity is getting the better of her.

"Sure, you can come over," Jess says.

She looks at herself and considers changing out of her school outfit. Would it be too obvious if she changed into something more flattering? Abby would probably notice, and then Jess would be all out of luck.

Jess looks at her crumpled T-shirt and jeans: there's a stain from the dismal school spaghetti on her shirtfront.

Okay, changing it is.

She digs through her closet, pushes aside things that are too formal and clothes that don't fit anymore, grabs a few options. She tries on shirt after shirt.

This shirt's V-neck dips too low, and Jess blushes at how much cleavage shows; this shirt is out. She picks another tank top and throws over it a loose-fitting lace top, an impulse buy she's never worn; no, she can't pull this off. Jess scowls and finally settles on the last clean, and normal-ish shirt of hers—the "Master Mischief Was Right About the Cheese" graphic tee.

Ugh, she should have called Emma; she's always good at whipping up outfits from whatever's around.

The doorbell rings, and Jess races past her mother, who is just standing up from her chair in the office. "I got it, I got it!" Jess hurls herself down the stairs and flings the door open. "Hi," she says, breathlessly.

"Hey, Jess." Abby's changed from her school outfit, too, and looks comfortable in an old AHHS volleyball T-shirt and a loose pair of basketball shorts. She's carrying a large portfolio, the kind artists use to haul around paintings.

"Oh, hello, I don't think I've met you before," Li Hua says from the top of the stairs.

"Mom, this is Abby, Abby, this is my mom, we're just gonna go study—bye!"

Jess jerks her head for Abby to follow before the interrogation starts, but she's too late. Li Hua's eyes light up. "Abby! Oh, Jess talks about you all the time!"

Jess' cheeks turn red. Oh God, no, no, no. "Thanks, Mom. We have a big project, lots of work to do."

Abby chuckles and follows Jess to her bedroom. "Nice to meet you, Mrs. Tran."

"Likewise!" Li Hua says, and then adds, "Kai men, okay?" to Jess. Jess' jaw drops because she's never heard her mother ask to leave the door open when Emma or Bells visited, but there's no time to argue.

Abby looks around Jess' bedroom; her eyes flick over all the Captain Orion posters on the wall. "Fangirl, eh?" she teases, but there's no heat in it. "I'm a Bellevue girl myself, but the Captain's pretty cool."

"Ah, yes, um, I used to—I mean I still, okay." Jess' mind goes blank at the sight of Abby sprawling out on her bed.

Abby's hair is pulled back in a purple headband, vivid against her scarlet hair, which is springing out in a riot of curls to frame her face in a fluffy halo.

Abby opens the portfolio and pulls out posters preserved in collector's plastic. "My dad was an avid fan of Gravitus," she says. "He kept all the posters and comics, everything. He said there was a recall of the material, back when he was in college."

Abby hands a poster to Jess, who marvels at it. It's the same type of poster she's seen for Lieutenant Orion in the National History Museum in the Meta-Humans section; the same artist could have designed it. In vivid painted strokes, it depicts Gravitus in his solid gray costume, holding his arms aloft, with columns of earth lifting him toward the sky.

"I knew it! He was a hero!" Jess says. "Then why all the erasure? Why go to all this trouble to make sure we forgot him?"

"It's definitely fishy. Gravitus isn't the only one, you know. The whole origin of the Heroes' League of Heroes is really interesting, and by interesting I mean, we only know the nice, neat packaged story we get in the textbooks. And this wasn't all that long ago. But when you think about spin and how people can twist things... Like, think about X29, and all these people for the first time, all over the world, discovering their powers. I mean, different countries handled it in various ways, but for the most part, people went on with their lives. The ratio of meta-humans to those unaffected by the solar flare was so huge that there weren't enough metas to mean much to a government unless they could be useful on the battlefield. Except when they started to interfere in government plans like the decision to invade

Constavia, and then the government started getting all the meta-humans to register—"

"To keep track of them, to provide them with resources and then training," Jess says, repeating what her parents have told her time and time again.

Abby huffs and crosses her arms. "I'm not saying the system doesn't work, but it has its flaws, you know? Have you ever thought about the people in Meta-Human Training who go through the program but *don't* become superheroes?"

Jess' parents barely made it onto the C-list because their power level was so low. They wax nostalgic about how fun the program was: how it was great to meet everyone, the friendships formed, living on the campus, learning the extent of their powers, research. But they've never talked much about the other people. They're not supposed to, especially since everyone had their secret identities, but it probably isn't hard for someone to guess who their old roommate is now, and she's seen her parents chuckle when people they used to know are in the news.

But the power ranking system ensured that everyone got the amount of training they needed; and there were powers that weren't appropriate for battle. Those people would be shifted to jobs specific to their nature where they could still help the country.

"I guess they went back to their lives, and they're just living among us," Jess says. "I mean, anyone could have a low-level power and not be a superhero, you know. It's not like the Meta-Human Training program puts out Captain Orions every class."

"Yeah, okay, but there's a chance that there are a number of A-class people who don't become heroes, right? Also, you don't really look comfortable. Am I taking up too much space?"

"No, no, you're fine." Jess sits on the edge of the bed.

Abby looks at her. Jess can't figure out what that expression is, but her own heart is thudding loudly.

"Here, look," Abby says. She takes out an old comic book and flips through it until she stops on a page where Lieutenant Orion and Gravitus are working together to help put out a disastrous forest fire in the San Bernardino's.

"This happened?" Jess scoots closer. She ends up on her stomach next to Abby as the two of them pore over the old comics. Jess bites her lip, grateful that Abby collects print comics—she can't imagine huddling this close to her flicking through a holobook.

"Pretty sure the comic artists were all inspired by actual events." Abby shows Jess how all the comics start: Lieutenant Orion finding Gravitus at the scene, Gravitus creating a natural firebreak with his earth powers, and Orion flying firefighters to safety. "There aren't holos of these things anymore, though, not of Gravitus being heroic. I mean, there is a record of this particular fire and Lieutenant Orion being there, but—"

"They wrote Gravitus out of it," Jess says.

"Exactly."

Abby leans close. Their shoulders touch. Abby's close enough for Jess to smell her shampoo—apple and cinnamon.

Abby looks up, and their eyes meet; Jess is too afraid to look away, too nervous to move closer. She hangs in the moment, wondering, wondering. It's the worst part about being attracted to girls—she doesn't know how to flirt. Will Abby think she's just being friendly? Should she just say it? But then if she says something, their whole friendship will change, and they only just started being close. And Jess likes that a lot. The chances that Abby is straight are high, and asking might ruin everything.

Abby's eyelashes and eyebrows are a darker red than her hair, and there's a faint scar running down her left cheek. Jess takes in all the details of her face so she can look back on this moment and remember—*one time Abby Jones was on my bed and was this close, close enough to kiss—*

There's a knock on the open door. "You girls ready for dinner?"

Jess scoots back away from Abby. As much as she likes to dream about kissing Abby, the reality is that she's not ready to find out whether Abby wants to kiss her back. Better not to risk certain rejection and stay in this realm of infinite possibility.

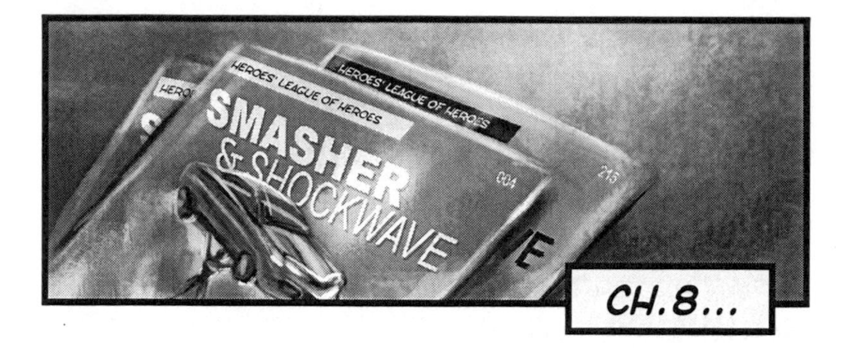

Brendan, who usually reads at the table, looks up from his DED and peers curiously around his holobook with the projected text flickering on his face. He blinks at Abby. "Who're you?"

"Abby Jones," Abby says. "I'm friends with Jess, from school."

Brendan scrunches up his face. "Are you a new student?"

Abby takes the plate of vegetables and tofu from Li Hua. "No, been attending AHHS since freshman year."

"So why are you friends now?" Brendan asks. "Jess only has had two friends since freshman year. If you've gone to the same school, you knew each other, so why start being friends now?"

Jess looks at her plate and wishes she could disappear.

"Brendan, stop being rude," Victor says. "People can start being friends any time they want. When I was in M—college, there were quite a few people I didn't start talking to until two years into the program. It's perfectly normal."

"Thanks, Dad," Jess says.

"Well, I didn't know Jess until we started AP English together this year," Abby says. "That's all."

"Ah, what classes are you taking?" Li Hua asks.

Abby rattles off her schedule, which sounds startlingly similar—just exchange volleyball for tennis and she'd be another Claudia.

AP everything, including Student Leadership, the elective for student government.

"Oh, you're so involved!" Li Hua says. "You should encourage Jess to try for something; she's never really shown more than a passing interest in sports or any extracurriculars."

"That's because I didn't like any of them," Jess says, picking at the vegetables on her plate.

"But you come to the volleyball games!" Abby says. She knits her eyebrows. "I've seen you in the stands a lot."

"Oh—you noticed?" Jess says. Hope flutters in her chest, a fragile and new thing. It could be just friendship, but Abby *noticed* her even before they started working together. She likes spending time with Jess; she stayed for dinner.

"Well, aside from the parents and the friends, I mean, the prelim games don't really draw a lot of attention, so it's not like I wouldn't see you," Abby says. "Emma is on the team, though. That makes sense, that you're really supportive."

Jess nods, eager for a way out. Emma laughed at her when she first started going to all the games; she told her that the preseason games were probably going to be pretty boring, but Jess wanted to go.

Brendan laughs. "Jess and sports? Never."

Jess colors. She's not bad in P.E.; she just gets bored easily. She does the assigned exercise at school because she has to, but she's never figured out the whole team thing. And she's not good with hand-eye coordination.

"Um, well, student elections are up soon if you wanna run for anything. I think pretty much any position other than president and vice would be easy. You'd only run against one person, probably someone who already held that position. Or you can do student affairs, that's a position," Abby says. "It's really easy, winning the election if you're the only one running, and the whole responsibility thing isn't bad either. You get a whole period with all the other officers to plan the school dances and stuff."

Jess pokes at her food. "I don't know. Maybe. I'm not really into planning the pep rallies and dances and everything."

Abby shrugs. "It looks good on college apps, if that's what you're into. But personally I think Jess has a strong application anyway. She does well in her classes, she really is good at writing, and she's got this story that will probably win this short story contest, if she actually enters it. And she's got a job as an executive assistant at Monroe Industries. I mean, how many high schoolers can say they do that?"

Jess stares.

Abby turns to her and nods.

"I—ah—thanks, Abby," Jess says.

"Well, of course we knew about the job; we're so proud of you," Li Hua says. "But doing a sport would really help you be well rounded."

Abby and Jess catch each other's gaze and Abby gives a little shrug, *I tried.*

Jess nods back.

After dinner, back in Jess' room Abby asks, "Do you wanna try to work on our story while I'm here?"

"Sure."

They work on their short story, and the pleasant sound of their pens on paper makes a nice rhythm. Every so often one of them asks about a word or where this sentence should go, but it's just nice, companionable. By the time Jess thinks to check the clock, it's already past ten.

Abby yawns.

Jess looks at her, thinking about her big empty house, all cold glass and steel. "Are you okay to drive home?"

"It'll be cool," Abby says, rubbing at her eyes.

"You can sleep over, if you want." Abby lifts an eyebrow, and Jess tries not to blush. "If you want to! It could be fun! I have extra pajamas and stuff, and um, usually when Emma and Bells stay over we just all crash on the bed, but we have a guest room if you'd be more comfortable."

"Okay," Abby says, with a small, pleased smile. "Sure. I'd love to. It sounds like fun."

"Um, okay." Jess roots around in her drawers for a clean pair of pajamas, finds a blue fleece set with fluffy clouds on them, and hands them to Abby. "I'll get you a toothbrush."

Jess is in the main bathroom, looking for the new spares, when Brendan walks by, singing loudly, "Jess and Abby sitting in a tree—"

Jess grabs her little brother and claps a hand over his mouth. "Do not finish that," she hisses in a fierce whisper, eyeing her open bedroom door. "Otherwise I'm telling Mom and Dad where all the missing parts from Mom's Smashmobile went last year, conveniently right before you finished your Young Inventors project."

"Fine, fine." Brendan rolls his eyes, but continues to whistle the song as he walks down the hall.

Jess ignores him, finds what she needs, and walks back to her bedroom with a new toothbrush. Her mouth goes dry. Abby is sitting in her bed, wearing her pajamas. The top button is undone, revealing a hint of collarbone and the slope of her long, graceful neck.

Abby's thumbing through one of Jess' comic books. "Not too many people have Smasher and Shockwave comics," she says. "You've got the entire collection."

Jess has them because she loves comics and is supportive of her parents. She wants to have something to show their legacy, even if it's just stopping a few robberies in their city.

Abby turns the book around to show an illustration of Master Mischief and Mistress Mischief flying in the air in their mecha-suits. "This is funny; Mistress Mischief doesn't wear a mecha-suit. She doesn't need to."

Jess looks at the panel; the artist even got the colors wrong. Their outfits are nowhere near as garish. "Yeah, well, artistic license I guess. I mean, they always draw Smasher with these huge boobs, and her outfit isn't that tight. Look, that's not even how fabric works." Jess points at another panel where it looks as if her mom's outfit has an unnatural focus and shading on the chest. "They don't really bother getting all the facts of these things right either. I mean, I was at this battle, I saw it happen, and Mistress Mischief definitely didn't make that store's holo display malfunction."

"Yeah, it's like the writers think she's a technopath like Master Mischief." Abby chuckles.

"Or maybe it's just that they work together seamlessly, so people always think their powers are the same."

She looks fondly at the comic book; there's a panel where the artist draw the Mischiefs together giving each other sly, cunning looks.

"You can keep it, if you like it so much," Jess says. "I have a bunch."

It's true. Her parents have a box of each print issue in the basement. The Mischiefs don't have their own comic; comics are named after the heroes. Jess makes a note to ask M if there's a record-keeping project, or whether the Mischiefs care if they're in the comic.

Abby's fingers curl around the edge of the pages as she looks at the art.

"Thanks." Abby puts the comic in her backpack and then gets back on the bed.

"We could work more, but I think we're ahead enough on our project that we can like watch a movie if you want."

"Sure."

Jess activates her desktop projector and brings it to her bed. The holos dance, and her DED flashes her last-used programs. She rarely uses the larger projector when she's in bed, preferring to just look at the smaller holos on her DED, but this is a special occasion. Jess pulls up a list of the movies she has as well as what's currently streaming on the community data exchange. Jess flicks at the list, letting the titles scroll lazily in the air. There are some romances, some adventure movies… and Jess wonders if Abby would like any of those twenty-first century movies, with old ideas of superheroes—maybe another time when she has a feel for what Abby would think of the contraband media. "Here, you can look through what I have and pick something out. I'm good with anything, just nothing scary."

Abby grins at her. "You don't like scary movies?"

Jess shrugs. "It's just the gore and all the... Yeah, they're dumb, and I don't like being jumped at."

Abby flicks the projected cover of *Vindicated 3* and it spins in the air, ready to be played. She quirks her eyebrow at Jess when the menu displays that Jess has watched it seventeen times. "You like thrillers like the *Vindicated* series, though."

"That's different! I like mysteries and... there's no ridiculous monster waiting to carve up people, okay," Jess says.

Abby grins. "What about really terrible horror movies? Sometimes they're so bad they're good. And it's fun to watch with someone; that's the best part."

"Okay. Find something you like; I can't promise that I'll enjoy it but I'm willing to give it a shot."

Jess grabs her own pajamas, and goes to change in the bathroom. When she's changed and brushing her teeth, Abby knocks on the door, looking shy and nervous, and Jess jerks her head for her to come in. Brushing her teeth next to Abby is oddly intimate. She is softer somehow, in her pajamas, than when she's wearing her usual outfits.

Abby giggles as they walk back to the bedroom. "I really hope you like this."

Jess can't tell if she's ever seen Abby so excited—not when her volleyball team won, not at work when she solved a successful problem.

They get into bed and bump into each other when they both go for the right side, where Jess normally sleeps. Jess scoots to the left and gives Abby the nicer of the pillows. She doesn't mind giving up her favorite side of the bed really.

"All right, what do you have for us to watch?" Jess asks. The paused projection looks like an old black and white film showing goo leaking from a building.

"*The Blob from Ivan Lake*. It's ridiculously awesome."

"Is the Blob the monster?" Jess has never heard of this movie and wonders if it's from Old America, and then dismisses that notion. The Collective had a phase a few years back where they made everything in black and white because it was in vogue. Abby's head bobs; her eyes light up. "Okay, let's go," Jess says, and pulls the covers up over her knees.

They sit close together, with the three-dimensional movie playing in front of them. They keep pausing to readjust the projector to bring the holos closer, and soon enough there's a comfortable nest of pillows with Abby and Jess sprawled in the midst of them. Their shoulders touch, and each brush sends a thrill down Jess' spine.

Jess finds herself laughing throughout the movie because it's *terrible* and not scary at all. Abby watches her more than the movie, points things out, and tells her more about the weird stunts.

After the movie Abby puts on another one, which stars a giant mutant grizzly bear, and they laugh their way through this one as well.

Jess can't look away, wanting to see how the plucky protagonist figures out how to escape from the bear, when she notices Abby hasn't said anything for a while.

A soft weight falls on her shoulder, and Jess turns to see Abby breathing rhythmically, fast asleep.

Jess smiles and watches her for a bit, and then gently lays Abby down and puts her head on a pillow. She turns off the desktop projector, and she should really put her DED in the charging dock, but she doesn't want to move.

Abby's eyelashes are dark against her skin and fluttering every time she breathes. Jess closes her eyes and drifts off to a contented sleep.

JESS WAKES UP INCREDIBLY WARM. Somewhere downstairs, her mom and younger brother are talking loudly about cereal. It must be time to wake up, almost; she still has time if they haven't left yet.

She turns, sighing happily at the how comfortable her bed is, eager for a few more minutes of sleep before her alarm goes off, and finds a heavy weight draped across her stomach.

Jess opens her eyes.

Abby is sound asleep with her arm curled around Jess' waist, holding on to her tightly. Under the covers Abby threw a leg over her, like an anchor. There's a faint smile on Abby's lips, as if she's dreaming of something special.

Sometime during the night, Jess' pajama shirt rucked up. Abby's hand rests on Jess' bare skin, and Jess stares at it. Abby's fingers move a bit every time she takes a breath, and every brush seems to radiate to Jess' core.

Downstairs there's a loud thump, and Abby stirs, curling closer to Jess. Jess closes her eyes and takes shallow breaths, not wanting to break the spell—

Her alarm sounds like blaring foghorns; her DED shines colored lights all about the room as it bounces on her desk.

"Gah!" Abby jolts up and falls off the bed, taking all the sheets and covers with her. "Abby!" Jess calls out, peering over the edge of the bed. "Are you okay?"

"Ah, just surprised. That alarm is... really something," Abby says, turning bright red as she looks at Jess. "Last night, did we finish the bear movie?"

"You fell asleep. I turned it off; you looked like you needed the rest."

Abby blinks. There's a pillow crease on her face, and her hair is everywhere.

The alarm horns are still going; the DED vibrates in a furious rhythm before it falls onto the jumble of blankets on the floor. It continues to make muffled shrieks until Jess reaches off the bed to flick the manual off switch on the display. The DED's holos flicker weakly as she checks the time. The battery must be drained.

"We've got an hour before school starts—"

Abby gets up. "I can drive, so we have enough time."

"Do you want to borrow some clothes?" Jess gets out of bed and from her closet picks out a button-down shirt that's loose on her. "I'm not sure they will fit." Pajamas are easy, but Abby's hips are wider, her shoulders are broader, and she's taller too.

Abby takes a look at the shirt Jess has picked out and shakes her head. "Thanks, but I'd probably pop all the buttons off that one. Boob problems."

Jess glances and then quickly looks away, shaking the idea out of her mind. In the back of her closet, she finds a bigger T-shirt, a Captain Orion one she wears to sleep sometimes.

Abby takes it, and she doesn't wait for Jess to leave the room before she shucks off her pajama top.

Jess turns away from the sight of Abby's bare back, grabs her own clothes, and runs for the bathroom. Her face burns.

Jess changes into her outfit—jeans and a T-shirt that's seen better days—but whatever. Thinking about Abby changing in her room makes her a bit lightheaded, but the night spent together makes her happy, and she can hardly believe it was real.

She finds Abby tying her hair back in a simple ponytail, wearing her basketball shorts and the Captain Orion T-shirt. She turns to Jess and smiles.

"Hey, thanks for letting me stay the night," Abby says.

"No problem. What are friends for?"

Abby laughs. "Oh, here. Your DED fell on the floor during that terrible alarm."

"Thanks!" Jess attaches it to her wrist, noticing that it's at half-battery. Huh, it must have had more charge than she thought. She realizes that she's being a terrible host. "Oh, is your DED dead or anything? You can charge it while we eat, I mean it won't be much but—"

"I'm good, thanks," Abby says, waving her own wrist. Her DED is fully charged, judging by the strength of the projections.

"Your batteries must be amazing," Jess mutters.

Abby shrugs and follows Jess out the room.

Li Hua has already left to take Brendan to his college, and Jess grabs a box of Captain Orion's Favorite™ Breakfast Pastries out of the pantry. "Chocolate or strawberry?"

"Oooh, chocolate," Abby says.

Jess toasts two chocolate pastries, and then they're off in Abby's shiny Mercedes.

"I'm sorry that, um, you have to wear my clothes. I know you usually like to dress up for school."

Abby shrugs. "It's no big deal. I mean, this year I've thought a lot about things and like... it's hard work, being student body president and captain of the volleyball team. I mean, people expect so much of you, and I always have to be *on* all the time, and then earlier this year... um... well, my mom got sick..."

"Oh. I'm sorry. Do you know... Do you know what it is?" She remembers Abby's parents were at a conference, or maybe it was just Abby's dad?

"No, not yet, but it's serious. It's why I quit the president gig and stopped playing volleyball."

"Don't worry about it. The pressure stuff. You're doing you, you know? I mean, taking time for yourself is important. I know."

Abby pats Jess on the arm.

They arrive at school and Abby parks. Jess trails behind Abby as they enter the campus.

Abby walks ahead, as confident wearing a T-shirt and shorts as she is in any of her designer clothes. They get a few looks but no one says anything, and then Jess spots Bells.

"Hey, I'm gonna get to class, I'll see you later," Jess says.

"See you later," Abby says, and she steps a little closer, as if she's about to say something.

The bell rings.

Abby steps back and gives Jess a small smile and a funny little wave before she walks away.

Jess watches her go and then rushes to catch up with Bells so they can get to class.

"Oh my God, did I just see what I thought I saw?" Bells asks, his eyebrows nearly reaching his hairline. "You and Abby came to school together!?"

"Yeah, she gave me a ride. I like your hair today, it's blue! When did you dye it? Did you have to do a complicated thing with bleach or something, because it was purple yesterday."

"Don't change the subject." Bells grins wildly. "My hair always looks amazing. Now okay, maybe I might buy that your new friend gave you a lift to school, but, but, but! She is also wearing your favorite T-shirt. Explain that!"

Jess shrugs. "We were working late on Rhinehart's assignment last night, and Abby stayed over, no big deal. You and Emma stay over all the time. You have totally worn my clothes before."

"Okay but, you don't want to date me or Emma," Bells says, bouncing a little. "Oh my God, please tell me all the details."

Jess turns red as they walk into the classroom. She whispers, "Later, at lunch."

THEY DON'T GET TO TALK about it at lunch because Abby's already joined them. She's in an intense conversation with Emma about Captain Orion and Lilliputian, Emma's favorite superhero.

Abby grins and waves at them. "Hey, settle this, Jess, you're the superhero expert. Caption Orion or Lilliputian?"

"Captain Orion," Jess says.

Emma gasps. "No way. Lilliputian can shrink to the molecular level. That is way cool, okay?"

"Yeah, but she can't fly. And it takes her forever to get anywhere in that size! She always needs assistance when she's at the atomic level, too. Her power is practically useless. And you forgot that even at the A-class, Lilliputian can only use her powers for about three hours a day, so whatever she does has to be planned out perfectly."

Abby hands Jess her lunch tray, complete with steaming hot tater tots. "For you, I got extra."

Bells laughs. "Oh man, I should get a girlfriend, too!"

Abby doesn't say anything, just hands Jess the ketchup.

Jess' cheeks heat up but Emma turns the conversation away from Bells' joke toward volleyball.

On their way to fifth period, Jess coughs, taking advantage of the hustle and bustle of the crowd leaving the open quad to have a private conversation. They're away from her friends, at least. "Hey. I'm sorry if that was weird, Bells calling you my girlfriend."

"Why would it be weird?" Abby asks.

"I, uh…" Jess stops in her tracks. "Because we… um…"

"I'd be pretty lucky to be your girlfriend; I don't think there's anything bad about that statement," Abby says. "It was cute."

Jess is frozen to the floor; it's as if time has stopped. Students walk past them trying to get to their classes. Most of them have already filed into the buildings, but there's a mad rush to make it before the tardy bell rings. Bodies move in a hurry, and the noise of conversation fades to nothing more than a dull roar. The sky is a bright, bright blue. Her heart thuds, still beating; blood still rushes through her veins. Jess is breathing, but she can't move. Abby's smile is overwhelming, and Jess is too big for her skin, as if she might float away in the exhilarating possibility of the moment.

"Oh, you, um," Jess says. "I would love to ask… if you, do you want to…"

The bell rings, and Jess' heart sinks. Could she work up the courage to ask again later? It was hard enough trying now. *It'll be fine to be friends.* Last year, she couldn't have imagined being friends with her crush, and now they hang out all the time. "Never mind," Jess adds in a small voice and starts to walk away. "I'll see you later."

"Jess!" Abby calls back. "To what you were asking—yes! I'll go out with you! That is what you were asking, right? Otherwise I'm gonna feel really dumb."

"Oh!" Jess blushes and nods. "Yes, I um, okay. A date. Yes?"

Abby chuckles. "Okay, we can talk about it on the way to work, yeah? Make plans then?"

Jess nods and watches Abby rush off to her own class, wearing Jess' T-shirt.

Jess walks on clouds for the rest of the day.

Abby is humming when they meet in the parking lot. She bounces on the edges of her feet when she sees Jess. "Ooh, okay, so do you like plays? Or museums? We can go to the modern art museum downtown, or the national history museum has this really neat butterfly exhibit. Have you ever had the chili cheese fries in that new diner off Seventh Street?"

Abby even opens the door for Jess to get in the car, which makes her giggle.

"Uh, yeah, all of that sounds awesome," Jess says. "Actually, I've been wanting to go to this thing—Captain Orion is coming to town and she's giving a speech at the Andover Museum of Modern Art. There are a limited number of tickets, but I managed to get two. Do you want to come with me?"

"Captain Orion is going to be here? In this city?"

"Yeah! It's awesome! It hasn't been announced publicly yet, only to those in the fan club but—"

"When?"

All the warmth and excitement has gone out of Abby's tone, and Jess' heart sinks before she says, "Friday night."

Abby starts the car. "Oh, I'm sorry, I think I… might be busy then."

They drive to Monroe Industries in silence, and Jess steals glances at Abby. She'd been so excited about the date a few moments ago, but now her face is taut. Unlike their other rides when they've laughed or joked, Abby pays attention to the road and not much else.

Maybe Abby regrets saying yes. Maybe it was a spur-of-the-moment decision and then when we tried to make it official, make plans, it wasn't really what Abby wanted.

Abby parks in the Monroe Industries parking lot, and they walk into the building. It's so awkward; clearly Abby is consumed by some dilemma.

Finally, in the elevator, Jess manages to say, "It's okay, we don't have to go out, if you're second-guessing it."

"No, it's not that, I just… guh, it's not you…" Abby looks at her feet.

"It's fine."

Jess rushes out the door as soon as it pings. She goes right to her office, shuts the door, and presses her head against it. She takes a deep breath; her disappointment surges.

"I'm not going to cry," Jess says to no one.

People are rejected every day. Maybe having that little glimmer of hope was worse than if Abby just outright said no. *Why didn't Abby just say no to begin with?*

Jess starts with the first item on her task list instead of taking the usual few minutes to settle in and check messages. She hasn't seen M yet, but that isn't unusual. Sometimes M will come in and say hello, sometimes not. Jess enjoys their conversations, but she's not in the mood right now. She doesn't want anyone to see her.

Jess hiccups and hastily wipes away the stray tears that leaked from her eyes when there's a knock at the door.

"Come in," she says.

M, visor dark and devoid of any lights, lingers in the door; her mecha-suit casts a long shadow into the office. "Hey."

"Hey. I'm almost done with this box, and then I have some—"

"Okay, that's not a priority right now," M says. "I want to talk to you about something. Something important. The future of this division of Monroe Industries. And the future of the Mischiefs."

"Oh, sure." Jess sits up taller. She looks up expectantly, and the panel in M's face starts to glitter with bouncing red lights. Jess hasn't seen red before. "Is this for everyone in the lab? Do we need Abby?"

"I already talked to Abby."

"Oh." Jess fiddles with her ponytail. It would seem more efficient for their supervisor to tell both of them at once, but Abby probably doesn't want to see her right now.

"So, I have heard that Captain Orion is going to be in town this Friday," M says. She steeples her fingers and the metal's clinking echoes in the room. "I have reason to believe that Orion's DED or MonRobot has important information that we need. I have developed a plan to commandeer one or both of those during this fan event."

"We're stealing Captain Orion's DED?" Eyes widening, Jess leans forward.

"I think it's necessary. I know that you've expressed admiration for the superhero, and I certainly respect that, but I know she knows *something* and if I don't try, I'll regret it forever. Please. Will you help?"

Jess is stricken by the emotion in M's voice, the desperate plea. She's never heard her sound like this; the electronic voice is different, much more human. *Is it a voice modifier that M has to consciously control and sometimes forgets?*

"Are we going to give it back?" Jess asks. "And why do we need it?"

"It's... I'm looking for someone. Two someones. They went missing a while ago, and it's not something the Collective's police could help with. I just know that Orion knows something, and I need to find out what."

The desktop projector next to Jess sparks; holos blink out of focus as if there's interference in the signal, and M coughs. "I'm sorry, I'm a bit on edge over this, it might be our last chance, that, um, well, Master Mischief left specific instructions while they were gone, that Orion was likely to be involved, and if she was nearby, not that I should go steal it, but I just need to know."

Jess has come to think of M as a friend, too, but she's been so wrapped up in getting to know Abby and hanging out with her that they haven't had many conversations in the office lately. Jess feels guilty about that. And these missing people—they must be important to M.

But stealing? And looking through someone else's DED, *Captain Orion's* personal information? She can't do it. Sure, she thought signing up to work with Master Mischief was a fun act of rebellion, but Captain Orion is a hero. She's Jess' hero, always has been. There's no way she could be involved with M's missing people.

Jess thinks of the date-that-could-have-been. Abby would have teased her for knowing all the trivia, and they would get autographs and take photos with Captain Orion, and Captain Orion might smile and wink at Jess and recognize her from the articles she's written for the fan club. And then Abby and Jess would have wandered through the museum, maybe holding hands, taking photos in front of all the exhibits, and had ice cream afterward.

"I'm sorry, I..." Jess shrinks backward. "I just don't think I could do it. Captain Orion's a good person. I know it."

"Look, there's *something* going on, and you're just on the cusp of seeing it, if you could only—" M throws up her hands. She gestures, and a holo projection appears in her hands. Jess can't see a DED, but it must be a part of the mecha-suit. The projections flash, images and videos and articles, one after another: proof of the changed history of Gravitus; the strange pattern of all the public fights broadcast on the news; and then just articles, from smaller town newsholos all around the NAC. There's one from the *Gazette* that remarks on the lack of activity from the Mischiefs, then a report from Turner City that Plasmaman hasn't been seen in five months, and another brief mention from Redwood County that Tree Frog hasn't gotten up to her usual hijinks.

"Yes, I see, but it doesn't mean Captain Orion is at the heart of it," Jess says. She takes a deep breath. She doesn't have the energy to figure it out; can't she just wallow in her misery? "I know that the Mischiefs were suspicious but like, isn't that just like a hero-villain thing?"

M's visor panel blinks red, once, and then it's completely dark. "A hero-villain thing," she says flatly. "I thought you—Jess, I thought you were different."

M turns around and shuts the door. It clicks with a solemn finality just as Jess says, "M—"

The apology dies on her lips as the door closes.

Great. Her friend M is upset, and Abby doesn't want to go on a date with her.

Jess gets back to work.

Jess is at her wit's end. She tries to focus on schoolwork, but didn't realize how intrinsic Abby was to her day-to-day school life until she suddenly isn't there. Every moment stands out to Jess, like the vivid colors of a holo projection, constantly dancing in front of her. Abby is absent from the lunch table. She still sits with Jess during English, but there's barely a nod of acknowledgment—no more glances during class or shared smiles over Rhinehart's jokes. Abby doesn't ask Jess if she wants to work on their project as they normally do on Thursdays. She isn't waiting outside Jess' sixth period when the day ends. Jess finds herself standing in the hallway, waits until she realized Abby isn't coming, and then shakes herself and rushes to catch the bus home.

She did more research on the missing villains that M brought up; her doubt grows as she finds even more. There aren't any specifics on any of the incidents, just a vagueness that Jess finds unsettling. Tree Frog, the colorful climbing villain whose signature move is to scale the redwoods in the Northern California region and hang ludicrous signs, hasn't put up a new sign in over seven months. *It is probably coincidence, right? Maybe the inactive ones aren't missing; they're in the Meta-Human Corrections center.* But there aren't been any reports of Tree Frog being captured, or even fighting with the local Redwood City hero, Arête.

Jess finishes her homework and finds a message from her dad that her parents are downtown for a meeting with the Associated League and to take care of dinner for her and Brendan.

Brendan is in the middle of an experiment, but gladly shouts out his expensive and ridiculous requests for food through the door. Jess refuses to drive all the way to Las Vegas to pick him up a steak, and they argue until compromising on an order of jambalaya from the Broussard restaurant.

It's quiet today, so Jess just slides into an empty booth and waits for Bells. "Just two orders of jambalaya to go," she says, slumping in the seat

Bells sits next to her. "Thought you hung out with your girl on Thursdays."

"Not today," Jess says, laying her head on the table.

Bells doesn't push, just throws an arm around her shoulders. After a moment, he blurts, "Do you want some cheesecake?"

"Dessert before dinner." Jess laughs. It's a small, mirthless sound. "Sure."

Bells comes back with a slice and two spoons, and they eat silently until Bells starts talking aimlessly about the gossip surrounding *Vindicated 7*. It's easy to relax with the sweet dessert and his comforting voice, and soon enough Jess sighs and places her spoon on the empty plate. "I, ah, I asked Abby out on a date yesterday."

Bells nods, his spoon in his mouth. "Good job. Knew you could do it."

"She said yes... but then she freaked out once we started making plans." Jess buries her face in her hands.

Bells licks his spoon. "Well, we're out of cheesecake, but I'm sure I could find you some pie."

"Thanks, Bells."

The hug is a lifeline, and Jess clings to it, breathing in the spicy scent of Bells' cologne.

"That's not the only thing bothering me," she says when they let go. "I don't even know how to say it. I, um, I signed a non-disclosure agreement."

"For work?"

"Yeah. My coworker asked for help on this project, and I couldn't... I mean, it's technically stealing?"

"Oh. Like corporate espionage?" Bells quirks his eyebrows. "I mean, picking the teenage intern to do it is genius, by the way. No one would think to look at the kid, right? Is it Hale Tech? Oh, right, you can't tell me. Blink once if you're sneaking into Hale Tech, blink twice if you're going for—"

Jess huffs and bumps Bells in the shoulder.

"Well, sometimes the wrong action for the right reason can be right," Bells says. His eyes are glassy and it seems as if he's quoting someone.

"What's that from? Some vintage superhero movie we haven't watched yet? Bells, you holding out on me? You've got your own contraband media?"

"Shut up, you know I wouldn't watch those without you guys." Bells scrunches his face. "Well, is stealing the only way to get the thing? I mean, that's kind of a lot to ask. You've only been there, what, a few months?"

"Not really stealing a thing," Jess says. She's thought about it for a while. "More like getting information I wouldn't normally have access to. But getting that information could help people."

"Hmm. You know that the NAC sees everything, right? On our DED's, all our messages and what we search and all that. All that information is out there for the government to look at any time, as well as for anyone clever enough to try and get it. What's the difference between you reading something you're not supposed to and the NAC looking at all the weird cat holos I send you?" Bells gives her a knowing look. "Look, is it like a personal secret?"

"No. I think it's company stuff."

"So, there's a big difference; it's not like if I told you—"

"Told me what?" Jess turns to eye Bells.

He coughs, wheezes, and practically falls out of the booth. "Nothing. I don't know anything. I, uh, I see your food is ready."

Jess sits at the table, dumbfounded. When Bells' older brother brings her the jambalaya, he just shrugs and says Bells had to go. School stuff, something like that.

Everyone is acting strange. Of course. It's that kind of week.

JESS HAS BEEN LOOKING FORWARD to this event for a month, and on the day, she can barely muster excitement. She'd gotten the two tickets a while ago in the hope that she could work up the courage to ask Abby out. Well, she did, and that worked out *so* well.

It's last minute, so Bells wasn't able to get out of his Friday shift, and Emma's cousins are in town again so she can't make it either. So when the bell rings after her last class, she walks down the block to wait for the downtown city bus by herself.

Jess makes it to the Andover Museum of Modern Art with a few minutes to spare. There's a huge poster swathing the wall that shows Captain Orion in flight with a span of glimmering stars behind her and the constellation she's named for.

Jess waits, watching the security guard check the people ahead of her in line. She pulls at her shirt collar. The man ahead of her has to give up his water bottle—no foreign liquids in the museum, apparently. Finally it's Jess' turn. The guard at the museum simply scans her DED and waves her on in.

Jess joins the group in the Lieutenant Orion exhibit, featuring the new display of Captain Orion's latest adventures in New Bright City. A whole section of the exhibit is dedicated to Captain Orion, with new art that the museum is auctioning off today.

Elizabeth and Denise are here, too. Jess nods at them, earning a nod back from Denise. She and Elizabeth whisper to each other and giggle. Another time, Jess might have tried hard to ignore them and then been laughed at, but today she just doesn't care.

She picks a seat in the back of the exhibit hall. Jess' hands find her way to her pocket and toy with a frayed bit of thread. She gulps when she counts four armed security guards. Is M still going through with her plan? How would she get access to Orion's personal DED? Orion doesn't wear it often; it clashes with her outfit. The device is probably on a charging dock somewhere.

Jess shakes off all ideas about M and her plans and tries to focus on having fun. She's about to see her hero in person for the first time!

A curtain behind the stage suggests Captain Orion will appear from behind it, but she flies in through an open window with her cape flapping behind her. After landing, she stands tall as the audience erupts in applause.

Captain Orion dominates the stage, in full regalia: blue and silver body suit, shining blonde hair. Her blue eyes gleam at the audience. Unlike most superheroes, Orion doesn't wear a mask. She was raised in the public eye and long since stopped using her name, preferring to be called only by her superhero title.

She looks stunning, and a bit smaller in person. A month ago Jess would have been thrilled to be in the same room with Captain Orion, let alone have the chance to get an actual autograph, not a stamped one. Orion is amazing, and the years of loving her adventures and collecting her comic books yield a sense of awe at seeing her hero in person. She still likes the Captain, but she's gone from full-blown obsession to just mild interest.

Jess thinks about Gravitus and the countless other strange things she's discovered: about the villains disappearing all over the country; about where Andover's own two villains are. The Mischiefs aren't on an extended vacation either; there *is* something else at work here.

"Well, hello, hello, my nearest and dearest fans!" Captain Orion says, her voice bright and syrupy. She sounds exactly like she does on her commercials; every sweet inflection is the same. Even the little quirk in her smile that Jess used to swoon over looks as if Jess is watching a recorded holovid. Orion stands with her hands on her hips, poised for battle. Somewhere in the orchestra pit there must be a person with a fan because Orion's hair flutters spectacularly, just like in her commercial for Orion Approved™ Volumizer.

She waves, and the people in the audience cheer, scream, and shout praise. Everyone loves Orion. Tickets to any of her events are almost impossible to get. Jess has been on the waitlist for this event for months. She had to trade her limited first edition Captain Orion comic to one of the forum moderators to get tickets.

Orion waves offstage, pointing at her microphone with a harried expression. A stagehand tries to raise it to her height and fails, staring at her in awe. The microphone falls, and he blushes and fixes it. Orion waves him off, and he bows awkwardly, apologizing profusely.

"Thank you for coming here today. I'm going to read aloud from my latest book, *The Life and Times of Captain Orion,* which has a corresponding comic book, available today in the gift shop!"

The audience cheers. Cameras flash, and Jess is struck by how posed it all seems to be. Live, Orion seems as though she's acting out a script as she carefully turns left and right to face the audience.

"Marry me, Captain!" a woman yells from the front row.

"Captain, Captain, are we safe from Coldfront?" a man yells.

Captain Orion clutches her hand to her chest with an affected sigh. "I can assure you that Coldfront is in a maximum security Meta-Humans Corrections center, secured by the special forces of the North American Collective. You and the general public are safe." She ducks her head in a little bow.

"Is he okay, though?" Denise asks, surprising Jess. "I mean, you, like, lightninged him in the chest."

Orion frowns; it's the first expression that isn't carefully composed. "Of course," she says, a little too brightly.

"What about Tree Frog?" Jess asks, not bothering to raise her hand.

"Tree Frog is also in Corrections," Orion says. She narrows her eyes at Jess and *tsks* in annoyance. "Now does anyone else have a question that could be answered on the League's official holo, or can I get on with the program?"

The audience laughs, and a few people turn around to titter at Jess.

Jess might have been bothered by how rude Orion was, but she's too focused on the fact that Orion said Tree Frog was in *Corrections*. There's no record of Tree Frog ever being captured after a fight. The last time she was in the media she was atop one of her signs aloft in the trees laughing at Arête.

Shock pours over Jess, and she hears M's voice, in that sad tone, asking for help.

"Now, are you ready?" Captain Orion smirks and tosses her hair.

Orion only gets as far as "I was born in…" when the nearest window shatters with a small burst of energy. Jess recognizes electronic pulses from M's mecha-suit.

M flies into the exhibit hall and stands tall on the stage.

Maybe it's because Jess knows M now, but though she's found the colors laughable on the Mischiefs, she finds the contrast between M's darker colors and the overly saturated brights of Orion's suit visually compelling.

"You!" Captain Orion gasps. Her book clatters to the floor, and she adopts a fighting stance. "You escaped?! How!"

M's voice modulator drops to a low pitch that's reminiscent of Master Mischief, and then M seizes a large canvas painting of Orion and flies out the window, cackling.

A man in a suit rushes forward, whispers in Orion's ear, and hands her a metal bottle. She takes a long drink, wipes her mouth, and then gets into a ready position. "You won't get away with this!" she says, flipping her hair. Her teeth sparkle.

Someone yells, "Go get him, Cap!"

Orion flies out the window; her cape flaps heroically behind her.

The audience whispers, and then everyone gets up to go look with their DED's raised high to snap pictures. The guards stand their ground.

Jess sneaks out the back. She can still help. Adrenaline rushing through her, Jess starts down the hallway. On impulse, she spins about and heads in the other direction. She rounds the corner and spots a MonRobot. It goes forward and then hovers, shakes and spins, heads in another direction, like... like whoever is directing it is *distracted.*

"Hey! Hey!" Jess whispers, looking left and right. This area is devoid of security guards; most of them are at the exhibit hall protecting the art. She tries to be as quiet as she can, rushing over to the MonRobot. "Hey, are you here with M?"

It cheeps at her, and lights up as it scans her face. "Jessica Tran, Experimental Divisions Intern—"

"Yes, yes, come on, can you open up a comm link to M?" Jess grabs it and shakes it. Her fingers tremble as the MonRobot processes the request.

A crackle of static bursts, and there's a searing sound of energy crackling. "M! It's Jess, let me know how I can help!" Jess hopes she can be heard over the firefight.

"Jess?"

Jess thinks her heart might explode; M's voice is so full of hope.

Another piercing noise; M must be dodging Orion's lightning blasts. "Okay, I'm keeping Orion busy, but I don't know where her DED is and I can't direct Jills at the same time—"

"Got it, got it. I'll find it. Don't worry," Jess says.

A security guard stands at the end of the hallway.

"Jills will have a chip for Orion's DED, just get the info and meet me back at the lab—"

"Hey! No unauthorized personal assistant bots in the museum!" A guard shouts at them and walks forward.

Jess picks up the MonRobot and runs. The oblong metal case bobs awkwardly in her hands, but she does her best. She ducks down another hallway and tries a door; it's unlocked. She waits until she hears the guard rushing down the hall. Jills cheeps in her arms.

"Hush," Jess whispers.

Jills. What a funny name for a MonRobot, kinda like—

She doesn't have time to finish the thought; she has to find Orion's DED. The hallway is silent, and Jess ventures out. The staging area must be here somewhere; there are a bunch of offices and labs for the museum staff.

Jess puts down the MonRobot and Jills trails behind her in the air as she tries every door until she finds one filled with flowers and well wishes for Captain Orion.

Orion doesn't have many personal things, but there's a little work area with some letters from the museum and a desktop projector with a DED charging in the dock.

Jess exhales and Jills holds out a chip to Jess. She plugs the chip into Orion's DED port. M said there was a program that would do everything automatically, and sure enough, a popup holo opens in the Mischief's trademark purple and a progress bar starts to load.

Jess watches the bar increase as she listens to the sounds of cheering and what sounds like energy blasts in the distance. Oh, she hopes M is okay. She sees the window blink "copy complete," and she removes the chip, picks up Jills, and races out the door.

When she returns to the exhibit hall, M and Captain Orion are flying about each other as M artfully dodges the lightning blasts from Orion.

Jess sits at the end of the hall, watching with a few fan club members who aren't taking pictures or hiding behind something. A few people are clapping, gasping in awe.

M spots Jess and her face panel lights up with the pink lights Jess has come to associate with happiness. She nods at her and puts down the painting. Jess smiles and gives her a small wave.

It's kind of thrilling, being part of a heist.

Jills is hovering at Jess' side. "Can you look less... obvious?" Jess mutters. She's the only one with a MonRobot. Assistant bots aren't uncommon, but usually people have a special permit for them.

Jills beeps once and then its panel rearranges itself; the case slides apart, and circuitry uncoils and refits itself. Jess has never seen anything like it; it must be incredibly advanced tech. *How handy, to have a MonRobot that can shrink!* Jills, now the size of a messenger bag, complete with a carrying strap, beeps again. Jess pats it and shoulders it, and then turns back to watch the fight.

M hovers, all of her panel lights flashing pink. Jess points to Jills and mouths, "Awesome," at her, and M shakes a little, as if she's laughing. And that's when it happens.

Captain Orion blasts M, and it hits her with a sizzling finality. Sparks fly across her torso. M drops ten feet, faltering in the air. Her suit sparks. Jess freezes, and then watches as M manages to fly out the window despite her injury.

Captain Orion laughs and puts her hands on her hips. "And that's how you do it! I'm going to go leave and take care of that pesky villain in a second—"

No, no, M needs time to get away.

Jess bumps into the group of girls next to her, jostling them into standing up. "Clearly he's no match for you," she calls out, keeping her face hidden. "I think part of the ticket package included autographs!" she adds in a slightly pitched voice.

The girls clamor and shout with her. "And photos! Please, please, please?"

Captain Orion holds her arm out for the crowd. "Why, of course, anything for my devoted fans."

Jess watches the crowd of fans swarm the superhero. There isn't going to be any immediate pursuit of M. Jess ducks out the exit with Jills. She just hopes they get back to the lab all right.

JESS CATCHES A BUS AT the corner and, a few stops later, she's in front of Monroe Industries. It's Friday evening but there are still employees moving about. The robot at the front desk beeps a greeting, and Jess heads right for the elevator.

"M?" Jess calls out, stepping onto her floor. She sets down Jills, and it automatically transitions back into orb shape, hovering behind her. "Abby?" Abby usually doesn't stay past five o'clock, because she takes Jess home, but maybe she's still here; they haven't talked much since Jess asked Abby out.

No response from Abby's office.

Jills flies after her, making meeping noises.

The whole lab is in disarray; wires and electronic paraphernalia are scattered everywhere. Jess notices a scuffed floor section, so it looks as though M made it back. Jess follows the scuff marks past Abby's office and toward M's office where she can hear electrical crackling.

The steel door is ajar; burn marks streak across it, and the handle is melted. A broken metal glove lies on the floor.

Jess rushes forward, throwing all M's "don't come back here, it's private" warnings out the window. M might be hurt.

"M! Are you okay?" Jess yells.

No answer. Jess rushes forward; the sound of her shoes echoes in the empty lab.

"M! M! I got the information! Are you hurt? Please tell me you're okay."

"Jess?" The voice is strained, as if desperate and in pain.

"You're here," Jess says as she turns the corner. An ominous rattle makes her stomach churn, but she can see M now at the end of the room. This must be where she works on the mecha-suit and also gets in and out of it.

M is on the floor. The suit crackles and sparks. M is caught between two large cables; the suit is tangled between the two arms of the machine. It looks as if M was trying to rush getting out of the suit and her injuries were too much. She's slumped forward, barely moving. One of her fingers twitches, and her helmet is cracked wide open. Panel lights blink. Yellow. The color of relief. Joy, maybe.

"Are you okay?" Jess asks, stepping carefully around the wires and tools scattered on the floor.

"Yeah, just, I need you to disconnect that cable by entering a sequence in the computer," M says. Her voice is familiar, and when Jess gets closer she can see why.

Abby is inside the suit.

Jess gasps. "Abby? *You're* M?"

"Just help me."

Jess types in the code Abby gives her, and the machine powers down. Abby gasps. Jess rushes to her side and disconnects the large cable that's securing her to the main server, and then helps her remove pieces of the armor one by one.

Under it all, Abby is wearing the outfit that is definitely not workout gear. The pattern on the pants is elaborate circuitry, wired all over the skintight fabric.

Careful to keep away from the sparking circuits, Jess helps Abby to a nearby bench. .

"Thank you," Abby says. "I'm really sorry I couldn't tell you."

"It's okay. The M—it's not a James Bond thing, is it?"

"Nah, it's for Abby Monroe. I mean, at school I go by my mom's last name, but, I'm actually, you know." She sighs. "My parents are Phillip and Genevieve Monroe. Otherwise known as Master Mischief and Mistress Mischief. I've been running the business ever since they disappeared."

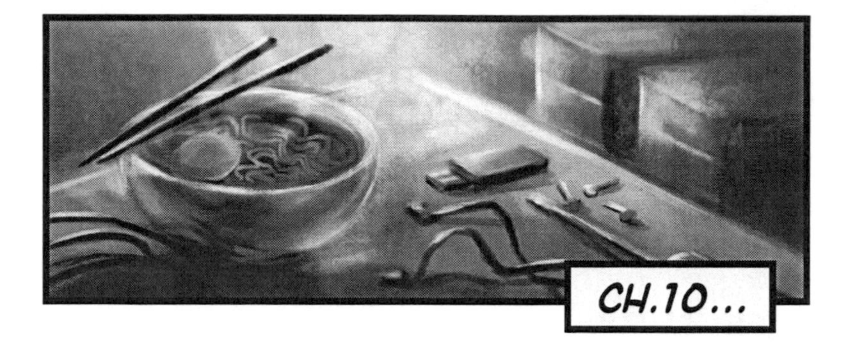

Abby has a huge bruise on her side where Orion zapped her. Jess wraps a stabilizing cloth bandage around it and then finds ice in the break room.

The story comes out in bits and pieces. Abby's parents disappeared a few months ago, and Abby needed to keep up appearances at Monroe Industries with her father's new MonRobot design. Monroe Industries is controlled by its board of directors—and Stone. They wanted to use the technology of the MonRobots to spy on the citizens of the North American Collective and feed that information back to the government.

Jess is still trying to wrap her head around the idea that the mild-mannered Phillip Monroe she'd seen on TV showing off a new gadget every now and then is also the colorfully costumed Master Mischief. And Genevieve Monroe, the high society heiress? The dynamic and powerful telekinetic Mistress Mischief?

"Yeah, they're amazing," Abby says. "They're also missing. I know my dad told Stone he didn't want to militarize the MonRobots—"

"What? They do household chores! They're not—they're not *soldiers!*"

"They could be, according to the board at Monroe Industries." Abby sighs. "Anyway, I found out that the government was involved. Apparently the newest model can do… quite a lot."

"Do people know that they can do more than just vacuum?"

Abby shakes her head. "It shouldn't matter, because no one but my dad would have been able to activate the other features. But he and my mom have been missing for a while now."

"Wait. You don't actually know where either of them are? What about all the times you've told me *it's not of import*?"

"Well, that was before I got to know you could be trusted! I thought you would just help with the filing and stuff, I didn't expect to—"

"To what?" Jess presses.

"To like you!" Abby says. "I like you, okay?"

Jess stares, and Abby's face turns red.

Jess still hasn't quite reconciled M in the mecha-suit she's come to know as a friend and Abby the girl she has a crush on and has been getting to know these past few months. She's told M so many things about how she feels about Abby—a flurry of embarrassing comments come back to her. Oh no, she talked about Abby's *butt* to M!

"How can you like me?" Jess says. "You just—you started hanging out with me after I told M I liked *you!*"

"Oh, come on! I told you to ask me out!"

"I didn't know you liked girls!"

"I do!"

"Good! I do too!"

The kiss is wet and quick. Jess doesn't know who moved first, just that Abby's lips taste like cinnamon with a touch of scorched metal and a thrilling otherness of ozone. She opens her eyes to see Abby's clear blue eyes staring back at her.

"Hi," Jess says, out of breath.

"Hi."

Abby moves first this time, and it's as if she's in slow motion. Jess notices the curve of Abby's dark eyelashes on her cheek, the gentle slope of her nose. Then they're kissing again, and Jess' eyes are closed, and it's just the warmth of her lips.

Jess' hands hang by her side until Abby takes them and laces their fingers together. She lets Abby take the lead, breathing in the metallic sweet scent of her.

"I've wanted to do that for a while," Abby says. "Ever since my house... your damn story with the girl... I really thought..." Abby blushes. "And you were so sure, and you were talking to M about how much you liked me, but then I wondered how much of it was just like... a superficial crush, and I got worried once we started hanging out you'd figure that I was really boring or something."

"You're not boring. Knowing you is a lot better than just the idea of you, you know. Like the whole thing you do at school with the... intimidatingly smart and glaring at everyone, but you're a huge marshmallow underneath."

Abby snorts. "I am not a marshmallow. You're the marshmallow." She pokes Jess in the shoulder.

At the mention of food, Jess realizes she hasn't eaten since lunch. A stomach rumbles, and it's not her own. "You need to get some rest, and also eat something. Come on, there's a kitchen in this lab and not just a break room with a lame microwave, right?"

She starts walking before she finishes asking the question, and turns right down a corridor she's never been in.

"Yeah, I've never told you about this hallway before. How'd you know it was here?"

"Lucky guess?" Jess tries an unmarked door, and it opens to a steel industrial kitchen, much bigger and better stocked than the break room where they usually have lunch. This one has a few homey touches: a crayon stick figure drawing in the familiar purple-and-reds of the Mischiefs with a younger girl between them. "Aw, this is cute. Done by you?"

"Yeah," Abby says, her cheeks almost as red as her hair.

Jess rummages through the pantry and finds a few bricks of ramen, sets water to boil, and looks for something to add to it.

Jess opens the last cupboard on the left and finds a can of corn and a real can of Spam.

"Jess. Jess!"

"What?" Jess looks up from slicing the Spam.

"There's no way you just happened to know where everything was."

Jess shrugs. "Luck, I guess."

"No, no," Abby says, her eyes lighting up. "Look, this is a weird question but, is there anyone in your family, parents, grandparents—anyone with meta-abilities at all?"

Jess opens her mouth. "I can't answer that question." She drops two bricks of ramen into the boiling water and opens the refrigerator, hiding her panicked expression.

Oh, eggs. Jess takes out the carton and shuts the refrigerator to find Abby staring wide-eyed at her.

"Your parents are meta-human, aren't they?"

Jess thinks quickly. Abby trusted her with her parents' identity She told Jess who her parents were, what's happened to them. The whole time Jess has worked here, she was trusted with so many secrets.

"Yes, they are," Jess says slowly. "My parents are Smasher and Shockwave."

Abby shrieks, "Oh my God, that's incredible—you—you—and you decided to work *here?* What about you? What can you do? Can you fly, like your dad? Are you super-strong like your mom? Oh, what about electro-magnetic field manipulation? I always thought that was amazing."

"No." The brief, happy buzz ends quickly. "I don't… I don't have anything."

Abby steps forward, and Jess thinks she'll get a sympathetic pat or a comforting hug. Instead, she kisses Jess again.

"What was that for?" Jess asks.

"You were making a face. It's my way of saying there's nothing wrong with you. Whether you have powers or not. You are wonderful."

"I—I—Thank you," Jess says. "You're pretty great yourself."

Abby nods, and they look at each other until Jess hears water boiling. She finishes the soup.

Jess says, "I was so worried when you got blasted. That data better be worth it."

"Let's take our food and go take a look at what's on that datachip."

THEY GO BACK TO ABBY'S lab. Jess has eaten a lot of ramen, but never quite like this, sitting in the midst of piles of circuits and computer consoles and bits of scrap metal, with tools scattered everywhere and half-finished projects out on tables. Several desktop projectors throw holos into the air: mecha-suit blueprints and MonRobot designs. The cool blue of the circuits casts a soft glow all around them.

Abby sits cross-legged next to Jess. Her chopsticks are forgotten on the floor as she picks up her bowl and slurps from it outright.

The makeshift meal is simple, just the noodle soup with a soft-boiled egg and the delicious novelty of fried Spam, but the company makes it Jess' favorite ramen meal ever.

They eat in companionable silence until both their bowls are empty.

"This was really good," Abby says, with a contented sigh. "I usually just crumble up the seasoning in the bag with the dry noodles."

Jess grins. "You ever try throwing some butter or oil on the noodle brick and then the seasoning and stick it in the toaster oven? It gets all crispy and makes a great snack, too."

The chip is still in Jess' jacket pocket. Jess takes it out; it's surprisingly light in her palm, considering how much effort has gone into getting it. She hands it to Abby, expecting her to drop it into a DED to look at the data, but she merely holds it in her hand and closes her eyes.

Jess hasn't seen much of Master Mischief's electronic manipulation on newsholos; they mostly show the aftermath of his pranks or show him doing battle with her parents and then getting captured and handed off to the authorities.

"Don't you need to recharge?" Glowing lines of light, flaring across her skin like luminescent veins, flow from the chip into Abby's arm and toward her head. "My parents can only use their powers like, an hour a day or so. Didn't you use your abilities during the exhibit—"

Abby's eyelids flutter as she processes the information.

"Oh, I'm sorry, I must be distracting you," Jess says.

Abby's eyes open. "Done."

Jess sees a flicker of that blue-white light in her pupils, and then it's gone. "So? What was the information? Was it worth it?"

Abby's eyes are shadowed. "I couldn't make sense of all of it, but it's not good. It confirms that Orion is at the center of all of this. Why else would she have..." Abby sighs.

"Here, let's get a bigger display," Jess mutters, waving at the electronic mess.

Jess follows Abby out of this room and to the nearest console, while Jess tries to apologize again for the distraction while Abby used her powers.

"Don't worry about it, I'm used to working with distractions. And I don't need to recharge all that much, I haven't tested my limits a lot but I can operate the suit and do a bunch of other tasks for most of the day," Abby says.

Jess is impressed. "Wow, that's like... better than A-class. And I thought Master Mischief was cool for using his technopath abilities for an hour a day."

"I, ah, I can do both, actually. I inherited both my parents' abilities." Abby blushes. Her hair is unruly and frames her face in a huge colorful cloud. It looks wonderfully fluffy, and Jess realizes she's staring.

Abby touches her curls self-consciously. "I ... yeah, I usually put a lot of product in it to keep it from going haywire like this. It's the heat from the suit, really," Abby says.

Jess yanks her hair out of its elastic and hands it to Abby. Her own hair falls about her face, but it's not as much of a mess as Abby's is right now.

Abby takes the elastic and tugs her hair into a sloppy ponytail. She closes her eyes and concentrates, and Jess watches in wonder as the machinery around them lights up.

"You're A-class," Jess says. "You have to be. Why aren't you in Meta-Human Training already? My older sister is only B-class and she got snapped up when she was fifteen."

Abby lifts her eyebrows, and a few circuits float and rearrange themselves around the broken mecha-suit. "I can't. My parents are both villains, and the government wanted me to be a villain too. They were promised if they did this one last project I'd be allowed to apply for hero track, but then both my parents just disappeared."

"They didn't say goodbye? Tell you where they went?"

Abby shakes her head. "We were very close. I'm an only child; they tell me everything. All their plans, what they want to do. I mean, I help a lot with the MonRobot design, and with my powers. My own suit is for protecting my identity, and to make sure that I have enough electronics to control and use while out and about."

Abby finishes bringing up all the documents on the screen and waves Jess over to look.

"What is all this?" Jess skims it but each file is like a wall of text. Locations, dates, logs of some sort. Someone's files, not Orion's; she was just reading them. Each one is annotated with insights like "not ready" and "will come around" and "needs more time."

At second glance, they look like health charts from a hospital. She doesn't recognize any of the names. There are photographs of grim-faced men and women who are vaguely familiar. "Who are these people? Why is Orion keeping track of them?"

"This is Fireheart." Abby points at a bearded man. His face is gaunt.

"No way!" Jess gasps. Fireheart is one of the most terrifying villains in Middleton. "Are all of these meta-humans?"

"Yeah, and all villains. Pretty sure these are the people who've been going missing the past few months. Not that many people in the Collective know or care."

Abby rattles off villain names, and then Jess startles.

"Wait, no, Cerberus was fighting Plasmaman last week. I saw it on the news," Jess says.

Abby raises her eyebrows. "Fighting? Really? Did you see Plasmaman use his powers last week? I've had a hunch that someone who just *looked* like Plasmaman was there."

"It's possible. But what are they doing with all these villains? And did you get any information on your parents?"

Abby brings up one of the last documents. *Phillip and Genevieve Monroe.* "They're alive," she says. "This doesn't say where they are, though. Just that someone—and Orion—has been keeping tabs on them."

"This isn't a health report. This looks like… something about mining?"

Abby reads the file Jess brought up and whistles. "Yeah, I thought as much. It's tantalum."

Jess' mouth falls open. Tantalum is incredibly rare, and is one of the few metals that dampen meta-abilities.

"My dad used to say whoever controlled the source would have the lead on creating any new technology. The North American Collective has some, but this report is from Constavia."

"And they're not part of the Global Federation," Jess says. "Aren't they at war with the Kravian Islands?"

Jess reads the report again. "This says the Collective sent them airships. And guns." A wave of nausea rushes over her, and Jess suddenly feels like being sick. "Are we... Our country is part of this?" The only thing she knows about the war in the Kravian Islands is that people are dying every day, are injured, are suffering, but the news reports only comment on how sad it is, and that the NAC isn't involved at all, and that the European Union should do something about it.

"The news. It's all about the heroes fighting the villains, all the time... no one would even know about any of this," Jess says. "Are these battles staged?"

"Pretty much. It's the way the NAC does things. I mean, I didn't know about the war in the Kravian Islands part, but yeah."

"Okay, we have to talk to Captain Orion. See what she knows about your parents and what all this means. What if she's being forced into it? Or maybe she's just carrying this information because the NAC told her to look at it? What if she's trying to stop it?"

Abby nods. "More information is good. We don't know where they are. But we don't know where Orion is, either."

Jess grins. "Social media does." She flicks at the DED on her wrist and quickly thumbs to the app for the Captain Orion Fan Club. A quick scroll shows excitement for the exhibit, and then news that Orion is going to a party in the fancy end of town.

There are already pictures of her shaking hands with the mayor at the country club up in the canyons. "So do you think you're ready to fly?"

FLYING WITH ABBY IS AN experience. Jess has flown before, remembers the thrill of the rush of wind and the exhilaration of being in the sky and the trust it takes. It's a quick flight, only ten minutes, but she remembers every second of Abby's metal arms circling her waist with the chill of the evening air surrounding them.

They land neatly in the back of the country club where caterers are preparing appetizers.

"Do you think she's all tapped out? Recharging for tomorrow?" Jess asks.

"She should be."

They hunker in the bushes, waiting. Jess checks her fan club feed; apparently Orion is leaving soon, she's already said goodbye to the mayor.

They drift unseen overhead as Orion, in a glamorous evening dress, clambers into her Town Car. They follow the car and wait until it's on a private road winding up the cliffside outside Andover. A light shines from a modern-looking building nestled into the rock face. *Orion's Andover home, perhaps?*

Abby concentrates, reaches out with her hands, and the car screeches to a halt. They land behind the car, their feet gently coming to rest on the concrete.

Abby steps forward, arms out in front of Jess, ready for action. Jess appreciates the gesture, but she isn't going to be left behind.

Powerless she may be, but she's not helpless. She can confront her… hero.

The driver gets out of the car and inspects the engine. Abby throws her arms out, huffing with effort, and car parts fly out of the hood and rearrange around her, trapping her where she stands before she can speak.

Jess walks forward and opens the back door.

"Good, are we almost there? I can't wait to—oh, you're not Minnie," Orion says, looking up from her DED.

"We need to talk," Jess says.

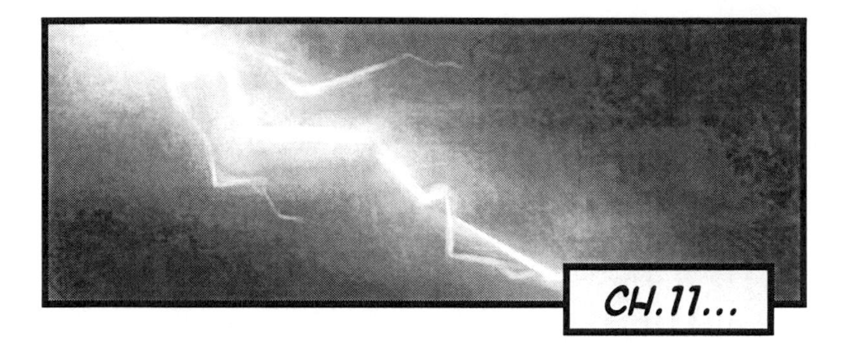

Orion blinks at Jess, and then her face widens in an automatic smile. "Oh, I remember you! You're from the Fan Club, right? Did you not leave with an autograph? Here, what can I sign for you?"

Jess pulls up a copy of the report on tantalum mining in Constavia on her DED and throws the projection at Orion. "What's this all about?"

Orion's face tightens, and her eyes narrow. "How'd you get that? And where did you… how did you know where I was?" She stands up, looming.

Jess walks backward as Orion gets out of the car. In the early evening light, she looks cold and menacing. Her hair flaps in the wind.

"Who are you?"

"I just want to know what this means. And where the Mischiefs are, and all the other villains who've disappeared the past few months," Jess says.

Orion's laugh is hard and shrill. "You must be one of those conspiracy theorists. They're getting younger and younger each year." She raises her hands and stretches her fingers. "What should I do with you? A little lightning zap should take care of that memory of yours. Then again, it's not an exact science. I might just fry all your brain cells. It'd be worth it, though."

Abby lands in front of Jess with a loud *clunk*. "Where are they? Tell us where they are!"

Orion's eyes widen. "You... Wait, you attacked me at the museum earlier! And you're not Master Mischief! Who are you?"

Abby holds out her arms, and the car behind them crunches into a twisted wreck, lifting up to surround Captain Orion. "Tell me where my parents are!"

"Oh, so you're the brat," Orion says. "Looks like you've inherited your mother's talent for telekinesis. Too bad, this little show must have depleted all your energy for today. And wearing your father's suit, how touching." She lifts her hands in her trademark lightning-zap move.

"And you're tapped out," Abby says.

Orion laughs. "That's what you think."

She lifts her finger and points, and all Jess can see is the burst of white-hot energy rushing toward them. A searing pain flares in her chest and then she knows no more.

JESS IS SUSPENDED IN THAT moment, hit by that lightning blast over and over again. Then she realizes the aching pain in her chest is residual, not active. The throbbing radiates outward up her neck and down to her belly button. Jess can still feel the heat resonating, and she tries not to move. Every breath is an ordeal.

The crackling of white-hot light in front of her is a crosshatch of energy, and Orion is standing behind it, giving her the disdainful look one might give to a bug trapped in a glass. Behind Orion is an impeccable living room with designer furniture and sheer glass walls that reveal a stunning view of Andover and the desert night. The moon has risen, casting ominous shapes from the cacti in the distance.

A shadow moves and Jess is terrified for a second until she sees the creature come into the light—a cat. She has no idea what breed it is, but it looks like one of the fancier ones, not that any carnivorous pet isn't a ridiculous luxury only for the rich and powerful. This one has immaculate white fur and is wearing a gleaming blue collar with a tag in the shape of a star.

Something inside Jess bristles; she's never met *anyone* who had an actual pet before, even the wealthy Robledos don't have one. There are plenty of feral dogs and cats roaming the wilds outside cities, but keeping domesticated ones fell out of practice in the time of the Disasters. Most of the holos that circulate on the Net are fascinating pieces of history, showing the way people used to document their pets' antics. In the past few decades, a pet has become a status symbol among the affluent.

The cat licks its paws and regales Jess with a scornful look before turning around and walking away, tail raised high in the air. It pauses to lap at a delicate trickling water feature in the center of the room.

Jess is appalled. Orion's home has a *fountain* in it, and she doesn't even live in Andover. How much time does she spend here, anyway?

In the middle of the living room, out of place among the clean lines of the designer furniture, is a grim-looking metal chair. Abby is sitting in it, secured to it by metal cuffs on her wrists and ankles. She isn't wearing her suit, and Jess can't see it anywhere in the room. Orion must have gotten rid of it.

Abby doesn't look injured, but there's weariness on her face and defiant determination in the set of her jaw.

Abby and Orion glare at each other.

"That doesn't even make sense," Abby says.

It seems they've been talking for a while.

Captain Orion paces as she talks. "Oh, of course it makes sense, brat. I mean, you are nothing more than part of the NAC plan for creating more meta-humans and controlling the ones we have. Of course, we can play with radiation all we like, but we can't come close to duplicating the effects of X29. All we can count on is that meta-humans will continue to propagate, especially with each other, so we can have more meta-humans in the future. The meta-gene has been studied by many scientists, but so far they can't figure out how to make it express itself one hundred percent of the time."

Jess reaches out for Abby, wanting to do something, anything, to make a gesture of comfort somehow. The barrier crackles like hot electricity when her fingers near it, and she draws back immediately.

It's gonna be okay, Abby mouths at her. Jess nods and then notices Abby's DED sticking out of her pocket, recording Orion as she talks.

Orion isn't even looking at them now; she just stares off into the gleaming lights of Andover in the distance. A poster spanning the length of the wall behind her depicts her in almost the exact same pose.

"The most we can do to ensure meta-humans in the future is to pair two and see if their child will exhibit any meta-abilities. However, this isn't foolproof, as even if you have high-powered parents, you could still have a low-powered child or a child without any powers at all. Furthermore, no one really understands how to control—if there is a way to control the extent of the powers—how long you can use your powers without rest, or what abilities get passed on."

"I was lucky to inherit all my grandfather's powers," Orion continues, "but I'll let you in on a little secret: I'm not A-class. I'm C-class, and I take supplements to help me maintain my level of ability. It gives me a certain advantage, you know, especially when someone thinks my power resources have been tapped out. The supplements are created by NAC research and are only available to a select few."

Jess gasps. *Captain Orion has been modifying her own powers with the help of the government?*

"The NAC needs to have a clear understanding of all meta-humans in its jurisdiction, to know that it can employ any number of them at any time, and to know the extent of all abilities. Now, take Smasher and Shockwave, for example."

Jess grits her teeth. *Are they targeting my parents? Are my parents in danger?*

"Now, we don't have any history of their gene pool to see how much of the meta-gene is present in their family history. What we do know is that they have formidable powers, but are severely limited by how much they can use their powers at any given time. They need to recharge. It's the problem with the C-class, it's unpredictable—how much time they will need to get their powers back. I've see Smasher pick up the Brooklyn Bridge on her own, but then I didn't see her for two months. Supposedly, she was recuperating."

Jess remembers this. Three years ago, her mom had used a huge amount of effort to stop that bridge from collapsing, and was sick in bed for ages afterward. She was so weak and tired, she couldn't even walk very far.

"It's preposterous," Captain Orion continues. "New Bright City is *my* town. I don't know what she was doing there, but I was on a mission and all of a sudden she said, '*Oh, Captain Orion, the League didn't send me but I can help!*'" Orion shakes her head, sneering.

Li Hua had gone to New Bright City for a real estate conference, and not hero work at all. She was trying to get better at her cover job. Jess clenches her fists. *What is that accent? Her mother doesn't talk like that.*

"The Heroes' League was generous enough to let Smasher have her own little city. They should be grateful that we let them in the Associated League; I'm appalled they even applied. Can you imagine? Refugees from the Southeast Asian Alliance in the League? Please. How would that look on the cereal boxes? I mean, we've got Copycat, but he wears a full-face mask. But Smasher and Shockwave go gallivanting all over Andover with just flimsy eye masks; everyone knows that they aren't—well, you know. The ideal."

Orion flips her hair and grins. Her teeth sparkle ominously.

Jess rushes forward to push against the barrier and gets shocked for her trouble. She gasps, shaking with pain, and Orion just keeps talking.

"And the rule is they stick to their town. They take care of the antics from that villain couple—those Mischiefs. Another waste of talent gone to C-class. Can you imagine how powerful a technopath and a telekinetic could be together if they weren't limited to using their powers every once in a blue moon?"

Jess wants to scream, but her mouth is numb.

Captain Orion laughs. "The solution seemed easy. All we needed were meta-humans to test on. The Registration act was a godsend—my father took care of that. But after that we needed to keep the meta-humans in line, to make sure that those with the power to create an uprising never got around to that. We did what was easy. Divide and conquer. Make sure a few people got a slice of the pie, and everyone else worked hard and had someone to blame for their losses."

"The villains," Jess says. "It's all—It's all a setup, nothing is real."

Orion glances at her, but doesn't give her more acknowledgment than a slight huff before turning back to Abby. "Well, some things are, more or less. The Mischiefs, all they had to do was keep to their town. Phillip Monroe, what a blessing in disguise—we had his patents, his technological knowhow, and he was already making so much money with his dumb MonRobots. How uninspired, using this amazing technology to do menial chores!"

"MonRobots are for everyone!" Abby shouts. "Everyone deserves the chance to have affordable help around the house."

"We needed *more*. We knew that Philip had created plans for the MonRobots to do everything from cooking to cleaning to acting as personal assistants. But he scrapped the best idea, the home security feature. What a waste. Imagine having a capable A.I. follow you, ready to take down any threat. Of course, Phillip said the project was too risky."

Abby shakes her head; her mouth is slack. "What did you do to my dad? Where's my mom? You better not have hurt them, you better not—"

Orion laughs. "You're in no position to do anything about it," she says.

She steps closer, grin widening. Jess is reminded of that commercial that played on repeat: Captain Orion's dazzling smile here to sell you everything from toothpaste to makeup. It's always seemed so bright and cheery. In person, it's terrifying.

Orion leans over to look at Abby. "You were actually the kicker. We had you picked for Meta-Human Training very early, but always were set to send you down the villain path. Your parents only wanted the best for you. We promised them that you would be put on the hero track if they cooperated with us on the MonRobots. This only worked for a short while, and then Philip wouldn't give us his codes."

"It's a shame. Abby Monroe, once this gets out, you're going to be the biggest villain in the world. After all, capturing North American Collective's favorite, Captain Orion, and then trying to kill her in her own home? You were perfect for this role. You're the spitting image of your mother, right down to your C-class telekinesis."

"That's where you have me wrong," Abby says. She takes a deep breath, and then closes her eyes.

"Jess, *run!*"

And then all hell breaks loose.

Abby's restraints fall to the ground, metal and circuits crackle everywhere, and then bits and pieces rearrange in mid-air. Metal panels rip off the wall. Orion's desktop projector disassembles itself, and the computer console falls apart and remakes itself. Abby is at the center of a vortex of circuits. Whirling parts come together to create another mecha-suit.

"Let's go," Abby says. She picks Jess up and flies out the window. The mismatched metal fragments of her makeshift suit rattle and quake in the oncoming wind.

"Orion's gonna chase us. How far can we get?" Jess asks.

"Far enough to hide. And hopefully somewhere where I will have enough time and parts to make a better suit. Also, Orion's a C-class, even if she was taking supplements. She was talking a whole bunch before you woke up, and I know how that stuff works. You have to constantly boost yourself, otherwise you'll fall back to whatever level you were before. And your body builds up an immunity to it after time, so she'd have to take more and more, at shorter intervals," Abby says. "She needs to rest. She can't fly right now, after all that, and she hasn't been boosting since she got back to her place. We can get out of here."

"You're amazing."

"Compliment me later; we have to get somewhere safe. Somewhere without the government tracking, where she can't find us, or anyone else."

Jess takes a deep breath, wincing as her pain amplifies on the inhale. "Okay. Let's go to my house."

"Your house? Look, unless you have a ton of blocking software and scramblers all around your information, they'll be able to find us—"

"We do. My parents are—"

"Oh my God, you totally told me earlier. It just hasn't sunk in yet. I bet your family does have all that and more. I mean,

Shockwave and Smasher are kind of the named protectors of Andover."

The town looks small from here, and the red canyons loom in the distance. Jess has no idea how long they were at Orion's home, but it's midday already; the sun is blazing hot all around them. They keep high in the sky until they approach Jess' home. She hopes everyone is focusing on their Saturday and no one will notice them dropping down from the sky. The descent is quick; Jess points them toward her house, and in a dizzying rush they're near the ground; Abby halts them and then gently sets them down.

"Come on, let's get inside." Jess waves her DED at the front door and it clicks open immediately. No one is home. *Right, it's Brendan's science fair today.* Jess exhales in relief; she's not sure she'd be ready to explain all of this. "Come on." She gestures for Abby to follow her in, and leads her upstairs. Abby peers into the open office door, at the posters of Smasher and Shockwave, and promptly starts chuckling.

"What's so funny? Is it because it's weird that, like our parents are fated enemies—"

"Please. This so not a Romeo and Juliet situation," Abby says. "Does this make you Romeo since you went after me? Am I Juliet? What was our balcony scene? I'm still . . . This is too much. I mean, I thought that your family could have some expression of the meta-gene, like maybe your grandparents, and then probably just in your line, but this is great. I haven't thought about it that much since today's been a ridiculous chaos of Orion and everything, but this is just—our parents. It's hilarious. I love it."

"Way to lighten the mood."

Abby laughs, but there's a bit of a desperate edge to it. She flops on Jess' bed; her body shakes as the laughter dies. "I'm not sure it worked entirely."

Jess sits. "Yeah."

There's nothing but the sound of their breathing, Abby's rhythmic breaths and Jess' slower, labored huffs through the pain. Abby laces their fingers together.

Jess sighs, closing her eyes. She leans back and meets not her pillow, but the curves of Abby's body. Arms wrap around her and Jess forgets about the current crisis, how much her chest hurts, the worry over what they're going to do next.

Here is safe.

Soft lips press against her temple, and Jess can't help but smile. She turns around and buries her face in Abby's neck, breathing her in.

"Jess, your neck," Abby says, wide-eyed.

"What?" Jess blinks wearily.

Abby gingerly touches her throat; it stings a little, probably leftover pain from Orion's lightning zap. "The lightning… I was wearing the suit but you… you've got a scar," she says. Somehow the word *scar* sounds full of awe. "Does it hurt?"

"Not anymore."

Abby runs a finger down the hollow of her throat, grazes her collarbone and skirts the neck of Jess' t-shirt.

Jess forgets to breathe. She lays still, hyper-aware of the way their bodies fit together, and of how Abby's pupils are blown so wide there's barely a trace of blue around the iris. Abby's just watching her, with a pleased, soft smile, fingers brushing against her skin, as if she'd be content to just do this forever.

"It's beautiful," Abby whispers. "Like you."

Jess kisses her.

It's as easy as breathing. Slow and appreciative, and this time Jess can take the time to notice little things, like the way Abby's body tucks around hers, the firmness of the thigh casually thrown over Jess' legs, how Abby has to tilt her head down a little to reach Jess' lips. Jess runs her hand down Abby's back, traces the curve of her spine, and delights in the way Abby exhales and trembles under her touch.

Jess can feel Abby smiling into the kiss, and she has to pull back to see. Abby's eyes are still closed, her lips are raw and shiny, and a smile is just starting at the corners of her mouth. A pink flush stands out on her cheeks. She opens her eyes, and they look at each other before grinning at each other, and Jess leans forward so their foreheads touch.

Abby traces the edges of her collarbone again and drops a light kiss there.

An image springs to Jess' mind from their writing assignment, Abby's looping handwriting describing bare skin and—

"Are you okay?"

"Yeah," Jess says, heart racing. She thinks she—she's not sure, actually.

"You made a noise."

"Was it a good noise?"

Abby kisses her forehead and sits up. "Yes." She takes Jess by the shoulders and guides her to turn to the mirror. "Here, you should check it out; it turned out really cool."

Jess' reflection stares back at her, and for a second she doesn't recognize the pretty girl on her bedspread sitting with her crush—girlfriend? Abby nudges her, beaming.

It's strange, how Jess realizes she looks very much the same; she just feels different. Her hair is the same, albeit mussed. Strands are sticking out everywhere, and usually that would bother her, but she blushes, thinking of *how* it got that way.

Standing out from her dark brown skin is a network of pale scars, stretching out from under her shirt in a fractal pattern, like the outline of a wandering river or the infinite, inestimable beauty of tree branches reaching for the sky.

It still hurts, but the pain has receded now to a light, residual throbbing.

"You should probably put burn cream on it," Abby says. "Do you have some?"

"Yeah, there's a first aid kit Brendan uses all the time," Jess says. She swallows, wondering if Abby is asking to *help,* and she flushes, thinking about Abby's hands on her skin.

Abby smiles and squeezes her shoulders. "Go on, I'll be here."

Jess gives her a wry smile and gets to her feet, ambles to the bathroom, shucks off her shirt. The burn cream is a cool relief on her skin, and she traces the outline of the scar. It starts a few inches below her left collarbone and spirals out, wrapping around her neck and creeping down her breast and petering out by her belly button. It is strange, but she can see why Abby thought it was beautiful.

Inside the bathroom cupboard is the makeup Jess uses from time to time. Her fingers linger on a bottle of foundation.

She closes the cupboard and puts her shirt back on, eyeing the way the scar protrudes from under it.

It's a souvenir. *I survived*.

Back in her bedroom, Abby is lying on her bed with a comic book open in front of her. It's a vintage print copy of *Magnus, Robot Fighter.* She traces the hard plastic of the laminated page, holding up the terrifying illustration of the rogue robots.

"It's funny how people used to picture the future," Jess says, hoping to lighten the mood. "Then again, maybe robots will look like this in the year… four thousand." She closes the comic book and sets it back on her shelf.

Abby gives her a glum smile. "Captain Orion said she and the government kidnapped my parents because they wouldn't make soldier-bots for them."

"They were looking for codes to do something to all the robots. Do you know what it was for?"

"My dad designed this project a while ago, like a home security program, but then he found so many flaws. Like, the MonRobot could be programmed to recognize certain people, but the cost of developing the A.I. to recognize who was an enemy, who wasn't… it wasn't worth it. So he discontinued it. But there was a line of MonRobots that went out, the most current one, that have the capability for this defense-type program. But I think the government wants to use it, use the information. If there's a person they don't like or want to take down, and there's a MonRobot in the home, then…"

"There'd be a homicidal robot whose A.I. could be controlled remotely by the government? That's awful."

"Yeah, you can see why my parents didn't want this code going live," Abby says. "We just need to find out where they're keeping them. And it's not at Orion's Andover home. Unfortunately I still have no clue."

Jess nods. "That really sucks."

Abby's eyes light up. "Wait! This totally makes sense. You can use your power to find them!"

"My power? I don't have any meta-abilities, Abby."

"No, no, you *do,* and hearing about who your parents are just confirms my suspicions. I mean I thought you did, like, you're just not aware of it. And it's not a power that the Training Academy looks for—I mean, it's almost—"

"What is it that you think I have?"

"Okay, where was I born?" Abby asks.

"How would I know that? I don't know that. You haven't told me where."

"I know! But do you have a feeling? If I asked you to walk toward where I was born, what direction would you go?"

"I don't know!' Jess says, stepping to the side.

Abby yelps. "Okay, okay, I knew it!"

"Knew what?"

"Look, you subconsciously knew that direction was where you needed to go! I think your power has to do with direction, Jess, really."

"Direction? I've never heard of it."

"New powers are discovered all the time," Abby says. "I was born in Old Bright City, which just happens to be east of here. And you were walking east. Okay, now where is Captain Orion right now? Just point."

Jess points west. "That doesn't mean anything. We just came from there."

"No, it could be that she moved. Look, I really believe you are a meta-human. Like, think back. Haven't you ever noticed you've gone in the right direction without knowing why? Like you know where everything is, but you don't necessarily know that you know, you have to think about it."

"This is ridiculous! I don't have powers! I've tested for all of them!"

"The ones that you knew about, sure," Abby says. "So you can't fly and you don't have superstrength. But you have this *amazing* ability, Jess."

"Sure, say I have this direction power or whatever. It's still entirely useless. I wouldn't even be like, D-class. I would be an F. This power isn't even on the Registrar's list. It's useless. I can't fight anyone with this power."

"No, but you can *find people*."

Jess takes a sharp breath in, realizing what she means. "Okay, let's say you're right and I do have this ability for... direction, or whatever. Like I can't just say your parents are..." She closes her eyes, and then...

Jess knows. As soon as she asked the question, she knew what direction to go. It's not an address, but she knows. "Southeast."

Abby seizes her in a hug.

They spend about an hour in Jess' garage retrofitting a bunch of old electronics to build Abby another suit.

Abby just—creates. Abby's powers seem limitless, and she manipulates every piece of electronics with a single thought; they travel in the air following her own design. It's captivating and powerful, in a much different way than Jess has seen any other meta-human powers—everyone she's seen before has used their abilities to fight each other, to destroy. This is creation. Invention.

Jess runs around the house, grabbing whatever spare electronics she can find. Her desktop projector and her parent's spare computers all disappear in a flurry. The bulk of the new mecha-suit is built from the minivan, with its ample computer and navigation technology. The stove is in pieces; Jess will have to explain to her parents later that it was an emergency.

Abby is almost finished, but there remains a complicated bit. It's found only in certain advanced tech, and she's already taken apart the minivan. "I know just the thing," Jess says.

She finds Chả at its docking station and picks it up with a fond pat. "Hey, little guy," she says.

Chả cheeps, little engine whirring, ready to vacuum.

"Not so much," Jess murmurs, carrying him to Abby.

"Oh no, I couldn't," Abby says, shaking her head. "It's your pet! It has a name."

Chả cheeps at Abby, rolls over to her, and bumps her on the foot in greeting.

"It's Monroe tech. Best of its kind. Chả, what do you think? Do you wanna help Abby out?"

Chả cheeps and spins about in a circle.

Abby takes a deep breath and holds her hands out. Chả's silver casing flies apart, revealing the circuitry underneath, and one slim shining piece flies into her hand. She holds the data chip aloft. "This is Chả's A.I.," Abby says solemnly. "We're gonna keep this safe, and when this is all over I'm gonna rebuild it for you."

The MonRobot becomes the chest piece and the main circuitry, and the new mecha-suit is complete. Abby's new suit should look ridiculous. It's the bare bones, just armor covering the body and thrusters so she can fly. It looks pretty amazing on Abby. Her dad's suit fit her awkwardly, and Abby moved hesitantly in it, but now she stands tall, waiting for Jess' approval. This suit doesn't have a logo, and it also doesn't have a helmet or an electronic panel covering Abby's face. Abby stands proud, her hair flying free.

"You look like a hero," Jess says.

Abby snorts. "Not so sure about that word anymore, but thank you. Let's go."

With some effort and the assistance of the suit, Abby carries her into the sky, and Jess points the way. Jess stands on Abby's feet as she flies, and Abby hooks an arm around her waist, holding her close.

Jess revels in the wind in her hair, the way the air rushes past her cheeks, sharp and biting, and Abby holding her securely as they travel, listening to her directions.

Jess remembers the last time she flew with Claudia. Jess was nine or ten, pointing out a path through the canyons where there wouldn't be so much headwind, and Claudia had told her to be quiet and let her fly. Even then, when they were closer, Claudia treated her as little more than a sidekick. Abby saw her as an equal, even when she thought Jess didn't have powers.

They head out into the desert and fly over the park past all of Jess' favorite trails, past the canyons. The view is lovely, but Jess concentrates on the feeling that keeps taking them toward their destination. The wind whistles against her hooded sweatshirt but, lost in her thoughts, she doesn't register how cold it is.

Could she really have a power? It makes sense: all those times she's known where things were but chalked it up to luck or chance; the times she's found herself moving to get in a line that then moves faster, or even told Bells where things were on sale.

All this time she's been using her power, but not in any useful way.

She's being useful now.

They fly toward a desolate area with fences and signs that read, "DANGER: DO NOT ENTER. CLASS FIVE UNMAINTAINED ZONE. RADIATION HAZARD" everywhere. Jess knows of this area. She thought it was a government testing area for hazardous waste or chemicals.

Now she knows what's really here. It's where they're holding Abby's parents, and maybe all the other villains they're holding hostage.

"They're gonna see us coming from a mile away," Abby says with a frown. "I can't land here."

Jess has to agree. Even if the only flying people they expect are Captain Orion and other heroes, they'd be watching the sky. They need a disguise. They need—

Chameleon.

They fly back to Jess' house, and Abby disassembles her suit, taking the time to perfect it while Jess paces.

"There's another hero, a young person. I don't think they're in league with Orion—they probably just finished Meta-Human Training, I'm not sure what they look like but they can shift and make themselves look like anyone! And I've seen them like touch something and change the appearance of that too—I don't think it's permanent, but it could be incredibly useful."

"Why would they help us?" Abby asks. "If they're in the League, what if Orion's brainwashed them already?"

"We won't know until we try. Orion kidnapped your parents. I'm sure we can figure it out."

"What about *your* parents?"

Jess sighs. "I don't know. I think they've been stuck in the mindset that your parents are their rivals for so long that it might take a lot longer to convince them." She takes a deep breath. "Maybe my sister. We used to be close. But I don't know where she might be."

Abby nods, stands up, and all the pieces of the suit fly around and fit her again. "All right let's start with the first idea. Where's Chameleon?"

Jess points east.

She's expecting to go a long distance, but they only fly a few blocks when Jess' instincts tell them to stop. Abby sets them down in front of a familiar-looking house.

"No way," Jess says, staring up at Bells' home.

Abby rings the doorbell. "Chameleon is inside?"

"I guess?" Jess says, trying to put the pieces together. They don't know much about Chameleon except that they're young, and Bells has been incredibly busy lately. It does make a ridiculous amount of sense, now that she thinks about it.

Bells answers the doorbell, his hair in a brilliant green mohawk today, wearing a new jacket he had his eye on in the mall last week but that was supposedly too expensive to buy.

"Hey, Bells," Jess says. "Um... do you have superpowers?"

"Me? No, why would you ask that? I totally don't." Bells shuffles back, his eyes darting between Jess and Abby. His eyes widen at the makeshift mecha-suit, and he lifts his eyebrows at Jess, as if to silently ask, *What is all this about?*

"Well, that's too bad," Abby says. She lifts a few inches off the ground and holds her hands up. The porch light flickers and then goes out. The entire glass and metal structure detaches itself from the wall, floats in the air, and all of it, metal, glass, wires, reconfigures to become a blooming rose in Abby's hand, a work of electronic art, floating in her palm. Abby smiles. "Jess totally thought you might be Chameleon, or well, that Chameleon is here. We could use some help."

Bells' mouth falls open. "What? You—you're—"

"I'm a meta-human," Abby says. "I'm thinking there might be three of us standing here. Am I right?"

"Three?" Bells eyes widen.

Jess sighs and says, "We should talk somewhere private."

SOMEWHERE PRIVATE TURNS OUT TO be Bells' bedroom. Jess is used to the warm, colorful space and the soft glow of twinkling light garlands strung up on the ceiling. She throws herself onto Bells' bed, sinking into the pillows. This could be just another day hanging out, except instead of the characters from *The Gentleman Detective* projected on Bells' holo, there's an open array of Bells' personal files, including blinking holobooks titled *META-HUMAN TRAINING 101* and *HEROES' LEAGUE OF HEROES OFFICIAL MANUAL AND GUIDEBOOK*. Bells waves his hand frantically and closes all the windows.

He rubs the back of his neck and the tips of his hair turn aquamarine.

"That's neat," Abby says, lingering by the door, giving him an impressed once-over. "Can you make it go curly or any texture?"

Bells nods; his mohawk falls down around his face in long, soft tendrils. "I mean, technically I shouldn't use my powers outside of actual hero work, but I can't help it. I've been altering myself ever since I learned how. It's just part of who I am." A corner of his mouth quirks up. "It took me a while to learn how to concentrate on *not* shifting accidentally, but today's full of surprises, so I think I'm allowed." He looks at Jess, as if he's waiting for her to react.

Jess gets up and pulls him into a hug. She's known Bells for years, knows that's probably the extent of how much he would want to get into it right now, especially considering how long he's known Abby. Instead, she throws all her love and appreciation into the embrace, hoping Bells knows she understands how much this means to her, how it's okay that he didn't tell her earlier, and what this power means to Bells. He closes his eyes and leans into the touch, hugging her back tightly.

"So that's how your hair got longer. I knew it wasn't hair extensions," Jess says, hoping to make Bells laugh.

He does, tossing his hair a little.

Abby paces back and forth, her mecha-suit clanking loudly as she goes. Her eyebrows are knit together. She narrows her eyes. "So you're in the League. What do you think of it?"

Bells shrugs. "I mean, I don't do much yet; my job until I finish school is just to help with public morale and do some reconnaissance, that's it." He glances at Jess. "I may have checked up on you once when I was on the clock. But the assignment was to 'do general good,' and I already rescued a cat, and making sure your walk to work was safe definitely fell in that category." He beams, the smile stretching from ear to ear.

"You walked me—" Jess gasps. "That was *you*! I thought there was something about that woman. Bells, what in the world kind of disguise was that? I spent forever trying to figure out how her hair was so shiny."

Bells hums in approval. "Well, I thought the hair would catch your attention. I was trying for Abby's shade, but I must have overdone it. Can't beat the original, you know." He holds out his fist for her to bump.

Abby gives Bells a small, pleased smile and taps his fist with hers.

"You've been tailing me all over town?"

"Oh no, I only did it until you started getting rides with Abby. The other time I was at Monroe Industries was an actual League recon mission, but I was glad I ran into you and said hi."

"Barry," Jess says suddenly. "Barry from Devonport."

Bells winks at her.

Abby looks affronted. "You were that punk that tried to look at my MonRobot designs!"

Bells laughs. "'Tried' being the key word. The security there is top-notch. Those security MonRobots chased me out; it took three different shape-shifts to get them off my tail. Anyway, the mission was super-vague. I have no idea what Captain Orion wanted to know. Figured it had something to do with… stocks, maybe? Wait, *your* designs?"

"Bells Broussard, meet Abby Jones, also known as Abby Monroe," Jess says.

It's Bells turn to look impressed, and he puts his hands on Abby's shoulders. "Okay. The latest update with the kitchen assistant model—genius. Saves so much time at the restaurant."

"Aren't they cool? Abby's MonRobot made me a grilled cheese and it—"

Abby coughs. Her cheeks are pink. "I appreciate the enthusiasm, but we've got a huge problem we'd love your help on. Can we get back to discussing the League and what you do there?"

Bells gives her an apologetic nod. "Sure. Like I said, some public morale tasks, a bit of recon, and there have been a few practice battles. I shifted into a popular villain and had to fight some of the other heroes, but it's mostly training. It's been kind of cool so far to meet the people the comic books are about, but I don't see them that often. They're always busy."

"Public morale," Jess says. "Is this what you were doing with all the rescuing cats and stuff? You've been driving my parents off the wall, especially since there's a limited amount of hero work in Andover to begin with."

"Your parents?"

"Shockwave and Smasher," Jess says. "Since we're coming clean about everything."

Bells gasps. "Oh gosh, really? That's so cool! I mean, I always thought your mom was amazing, but next time I see her I'm gonna have to really thank her for being awesome—ah! I never see them at League meetings, though. I just thought they're busy."

"They're in the Associated League, get a few missions from the big boys every now and then." Jess says. "I mean, technically they are part of the League, and my dad likes to say he is, but he hasn't had an official mission from them in years. I guess since the Mischiefs disappeared, they do what you do—public morale."

Abby scoffs. "Yeah, the League is gonna need public morale boosting after they've kidnapped all those villains."

"Wait, what?"

Abby folds her arms. "Where do you think all those people went? The 'villains' were the ones who disagreed with the current authority."

"Captain Orion wouldn't do that. Captain Orion does what's best for the North American Collective," Bells says, shrinking back.

"Look, that's what they want you to think," Jess says. "But do you know that our country is currently helping Constavia in their war with the Kravian Islands?"

Jess syncs her DED to Bells' desktop projector and pulls up the holos from the files she and Abby found, showing him all the evidence they've collected, the reports from Constavia, and the strange files on the villains. Bells scans through them, the furrow in his brow getting deeper and deeper.

"Okay, we have a presence there," he says slowly. "But I mean, the NAC isn't involved in a *war*. No one's even—" he splutters, as if the concept is too ridiculous to even think about. "Since World War III," Bells mutters. "There aren't any wars, okay? The Global Federation is stable. There's some conflict between the Kravian Islands and Constavia, and then over in the Southeast Asian Alliance, but definitely not with the NAC. Who would we be fighting? I mean, they would report it on the news if we were at war."

"Not if there were other news people care about more." Jess pulls up the latest news-holo and isn't disappointed; the current headlined article is about Captain Orion fighting the villain in Ore Town.

"Yeah, but that's important," Bells says.

"I know Plasmaman," Abby says. "He was like an uncle to me, used to come over for dinner all the time with me and my parents. Nicest guy ever. Made really good mashed potatoes. His whole job in the Villain's Guild was to show up where they told him to every once in a while and pick a fight."

Jess whistles. "And Plasmaman has been missing. And this report says he didn't actually use his powers in the fight. Didn't you say you… "

"Yeah, okay, that was me," Bells admits. "And last week fighting Cerebrus, too. But I—" He throws his hands up and sinks into a beanbag by the door. "It's training," he says, his voice flat. "It's good for me to practice not just my meta-abilities but also combat skills, and the public setting requires me to use my creativity and the environment." It sounds as if he's reciting, and he looks up. His voice wavers when he adds, "Plasmaman is in Corrections."

Abby flicks at the projections on Jess' DED, scrolling through the status reports on the "missing" villains, stopping on a profile of one Adam McVicar. "He isn't," she says gently.

"These are all… missing villains?" Bells looks at the multitudes of reports. "Why would Orion have this… where… why?"

"We don't know," Jess says. "But I do think that the big battles, everything that gets reported in the news-holos, it's just a huge distraction. The heroes and villains, all of it. Tell me, at Meta-Human Training, did they tell you that you were going to be a hero? You had to pass some sort of test, didn't you?" Abby asks.

Bells narrows his eyes. "I was good at my classes, okay! And I'm good at hero-ing, even if it's just small dumb stuff! It's important, it makes people feel good, and it's hard work, okay? Even if it's just returning a pet to some spoiled rich person. You know cats have so many claws and a lot of the time they don't want to leave the tree, and I don't—I don't even fly or have superstrength—most of my tasks involve trying to be creative and coming up with ways I actually can help! You try doing that and high school at the same time!"

"But the people you trained with, were all of you guys going to be heroes?"

Bells shrugs. "I mean, I finished the program. I don't know about the others. There were some people always getting held back for talking back and stuff."

"That's how it works," Abby says. "My parents… they were picked by the government to become villains."

"Wait, who are—"

"The Mischiefs," Abby says.

Bells takes a step back.

Jess touches his elbow. "Look, you know the Mischiefs have never hurt anyone. They do a bunch of harmless, elaborate pranks—"

"Because they're anti-government!" Bells cries out. "I'm gonna—I'm gonna—"

"With good reason, look! They're gone, they've been gone for a while, them and the other villains, Orion and the government are keeping them under wraps and it's wrong," Jess says. "Please, you know it's wrong."

"Captain Orion—"

"Held us captive," Abby says. "We confronted her earlier to ask about the Constavia thing and the missing villains, and she attacked us."

Bells claps his hands to his mouth in horror. "No way, she's the *Commander* of the Heroes' League of Heroes. They're the defenders of the innocent! The keepers of justice—"

Jess unzips her sweatshirt.

Bells stares, wide-eyed. "Đụ," he curses. He only borrows this word from Jess when the English one won't do. "Jess, what happened to your neck?"

"Captain Orion zapped me with lightning today," Jess says. "I asked her a *question* and she attacked us, like I said. And then I woke up in a cell at her house, and Abby was strapped to a chair as she questioned us. Like criminals."

Bells opens his mouth and then closes it. He pulls Jess close. "Oh God, does this hurt? I should have asked—"

"It's fine, Bells," Jess says, patting him on the back.

"I'm sorry, I didn't know she could—" Bells takes a deep breath. "I guess I just was so caught up in the idea of being a superhero that like, I mean, there were some questionable parts, and sometimes I'd get weirded out but… I was so excited about it, you know?"

"All right, Chameleon," Abby says with a grin. "Ready for a rescue mission?"

"And who are you supposed to be? I mean, I know you're Abby Jones, but like, when you're in… this mode?" He gestures at the mecha-suit. "Do you have a codename?"

Abby shrugs. "I haven't thought about it yet. My parents didn't get to pick for themselves, they were dubbed the Mischiefs by the Villain's Guild…"

Bells nods, and then turns to Jess. "Jess, you have powers? But I haven't seen you at Meta-Human Training!"

"I don't… well, I didn't think I did, not before today," Jess says. "And, um, I don't think I'll be applying there. My power isn't on the accepted list."

"What's your power?" Bells asks.

"Direction?" Jess gestures at nothing. "It's lame, I don't know why Abby—"

"It isn't lame," Abby says. "It's amazing. I bet you're at A-class, too; you must use it all the time without even thinking about it. Close your eyes, Jess. This is gonna be cool, Bells. So, I'm hungry. Does Bells have any oranges in his house?"

Jess shrugs. "I have no idea."

"Okay, Jess, where are the oranges in Bells' house?"

It's like something pulling her from her navel, familiar to her as the muscle memory of how to write. Jess stands up, thrilled that she can identify this sensation as an *ability,* and walks out of Bells' bedroom. She closes her eyes, testing herself. She can hear Abby and Bells follow her to the kitchen, where Jess lets her instinct guide her. Eyes still closed, she picks an orange from the fruit bowl. She opens her eyes and tosses it to Abby.

"Pretty cool," Bells says. "That's awesome!"

Jess ducks her head, pleased with herself.

"It is awesome; deal with it," Abby says. "Ready to go kick some butt?"

Bells takes a deep breath, and in an instant he's taller, wearing a rainbow-hued outfit of Chameleon's.

"Okay, good, the three of us, and maybe… "

Jess calls her sister. "Clauds, pick up, c'mon," she says, pacing back and forth as her DED shows the spinning wheel of doom.

"Wait, who's your sister?"

"Powerstorm," Jess says.

"Wow," Bells says. "She's awesome. She looked at me once and made eye contact, made my whole day. Do you think you can ask her what kind of conditioner she uses?"

"No!" Jess rolls her eyes.

"Sorry," Bells says. "It's kinda weird. I mean, I think it fits, like Claudia always was an overachiever, but I always thought the way she talked to you was weird… I mean, I don't talk to my siblings that way."

"Claudia got a big head when she got into the League," Jess says. "She isn't picking up. Let's go."

Now that they know where the facility is, they let Abby recharge her powers while they take the Trans' sedan into the desert. It's newer than the minivan and boots up in a reasonable amount of time, to Jess' relief. She's still not sure what she'll say when her parents get home and discover *both* cars are gone. At least one isn't gone permanently.

As they leave the city, the carefully maintained lawns and shiny buildings give way to the desolate landscape of the desert, marked by the tall mountains in the distance and the sparse shrubbery. The Joshua trees carve eerie silhouettes into the night sky.

Las Vegas shines in the distance, lighting up the skyline, and Jess can imagine the people going about their gambling and concerts without a care in the world.

Bells and Abby are caught up in a conversation about volleyball, of all things.

"Are we gonna tell Emma?" Jess asks. Abby's just talked about a game where she and Emma worked together to score a point.

Bells frowns. "I'm not sure. Maybe, we'll see. I mean, I wasn't going to tell you two—not because I didn't want to, but because the rules, you know, having a secret identity, and…"

"That's already out of the bag for me," Jess says. "And now that I know, you know it's gonna feel off to her. Not to mention that Abby's been hanging out with us too, and Emma's gonna feel really out of the loop."

"She's mad at me," Bells says, and sighs. "I don't know what to do."

Abby throws her hands up. "Hey, don't look at me. I don't really know what to do with close friends. Hanging out with you guys is a first, you know."

"But you're captain of the volleyball team," Bells says.

"*Was* captain," Abby corrects. "I stepped down after my parents were kidnapped. I wanted to focus everything on finding them.

And even before that, I didn't hang out with the girls from the team much. I talked to them, was friendly, but we weren't really friends, you know? I mean, it wasn't like I could invite people to my house. What if my parents were being weird, or what if they'd figure out our abilities, or if I forgot myself and began manipulating something… so yeah. I don't really know what to do with this. I mean I'm kinda jealous how close the three of you are."

"Friendship is pretty awesome," Jess says. "And now you're a part of this too. And yeah, Bells, you're overthinking it. I mean, Emma has been really hurt by all this lying and stuff, you know that, but once you tell her the truth, she'll understand. And the whole superhero thing and wanting it to be secret isn't the same as like when you have a crush on someone else and don't tell her."

Bells coughs. "So you know."

Jess chuckles. "Well, I suspected, but now I know!"

"Emma is awesome; you two would be so cute together," Abby says.

Bells looks at his feet. "I just… I dunno, I don't want to ruin our friendship."

"It'll be fine," Jess says. "Now we just have to… survive all this."

They park the car a good half-mile away from the facility and hike in. At the last moment, Bells disguises the three of them. He puts an arm on their shoulders and concentrates, and then they look like Captain Orion and two guards. Bells can only maintain the disguise for a short time, but the uniforms look impeccable and their features are forgettable.

Jess looks up at Bells, now in Orion's body. "Is this okay for you?"

"Not really," Bells says in Orion's voice. "I've gotten used to it, though. I shift into a lot of different people for the League. Part of having to use this power, I guess. But it's different when I *want* to do it to help my friends versus the League telling me to. Thanks for asking, though. Come on, the sooner we get through this, the sooner I can get out of this body."

They walk into the facility unchallenged until they get to the main door.

"Captain," the guard says at the door, surprised. "I didn't know you'd be back so quickly."

"Don't question me," Bells says, in Orion's commanding tone.

The guard lets them pass. "Of course."

The facility is a labyrinth, but Jess directs them forward, even though she doesn't consciously know where the path will go.

Even as Jess gets more and more comfortable with her power, they keep walking around in circles in search of Abby's parents. No amount of rephrasing the question aloud or Jess repeating it to herself gets them anywhere until Bells has the great idea of asking about depth.

They take the elevator down, down, down.

There isn't anyone else on the lower floors. Bells relaxes the disguises so he can recharge.

"That was pretty awesome," Abby says. "So you're a B-class then?"

"Yeah, the League likes me a lot, but I had to sign a lot of contracts with rules about when and what I could do," Bells says. "They didn't even like me randomly coloring my hair, like that was my favorite part after I figured out my powers. I can keep it up on myself pretty easily, especially if it's just a small thing like my hair, but to do the whole face and voice and clothes, that takes a lot more out of me."

"How long until you can put up the disguise again, if we need it?" Jess asks.

"I can do another disguise for the three of us in about twenty minutes, for about one more minute. And then I'll probably be done for the day."

"All right," Abby says. "Jess? Lead the way. My parents?"

Jess thinks about the question, then doesn't really understand what her instincts are saying. "I don't... uh, this is weird."

Bells perks up. "What's up, Jess?"

"Shush, I didn't even know I had powers yesterday," Jess says, trying to concentrate. "It's no use, I don't... I keep feeling like I'm being pulled in different directions. That can't be right."

"Or maybe it can," Abby says. "Okay, where's my mom?"

Jess points northeast.

"Ah. They're being held in different locations."

"Maybe we should split up?" Bells asks.

"No, no, that's the worst thing we could do. Besides, you're the only one with a disguise. One of us gets caught without you and all of us are dead meat," Abby says. "Let's go find my mom first."

Jess leads the way, and they get deeper and deeper into the winding hallways. There are no windows, and each hallway looks eerily similar to the last. The air gets colder as the building becomes more industrial. Exposed pipes line the ceilings; rusted paint peels from the walls.

"She better not be in a dungeon, or worse," Abby says.

"Stop right there!" a voice shouts from the distance.

"Bells—!" Jess says, but Abby grabs Bells' hand and shakes it before he can do the disguise.

"If we're already spotted, it would be a waste to use it now," Abby says.

They turn around to see their accuser. Abby stands at the forefront with her modified mecha-suit ready for blasting.

Jess stares at the figure flying down the hallway at them at full speed. "Claudia?"

"It's *Powerstorm!*" Claudia says, coming to a halt in front of them. "Jess, when Captain Orion told me you'd fallen in with these *villains* I could hardly believe it, but you were always simple and naïve. Of course, you would trust anyone."

Claudia shakes her blonde hair. Jess doesn't recognize the sister she's grown up with. She looks like a miniature Captain Orion, from the similar colors in her uniform to the hair, and even the blinding white smile.

"Surrender now, and we'll go easy on you," Claudia says, her hands on her hips. "Jess, it's okay if they brainwashed you somehow. We can pretend this never happened —"

"*Me* brainwashed?" Jess snorts. "You're the one who's brainwashed! Look, the League *kidnaps* people and does all these terrible experiments to try and make people's powers last longer!"

"In the name of the country," Claudia says. "It's for the good of the public. We need to believe in people who fight evil. We need to fight someone."

Abby shakes her fists. "What are you doing to my parents?"

"And what's this?" Claudia glances at Bells with disappointment. "You've got Chameleon believing this web of lies too?"

"Master and Mistress Mischief are my parents, and you've done them wrong. It could have been any toss of the dice, and it could have been your parents too, chosen to be villains," Abby says.

"*Chosen*? I knew you guys were off your rockers, but this whole idea is ridiculous. I'm bringing you all in." Claudia swoops forward, reaching out to grab them, but Abby waves her arms and the pipes above them burst, spilling water all over them. The broken pipes block their path, so they run the opposite direction until they come across a junction.

"Where are we going now?" Bells asks.

"I don't think my power works that way!" Jess says. "I don't know the answer, but if you ask me a specific question, I could figure it out!"

"Keep going toward my mom!" Abby says.

Jess directs them down the left hallway and then continues on, even as the hallway lights disappear. She reaches in the dark toward a door. She rattles it, until Abby waves her hand at it and they hear the lock click.

They push through the door, shut it behind them, and catch their breath.

The room is dark until Jess finds a switch and flicks it on. A light bulb turns on in the center of the room. A single figure sits on a chair, restrained with tantalum. Jess has only seen the heavy shining metal in newsholos. The tantalum seems to radiate a cold intensity that causes them all to pause where they stand.

"Mom?" Abby asks in a small voice.

"Abby!" The woman gasps and looks up. Her face is drawn and tired, but her eyes sparkle with hope that is visible even in the dim light. "What are you doing here? Who are—"

“Mom, this is Jess and Bells, my friends from school. We’re here to rescue you.”

Abby and her mom catch up while Jess figures out how to undo the restraints. She doesn't really know how the tantalum alloy will affect her, but she doesn't want to risk either Abby's or Bells' powers.

When Jess touches the metal, a cold heaviness weighs in her stomach, but it's not really noticeable. Better her than Abby or Bells, anyway. She finds a latch and presses it, and all the restraints unlock, pop free, and clatter to the ground. Mistress Mischief—Genevieve—stands up and seizes Abby in a hug, and then pulls Bells and Jess in as well.

"Thank you," she says.

"Of course," Abby says.

Jess lets them have their moment, holding on to the restraints.

Bells eyes her warily. "Isn't it affecting you?"

"I don't know," Jess says. "Ask me a question."

"Which way is north?"

Jess has nothing, no internal pull, no instinct. It's strange, having only known about her power for a day and now to miss it so much. How long will this last? The initial cold unsettling feeling disappeared when she stopped touching the tantalum, so maybe the rest of it will wear off soon.

"Phillip isn't here," Elizabeth says to the room. "They separated us a while ago."

"We need to get out of here," Jess says.

They race out of the room. Without Jess' sense of direction, it's difficult to navigate, but Bells recognizes the numbers on the hallways and gets them back to the elevators.

Abby pulls them into the stairwell. "Stairs, stairs, they'll be watching the elevators."

Their luck runs out three floors up. The stairwell is flooded with light and noise, and a rush of uniformed people comes down the stairs toward them. Claudia flies at them, and for a split second Jess is terrified.

Safety. We need to get out of here unobstructed.

"This way!" Jess opens the nearest door and flings herself down the hallway, running and following her instinct. *It's back!* She had no idea she missed it so much.

"You've already recovered from touching the tantalum cuffs," Genevieve says with awe. "Abby tells me your gift is amazing."

"Oh, thank you, I just found out about it today," Jess says, panting. "Come on, we have to get out of here before—"

The stairwell door bursts open, and Claudia flies down the hallway.

"She must have used the same supplements as Orion," Jess says. "She's never been able to use her abilities this much before."

"Chameleon, you traitor!" Claudia shouts. She picks up a hallway cabinet and throws it at Bells.

"Hey!" Abby steps in front of Bells. She lifts her hand, stops the cabinet in midair, and flings it back at Claudia, who just punches through it.

"Oh, I know who you are," Claudia says. "You're the one Orion says wanted to be on the hero track. Apparently you're A-class. Longest intensity level recorded, at least you would be if you were registered. Supposedly you're even stronger than me." Claudia sniffs, walking forward. "But I think you've been using your powers all day, and you should be just about tapped out by now." She advances, grabbing a broken piece of the cabinet and throwing it.

Abby can only duck, and the four of them back up, hugging the walls.

Jess cringes as the metal crashes to the floor.

Claudia gives them a sinister smile. "In the labs here we've been developing something that will revolutionize how we deal with uncooperative meta-humans. This batch isn't quite ready yet, but I think it will do. You're a threat, Abby Monroe, to me, the League, and the North American Collective. Can't have A-class meta-humans breaking into government facilities and aiding the escape of detainees, now can we?"

From her belt Claudia pulls out a syringe and uncaps it.

"No, no, no, what are you doing?" Jess yells, running forward.

Claudia shoves Jess aside, right into a wall, and Jess crumples to the ground in white-hot pain. Claudia injects the contents into Abby's neck and holds her by the wrist in a tight grip.

Abby's face goes ashen and she stumbles back. "What... what is—"

"You feel it, don't you, even if you're tapped out," Claudia says.

Bells has picked up a metal bar from the broken debris but stops when Claudia turns around. "I've got another one of these ready to go. You don't want to let go of your precious powers, now do you, Chameleon?" Claudia taunts.

Bells shrinks back.

"Leave him alone!" Jess says, fighting back the shock. She thought Claudia might have gotten a bit carried away with the fame of being in the League, but that she'd be able to listen to reason. Obviously she's so much in Orion's pocket that she doesn't see anything wrong with what she's just done to Abby. "I thought you were better than this."

"I *am* better," Claudia says. She gives Jess a long, considering look, purses her lips together, and for a second Jess is reminded of the way Claudia used to do that when they were kids; it's her thinking face, the same expression that preceded a new game or how to sneak sweets from their parents.

"What are you doing with these losers?" Claudia asks, jerking her head at Abby and Bells.

"They're my friends." Jess tries to stand up; her shoulder throbs from where she hit the wall and a new, throbbing ache has started in her chest from her scar.

"We're going to have to deal with them, you know. They're villains," Claudia says, shuddering with distaste. She looks down at Jess, still struggling on the floor, and then extends her hand. "Come on, Jessie Bessie. You don't have to be one of them. I'm very well established in the League now. Did you know Captain Orion is considering me for second in command? I've got a lot of say. And you're my *sister.*"

She leans forward with a conspiratorial smile, and suddenly Jess is reminded of the way it used to be between them.

"Look, remember what I said about hero support? You don't have to have powers to do that, but now that you've found this place and see what we've done with the meta-gene, there's just so many possibilities. I know you don't have powers, but you and I, we've got the same DNA. We're *legacies.* It would be so simple to activate the rest of your powers, Jessie Bessie. You could *fly.*"

Jess stares at Claudia from the floor, and a painful yearning in her heart leaps forward: those countless trials in the desert by herself, jumping off rocks, hoping for something, anything to show that she would inherit her parents' powers. The memory of flying above the canyons with Claudia holding her, the two of them laughing and joking like the friends they used to be changes to the present: Jess and Claudia wearing matching League emblems, flying *together.*

Flight. The rarest of abilities.

If Captain Orion found a way to make meta-abilities last beyond normal limits, it's entirely possible Jess could fly.

Claudia's hand is still outstretched before her. "It'll be great," she says.

Jess takes a deep breath; she'd always wanted to fly.

Behind Claudia she can see Abby's prone figure; Genevieve cradling her head and rocking back and forth. Bile rises in Jess' throat. Bells is cowering on the other end of the hall, still shaking from Claudia's threats.

The memories of Claudia and Jess together—they're just that; memories, in the past. Claudia is different now, and Jess knows the horrifying things Orion and the League have done.

"No," Jess says softly.

"What?"

"No." The word is louder this time, and Jess pushes herself off the ground, standing up on her own. She brushes aside Claudia's hand. "Orion and the League are wrong."

Jess holds up her fists and sets her feet apart in a fighting stance. She winces as her aching body protests, but she readies herself anyway.

Claudia's eyes flash and she flies up, seizing a pipe and breaking off a section from the ceiling with her considerable strength. The remaining pipes above her shake and groan.

"You're going to regret this," Claudia says coldly. "Corrections is not a fun place." Claudia shakes her head, hefting the heavy pipe. "I'm going to knock you all out now and take you back to Orion." She shakes her head at Jess. "I was so good to you; I took you flying and endured all your clingy little questions. You were going to be my sidekick, help me—"

"I am *not* your sidekick!" The volume of her own voice surprises even Jess, and it echoes in the hallway, but she stands by what she says, grabbing a stray bit of metal to protect herself. If it's going to be a fight, she might as well be ready. "I've *always* been in your shadow, Clauds. What makes you think I want to keep doing that? I want to be my own person, be liked for who I am, not just for copying you!"

Claudia laughs, loud and shrill. "*Your own person?* You're nothing but a byproduct of an experiment!"

Jess blinks. "What's that supposed to mean?"

"Maybe you should ask our *parents* what they've been keeping from you. I mean, they didn't seem surprised at all when you didn't get any powers, did they? Like they *knew* you wouldn't?"

Jess steps backward, stunned.

Claudia continues, voice hard as steel. "You'll never be a hero, never be anything—"

The debris above her shakes precariously. "Claudia, watch out!" Jess yells.

Claudia is still in the middle of her diatribe when a pipe lands on her, knocking her to the ground. Jess rushes forward; for all that Claudia has said and done, she's still her sister. "No, no, Claudia—"

Bells steps hesitantly forward. "She's got superhealing, right?" He reaches and tries to lift the pipe off Claudia. Jess struggles to help and the two of them finally push it aside.

Claudia's unconscious, and Jess tries her best to remember the first aid classes she's had and takes Claudia's pulse. It's steady, so she might just be out of it for a bit.

"Come on, we have to get her out of the way."

They take her to the cell where Abby's mom was kept and put the tantalum shackles on her to keep her from recharging.

"Orion will get her," Genevieve says.

Jess takes one more look at Claudia. With her eyes closed, she doesn't look angry anymore. Just young.

GENEVIEVE MONROE IS SHORT AND has a commanding presence. "Abby, you have to get off the base immediately. They'll want to keep you to monitor how the serum affects you—and how are you feeling?"

"Terrible," Abby says. "This is totally different from being tapped out."

"I haven't seen many of the test subjects, but a lot of them had very invasive tests," Genevieve says. "I need to get a message to your father as soon as possible. If I can get into the mainframe somehow—"

"I can get you there," Bells says. "I have enough strength to do one more disguise. We can look like two of the guards, get to a console close to the exit, and then we can walk out."

Genevieve nods. "Okay. Abby? Jess?"

Abby takes her DED out of her pocket and hands it to Bells. "Take this. There's a holo of Captain Orion talking about the experiments and all the horrible things the NAC have been doing with the League. Get it on the Net it as soon as you can after you contact my dad."

"I can definitely do that," Bells says. "How are you guys gonna get out? There are guards everywhere."

"We'll find our way," Abby says, looking at Jess.

Jess points at the hall behind them. "The safest exit route free from the guards or any other opposition is that way. Come on, Abby."

Jess hugs Bells tightly. "You're always a hero to me."

He chuckles and pats her back. "I'll see you back in town."

Abby and her mom are hugging, whispering to each other. "Ready?"

Jess takes her hand, and they make their way. It gets harder as they go, as Abby seems to get weaker and weaker. Finally Jess' instinct guides her to what looks like a garbage chute, and they crawl in, landing among soft garbage bags. They wait in the closed dumpster, and after what seems like an infinity of darkness, Jess can hear a machine moving them. Wheels. Concrete.

"Abby, it's going to be okay," Jess says. "We're getting out of here, and then your mom is gonna meet us back in Andover."

Abby squeezes Jess' hand weakly and then promptly vomits in the corner of the dumpster.

It's hot in the enclosed space, and the stench of vomit is more and more concentrated as they continue. Jess tries to keep track of how long they've been on the road, but she has no clue. She's tired and hungry and her eyelids are closing.

Jess wakes up to a shock of light and the sounds of more machines, and then she and Abby are among the trash bags in an open heap. They seem to be the last dumpster to be emptied. Jess hides among the bags just in case.

A bright morning sun bounces harsh rays off the canyon that serves as the dump. Jess waits until the truck drives away before she struggles to get free of the trash.

"Abby!" Jess calls. "Come on, let's go!"

Abby groans.

When Jess touches her, Abby's skin is pale and clammy. "Abby, how are you feeling?"

"Gross."

"We're literally sitting in trash, I would expect so. Come on, Andover is that way."

She manages to get Abby to her feet, and they clamber out of the trash pile and to the trail leading out of the dump.

Abby is sluggish and refuses to talk. She just nods and slings an arm around Jess. They walk in the heat, and Jess has to stop every now and then and remove the pieces of Abby's broken mecha-suit. They leave a trail of shining metal pieces behind them as they go, keeping a considerable distance from the road.

THE AIR SHIMMERS IN THE distance, but Andover isn't quite visible yet. There is only desert around them; Joshua trees twist toward the sky and creosote bushes dot the landscape.

A truck drives by on the road, whizzing loudly. Jess nearly trips over a rock, and they stumble, but Abby is the one who slumps to the ground.

"Abby!" Jess calls out, seeing Abby's prone form lying on the ground. "Please be okay, please be okay," she mutters as she rushes forward.

She turns Abby over and exhales when Abby's eyes flick open, and her chest heaves up and down.

"Abby." Jess holds her to her chest.

"I'm fine. I knew you cared, you dork."

"Of course I care!" Jess tucks the curl flopping in front of Abby's eyes behind her ear and pats her hair.

"You love me," Abby says, smiling.

Jess leans forward. "Yeah, I really do. This isn't our Romeo and Juliet moment. You're going to be okay. No one is dying."

"No, it's the end. I want a goodbye kiss."

"No." Jess refuses to believe it's that bad. Genevieve wouldn't have let them go if she didn't think they could make it out of the base. She doesn't know what that serum did, but for now she's just relieved Abby is still breathing and talking and doesn't have any visible injuries. "I'll kiss you when all this is over, okay? You're going to be fine."

Abby closes her eyes, breathing shallowly.

"Where is help? Where is someone who can help us?" Jess mutters to herself. "Come on, you stupid power, be useful. I can do this." She concentrates, but can't figure a direction.

Glancing at her wrist is an automatic reflex, but the display of her DED is shattered. It must have been damaged during the fight, and now is nothing more than a useless bit of metal and circuits. "I need someone who can help Abby get better. Where is the nearest person who can help Abby?"

Jess thinks and thinks and there's no direction that her heart is telling her to go, it just is…

That means the answer is Jess. Jess is that person.

The desert is vast and dry, and Jess' lips are already parched. They're going to need to find shade, and quick.

"Can you stand?" Jess asks. "If you can't move on your own, we can't go anywhere; you're going to get really sunburnt here and dehydrated. Let's try and get to that rock overhang."

Abby winces and lets Jess prop her up. Jess takes most of the weight. Together, the two of them struggle across the sand.

The gorgeous canyons all around mock them with the lack of shade; the few cacti rise tall and spindly with scant shadows. There is no wildlife, only the rustling of the wind, scattering dust clouds in the distance.

The wilderness outside Andover used to make Jess nervous whenever she left the city. Hardly anyone ever hiked out here, even for fun. There are plenty of recreational opportunities in Andover, and Las Vegas is only an hour's drive away.

They pass by an old sign that proclaims *DANGER: UNMAINTAINED AREA, CLASS THREE.* It's been over a hundred years since the Disasters, and there's no danger from the radiation, but the unknown, that huge "Unmaintained" label is the main reason no one wants to go outside the towns.

Even if there was a passing car, what's to say Orion hasn't alerted the League and everyone about what they've done? *Are they fugitives now? Are they in danger?*

Jess has always found the area intriguing, with bits and pieces of old America scattered throughout a vivid and beautiful landscape, but today she doesn't have the energy to appreciate it.

There's so much life here, all of it struggling to stay afloat, seizing sun and air and water where it can. Jess once memorized the shapes of cacti so she could learn their names on the Net. Supposedly there's one that can be sliced up and harvested for the juice, but Jess doesn't remember which one or how that process would work.

Jess concentrates on moving one foot in front of the other.

Water. She knows there is water close by. Behind that rock overhang, there will be water.

They make it to the overhang, and Jess sets Abby down.

"You should leave," Abby says. "I'm useless out here. That serum, whatever it did, I can't... Even if it didn't have an effect and only made me sick, I'm not charged enough to move anything, and there's nothing electronic for me to manipulate. Both of us don't have to die here. Go."

"I'm not leaving you. But I am going to get you some water. There's some close by. I can feel it."

"Go back to Andover," Abby says.

"Shh, I'll be right back." Jess kisses Abby on the forehead, then leaves her in the shade. She takes off her outer shirt and winds it around her head like a hat to keep the sun out of her eyes and follows her instincts. Water. Drinkable water.

Her instinct guides her to a sheer cliff, and Jess eyes the sandstone. "Đéo biết," Jess curses. Where is she supposed to go? Is the water embedded in the stone?

She looks around the outcrop she's standing on, searching for any sign of the water.

It's here. It has to be. She scans the area until she sees a pile of stacked rocks—someone made this formation. A cairn.

So, she's on the right track.

Jess turns back toward the cliff, looking at the way weather and time have carved the stone into jagged shapes, and how cracks mar the surface. Every so often, there's a dusting of white powder.

Chalk, Jess realizes, and a holovid of rock climbers coating their hands with the substance comes to mind.

"Okay," Jess says, taking a deep breath.

She grips the rock face, steadies herself on the tiny holds, and then finds the barest ledge for her toes. The sandstone is gritty and warm beneath her fingers; red dust coats her skin.

Jess is aware of nothing but the sky blazing pale blue behind her and the red rock in front of her as she climbs higher and higher. She loses her grip a few times and she barely catches herself before tumbling. Each inch is a victory.

The chalk is dusted generously in no apparent pattern, as if whoever was here—multiple whoevers, probably—skittered all over the rock for fun.

Ahead an overhang juts out above a dark hollow with another small cairn.

Jess rolls ungracefully, knocking the stacked pebbles aside; her body barely fits the small alcove. As her eyes adjust, she can see the shallow opening widens into a dark cavern. Pockets of light flick erratically inside the cave. *How deep does it go?*

She lies there on the cool stone catching her breath, and then wills herself to crawl forward until she can stand up.

Water.

She plods into the cave, and soon the hard stone gives way to softer sand, and then in a corner Jess falls to her knees. She picks up a sharp rock and digs. She keeps going until she hears a heavy metal klunk.

She finds a small barrel, someone's cache of survival supplies from the time of the Disasters, carefully squirreled away for later use. Jess pries open the lid. Inside is a backpack and a plastic jug of water. "Yes," she breathes out. She breaks off the seal and takes a swig of the cool liquid. She manages to stuff the jug into the backpack, not bothering to look at the other contents. She heaves the whole thing onto her back and picks her way carefully down the cliff. It's harder going down, but Jess only has one thought: *Get back to Abby.*

Jess wobbles forward once she reaches the ground. "Why is water so heavy?" she mutters. She shifts position, but any way she carries the pack is awkward; she cuddles the pack to her chest and waddles toward the rock overhang.

"Hey." Jess sets down the backpack and takes out the jug.

Abby doesn't respond.

"Abby," Jess says, crouching down. She takes her extra shirt and pours some of the water onto it, wiping Abby's forehead and then placing it on the back of her neck. *It's what we're supposed to do for people who are overheating, right? Is Abby overheating?* "Abby."

"Ah, that feels nice," Abby says, her voice barely a whisper.

"Drink some water." Jess pours from the jug into her cupped palm and holds it to Abby's lips. "C'mon, you got this." Jess tips her hands forward into Abby's mouth.

Abby drinks two handfuls of water, and then drifts off into an uneasy sleep. Jess drinks from the gallon jug, and then examines all the contents of the backpack.

So they have water and two reflective emergency heat blankets, five protein bars, and a glow stick. There's nothing electronic in the backpack, just the food and water. It must be a quick refueling spot, hidden out here all the way in the middle of nowhere.

It's not much, but it could be enough. Jess wishes her power was more specific because she could point them back to Andover, but they have no way of knowing how long it would take, or how far it is. It took an hour, maybe more, by car to get to the facility. That's probably what, eighty miles at the most? Jess knows in P.E. she barely managed a twelve-minute mile, and that was running. Walking would take longer, especially in unknown terrain. They only have enough water for the two of them for a day, maybe two if they stretch it. Should they leave the relative safety of this shelter?

Jess sighs.

Abby groans, still in pain. She twitches and reaches out. "Jess."

"I'm right here," Jess says.

"No, here."

Jess scoots closer. The ground is relatively cool, and Jess stays low and the two of them huddle there, Abby's fingers finding Jess' own and curling around them.

Jess falls asleep.

When she wakes up, the sunset is just leaving the horizon in streaks of warm oranges and reds.

Abby is awake already. She's got the contents of the backpack laid out in front of her and a half-eaten protein bar in her hand. She takes another bite and makes a face at the taste. "These things are dry and taste like cardboard, but they're edible. Where'd you get it?"

"Somebody's cache of supplies. Probably been here since the Disasters."

Abby makes a gagging noise. "Eating hundred year old protein. And I thought it couldn't get any worse. Wonderful."

"Hey, we're alive."

"We bought some time," Abby says. "I wish I could help, but my suit is gone, and even if I had it, I wouldn't be able to operate it without my powers."

Jess nods. "We can try and find our way toward Leichester. It's closer than Andover."

"What's there?"

"Nothing, really. It's an old way station between Nuevo Los Angeles and Las Vegas. There are pictures of aliens there. I've seen it when I used to come out here. It would be on the way. I wish I knew how far, but I don't. It's between here and Andover. We would get there sooner. I mean, I don't know if there's enough electronics there for you to make a new suit, but we could ask someone to use their DED to find out what happened to Bells."

"It's as good a plan as any," Abby says. "Let's get moving while it's dark."

Jess agrees.

By the light of the moon, they walk, keeping just off the main road. Occasionally a car drives by, its bright headlights shockingly blinding white against the looming darkness of the night. Jess hopes they aren't visible; she has no idea what Orion may have told the League about them or whether the authorities are looking for them.

Abby seems to have regained her physical strength at least and pushes away any question Jess has about her well-being. They walk in silence, the only sound their footsteps on the ground and the wind starting to pick up.

Jess puts her extra shirt back on, and she shivers in the cold desert night. Abby must be cold, too, in the thin skintight circuited bodysuit, but she doesn't say anything about it.

Temperatures here are so extreme. How did people live during the Disasters without heat or air conditioning to temper this harsh environment?

They walk through the night, silent and filled with determination. Jess begins to lose focus, just follows where Abby goes, puts one foot in front of the other; her body is starting to give up on her. It becomes routine; walk, walk, walk, hide when there's a car, take sips of water. Soon they abandon the empty water jug.

Abby walks as if her limbs are stiff. "Can you find us another shelter?"

Jess concentrates and points; there will be another overhang soon. The morning light peeks over the horizon, and they take out one of the emergency blankets; it shines in the moonlight, crinkles like aluminum foil, and they wrap themselves together.

THEY WAKE IN LATE AFTERNOON. Jess is groggy; sleeping during the day and walking through the night has messed with her natural sleep rhythm.

"How close are we?" Abby asks, and then sighs. "Sorry, I forgot."

"It's okay," Jess says.

"No, I mean, without you, we wouldn't have the food and water or know where we're going. You're doing all you can."

"Let's keep going."

They make a quick meal of the protein bars and then walk forward.

Sometime in the middle of the night, Jess sees the light of the way station and the neon green alien face, shining like a beacon. "Almost there!" she says.

Abby bristles. "I can sense the electronics… three cars… door locks… an old computer console… one DED… but I can't do anything."

"It's fine. We just need to get there and then we can call someone for help."

"Who would we call?"

"My parents, probably." Jess sighs. "I don't know how they'll take the news about Claudia."

They stumble into the way station looking like a mess, but no more so than the group of college-age kids fueling up on energy drinks and snacks, talking excitedly about their plans for a night of debauchery in Las Vegas.

Their flashy convertible speeds off before they can be approached, so Jess and Abby head right into the way station. They must be covered in dirt, but the attendant doesn't pay them any mind. He's incredibly old; lines weather his face and he's reading a novel at the register, gingerly turning a page at a painstakingly slow pace. A *MASTER MISCHIEF WAS RIGHT ABOUT THE CHEESE* trucker hat is perched on his head, and his long hair is gathered into a ponytail.

"Do you have a DED?" Jess asks. "We were hiking and got lost; our car battery died out in the canyons."

The attendant clucks his tongue. "Kids," he says, shaking his head. "Gotta charge those things up full before you leave the city. You know there ain't gonna be charging ports everywhere." He glances up and takes in their condition, and a trace of sympathy appears in his eyes. "My son gave me one to keep in touch, but it broke a few years ago. Never bothered fixing it. Now, cell phones, those I miss. A thing you can touch, you know, pictures stayed on the screen…"

Abby raises her eyebrows and whispers to Jess. "Think he's over a hundred?"

Jess shrugs. "It's possible." Emma's nana is a hundred and seven. This guy probably lived right through the Disasters, too.

"Those went out of style when I was a kid," he mutters, rummaging around under the counter. "Everyone had a cell phone, but companies didn't do the upkeep for them. This newfangled technology, all them pictures flying around in the air, everything is connected, but you lose one thing and it's a terrible inconvenience, a hazard—"

Finally he pulls out a DED. The model is at least a decade old; the screen is big and clunky. "You're welcome to try and get it to work."

"Thank you," Jess says, giving him a relieved smile.

"Can I borrow pliers?" Abby asks.

The man turns around and takes a dusty old toolkit off the shelf. "Don't really know what's in here," he admits. "Possible it hasn't been opened since this was the United States of America."

Abby grits her teeth. "All right, let's go see this thing."

They head out back, and Jess follows her, nervous. Didn't Abby just say her powers weren't working?

"I can fix it, powers or no powers," Abby says. "I still have my brain; I can still make this happen."

She wrenches open the back and stares at the inside of the DED, then starts pulling at wires. Jess watches as she uses a bit of duct tape to tease out a bit of circuitry and a chip, and then walks them over to the way station's small solar generator. She fiddles with the wires there, too, until the DED is attached. The screen lights up. "Got a network," she says. "Weak, but it's there."

Abby holds the DED out to Jess. "Try it."

Jess presses on the power button and it flickers to life with a few weak projections in the air. When she presses VOICE COMMUNICATION LINK: ENTER CITIZEN IDENTIFICATION #: there's a dial tone.

Jess whoops and jumps for joy. She wraps Abby close and kisses her ardently on the mouth.

Abby laughs. "It wasn't anything."

"We got this," Jess says. "We made it here and we're gonna get home. It'll be fine."

She calls her parent's emergency line, the one that goes to both their office and their personal DED's.

"Hello? Smasher here," her mom's voice says calmly over the line.

"Mom? It's me," Jess says.

"Jess! Where have you been?" her mom asks in a whisper. "Things are really terrible. I heard from the League that they're looking for a whole bunch of villains on the loose; they're out and about causing chaos, they already blew up this facility where… Oh gosh, where you've gone hiking before? Where are you now? Your friends are here; they're looking for you!"

"Can you come pick me up?" Jess says. "I'm at the alien way station. I'll explain everything later. I just need you and dad to come get me right now."

"Of course, Mei Mei," her mom says softly. "Your dad is all charged up. He'll fly your way and bring you right back home."

"I've got Abby with me. We both need to get back; I don't think dad can fly us both."

"I see. Well, you're only about forty minutes from the city. I'll take the Smashmobile. Be there soon."

AND THEN THERE'S NOTHING TO do but wait. The attendant takes pity on them and gives them bottles of water and a slice of hot pizza. She and Abby eat it quickly. It tastes heavenly after two days of nothing but water and protein bars, and they scarf it down, enjoying the cheese.

They sit so Abby can take a few moments to concentrate. "Anything?"

"Nothing," Abby says. "It's like my power's completely gone."

"This is horrible. If they have the power to turn off the gene and turn it on in anyone they want, they can do all sorts of ridiculous things."

"De-power people who threaten them, create more meta-humans whenever they want."

Jess spots the sleek black car pull up. Abby lets out a low whistle. "Wow. So you drive the minivan and your mom drives this, huh?"

Jess laughs. "Yeah, it's my mom's baby. I have a license, in case of emergencies, though."

"Was that a *be impressed with my driver's license* line?" Abby asks.

"Uh. Depends. Did it work?"

Abby shakes with laughter. "I'll tell you later."

Li Hua rushes out of the vehicle, in full Smasher attire, bright red body suit and the huge boxing gloves. "Here to rescue you," she says. "Hello, Abby. Jess."

They're in the car before Jess starts with the story; the beginning, all of it. Her mother listens quietly as she drives; her face betrays no emotion when Jess explains she's been working for her parents' archrival.

"I've been thinking something was fishy," she says. "I never liked the League much; it was always a huge name for your father, he was obsessed with getting to be a real hero. They kept promising all sorts of things, like upping our powers to A-level, and filling his head with dreams and promises that our powers and our contributions were useful and could help people."

"But we never were really helping people, I saw that. But it was easy; I spent so much time in Meta-Human Training that I didn't have a degree and couldn't go into another career if I wanted to. I had to rely completely on the government, and then I was pregnant with Claudia and we needed to make the right choices. Being a hero meant guaranteed housing and a salary, and that was important."

Abby is silent, and Jess nods. She knows how hard her parents have worked.

"Not everyone got that choice, though," Abby says quietly. "My parents were told to be villains from the very start. You guys got comic books and merchandise and people who look up to you, and my parents get booed whenever they go out in costume."

"It's not a fair system," Li Hua says. "I know it isn't. I'm just saying it was easy to stay rather than change. But I guess it's too late for that now. Whatever you did sparked a huge change. Nothing is going to be the same now."

"That much is true," Jess says. "Mom, have you heard from Bells?"

"Not since your birthday party, why?"

"Yeah, he has the footage of Orion—the real Orion, telling everyone about the terrible experiments. We're planning to just put it online for people to see."

The radio's pop station suddenly switches to news. "This just in. Chameleon has gone rogue and teamed up with the Villain's Guild. The general public especially in Andover must be immediately aware of Chameleon, who can disguise themselves as any person. Make sure who you're with is really who they should be, ask security questions only they would know. This is a public service announcement. Chameleon is at large and dangerous, and as far as the Heroes' League knows, he is fully charged and can maintain a disguise for at least ten minutes before recharging. This is a public service announcement."

Jess and Abby look at each other in horror.

"So that means Bells did escape with the information," Abby says.

"But we don't know where he and your mom are," Jess repeats. "Mom, you said my friends were at the house. Was it Emma and Bells?"

"Bells, Bells, no, just your friend Emma and one of your other friends, Denise. I haven't seen her at our house in a few years. It's so nice that all of you are getting along again."

Jess raises her eyebrows. As far as she knows, Emma still hasn't forgiven Denise for that incident in the seventh grade.

"Could that be Bells?" Abby asks.

"Probably. Step on it, Mom!"

THEY GET BACK TO THE Tran house, and Emma is indeed sitting in the living room with Jess' dad and also... Denise Ho.

"Bells?" Jess asks.

"How'd you know?" Bells asks with a grin.

"You always sit like this with Emma, with your hips tilted just so. Also, you left a tuft of pink in your hair, right here," Jess says, tugging the small lock.

"Ah, I couldn't resist. Your dad totally didn't notice, though!" Bells says, standing up. He drops the disguise, and then it's his usual face, dark brown skin and bright amber eyes looking curiously at them.

Victor and Li Hua look at Bells and then at each other in surprise. "Chameleon," Victor says, as if he's torn between asking Bells for his autograph and still wanting to treat him like Jess' best friend.

Bells beams. "So I've got the datachip. How do we blow this joint apart?"

"We were counting on Abby to use her powers to connect it to the Net and make sure it plays in every home," Jess says. "But Abby's powers aren't working."

"That serum really worked?" Bells asks in horror. "That means they can de-power anyone they want to!"

"What serum?" the parents both ask.

Jess explains about Orion's plan to control all the meta-humans.

"We have to stop them," Li Hua says.

Everyone starts talking at once. There are too many ideas to sort through, and no, Jess doesn't think "storm the castle" would work. Emma thinks it could be resolved by sitting Orion down to a nice dinner, while Victor and Li Hua don't seem very keen on the idea of facing down the superhero. Jess clears her throat.

"First, in order to get this video public, we need to find Abby's dad."

"Bells, where did my mom go?" Abby asks.

"Back to your house. Emma and I dropped her off. I think she wanted to get some stuff before she went back to look for your dad."

"No, no, no," Abby says. "She needs more time to recover; she can't be thinking about going to find him already! She won't be strong enough right now, they'll just capture her again, and it'll be awful."

Jess blinks. "We have to go!"

Her mom tosses her the keycard to the Smashmobile, and Jess looks up in surprise. "Really?"

"Yes, go ahead. Your father and I will fly. You four can go in the car."

The keycard is hot in Jess' hand, and she grips it, so ready. Jess starts the engine, and it purrs to life; the electronics whizz and crackle with energy. "Welcome, Smasher," the computer says smoothly, and the stylized fist logo lights up on the display.

"Very cool," Abby says, sliding into the passenger seat. Emma and Bells are still in the driveway. Bells has already shifted into his Chameleon outfit, his mask twitching as he scowls.

"We should take you home, it's too dangerous," Bells says.

Emma puts her hands on her hips, drawing herself up to her full height, which barely reaches Bells' shoulders. "Ex*cuse* me, what's *dangerous* is you gallivanting all over Andover and Devonport playing hero and not telling me! If you all are going, I'm going," she says.

Bells looks helplessly at the car.

"Just get in the car, we're wasting time," Jess says. "You guys can argue over who can protect who later."

They get back on the road, and head right for Abby's house.

"This is great," Emma says from the backseat. "I mean, the situation's not great, but this is pretty awesome, right? All of us going to save the day? We should have a team name."

Jess smiles to herself; next to her, she can see Abby's anxious face relax a little as Emma rattles off potential names and Bells shoots them down.

When they get to Abby's home, it's clear that they're too late.

The door is hanging open, and there's a distinct scent of ozone and burnt hair.

"Mom? Mom!" Abby yells and rushes inside.

The three of them rush in after her, picking their way around the destroyed living room.

"This is the last time you've been noncompliant with the League rules," Captain Orion yells from the hallway, tossing a statuette down the stairs. It shatters.

"Hey, I made that!" Abby says. "Don't touch my mother!"

Mistress Mischief rises triumphant from the basement, costume glittering and eyes hard as steel. Captain Orion is flung into the wall.

"Stay out of this, everyone!" Mischief yells.

Emma picks up a broken piece of the coffee table and hurls the chunk at Orion. "You're a fake and a liar and a kidnapper and—your dumb hair products *never work!*"

Orion snarls, her fingers crackling with energy, and she blasts a bolt of lightning at Emma.

"No!" Bells pushes Emma out of the way to safety, barely making it himself. The lightning grazes him, and Jess can smell singed hair.

"Stop, Mom!" Abby yells. "Just restrain her with the tantalum. We have some in storage!"

Jess runs downstairs, searching for the precious metal. There are boxes and boxes everywhere, but months at work has made her an expert in filing *and* she's got a knack for finding things.

Jess yanks open a lead safe, grabs the tantalum cuffs, and runs upstairs. "I got it, I got it!" Jess yells, shaking the cuffs.

Mistress Mischief levitates them and they float into the air, and for the first time Jess sees the amazing power of telekinesis used in a fight.

Mischief is brutal. She fights ruthlessly with Orion, whose superstrength damages the walls, and the entire house shakes with their battle.

Emma and Bells watch from the floor, curled around each other, as debris whirls. Jess holds onto the doorframe as Mistress Mischief uses her incredible strength to freeze Orion in the air.

"Come on, Mom," Abby mutters, and raises her hands too, concentrating as if she's trying to use her own telekinesis.

The cuffs snap on Orion's wrists, and she falls to the ground, shaking with anger.

"Where is my husband?" Mischief demands.

"You'll never find him," Orion says. "He's already given us the codes for all the MonRobots. This time tomorrow, we'll have eliminated all the targets we deem fit. And the rest of the League is coming. It doesn't matter if you have me. If you kill me, I'll be a martyr. You'll be known for killing the greatest superhero who ever lived."

Jess laughs. "You are *not* the greatest superhero who ever lived. You are a joke. You experimented on innocent people and caused countless suffering for your own power boost, and this whole system is a facade. The Collective is distracting the public from the little wars it's waging around the world. People have the right to know what's really going on, and the media needs to report what's actually happening. We *aren't* obsessed with these fake battles that you stage. And the people you force to be villains, that's not right either. What happens to those kids whose parents you promise so much? You promised Abby could be a hero and shackled her parents, and they willingly sacrificed themselves for her. No one should have to make that choice."

"No one wants to hear about those sad things," Orion says. "People have the right to focus on the amusement, the lighter side, and people should be able to hope and feel good that there are heroes protecting them."

"Yes, but we should have the *choice,*" Jess says. "It's not right that the only thing on the news is what's happening with you and your flirtation with Starscream, and soap operas and what's going on with your *hair.*"

"My hair *is* pretty awesome," Orion says.

"That's not the point," Jess says.

"You weren't here for the Disasters," Orion says. She clenches and unclenches her fists; the tantalum cuffs shake but hold fast. "Look, people don't want to watch the news if it's filled with awful things. Awful things happened all the time. The X29 solar flare could have ruined our planet, and it almost did. Even without the nuclear meltdowns, the ensuing battle for resources and food would have destroyed us. We needed something positive to focus on."

Jess realizes Orion wholeheartedly believes in her cause, in the Collective's cause. "It's not the time of the Disasters anymore. We've gotten past that; we've rebuilt as a society, moved forward. We need to be better."

"She isn't going to listen," Mistress Mischief says. She settles on the floor. "Come on, Cindy. It's time."

"No one's called me Cindy in years," Captain Orion—Cindy—says. "Even my dad calls me Captain."

"You don't remember me, but we were in Meta-Human Training together," Mistress Mischief says. "I'm Genevieve. You used to make fun of my teeth."

"I do remember," Captain Orion says. "Look, no hard feelings, okay? You were chosen for the Villain's Guild because you started to date Phillip. It could have been me, but I wanted to be a superhero. I chose that instead of the guy."

Abby narrows her eyes. "Wait a minute, you dated my *dad?*"

"Very briefly," Orion says. She tosses her head back, regarding Abby with a discerning look. "Philip was very interesting. I dumped him as soon as I knew he was on the villain track, though. The Collective likes to pair people up and make sure that spouses are on the same track; too many complications otherwise."

Bells pulls Emma to her feet, and they walk toward Orion. Bells stares at her, his lip curling in revulsion.

"And you, Chameleon," Orion says with a disdainful sniff. "I had such high hopes for you in the League. You have no idea what's in store for you now; things have already been set in motion."

"Oh, yeah?" Bells says, scowling. He pulls a chip out of his pocket. "This holovid of you admitting to experimenting on meta-humans, kidnapping all the missing villains, attacking and kidnapping *my friends*—I've got so many copies of this. Even without a technopath we can still be heard."

Orion shakes and laughs. It's a shrill, desperate sound, and her entire body shakes on the floor. "You think a holovid like that is enough proof for the people of the Collective? People *love* me."

Genevieve takes the chip from Bells, gently laying a hand on his shoulder. "Don't goad her, she'll start monologuing, and, even though she's the one restrained, we'll all be stuck here."

"Good point," Jess says, remembering the long rant she and Abby got back at Orion's home. "Can we do anything about the video right now?"

Genevieve nods. "I'm not an expert, and it won't be playing on every DED like we wanted, but at least we can get the word out."

One of Abby's computer consoles sits on the kitchen counter projector. She slides the chip into it and taps away at the screen. A holo springs to life: Orion pacing in her home, eyes glittering, saying, "*You are nothing more than part of the NAC plan for creating more meta-humans and controlling the ones we have. Of course, we can play with radiation all we like. but we can't come close to duplicating the effects of X29...*"

Glass shatters.

Jess doesn't have time to see what is happening before Abby pulls her behind the kitchen counter as shards fly everywhere. She peeks up; the beautiful floor-to-ceiling windows she admired so much on her first visit are in pieces, and *Claudia* is standing there, pulling Orion to her feet.

"I had to wait until I was sure Mistress Mischief here was tapped out, and I had to stop Smasher and Shockwave," she says.

"Late is better than never, Cora," Orion snaps.

Claudia grimaces at the incorrect name, but she gingerly takes Orion by the waist, careful to avoid the tantalum cuffs.

Jess lurches forward in horror. "Mom and Dad—what did you do—"

Claudia gives her a hard stare. "Just made sure Shockwave was tapped out. They're stuck on the other side of town, waiting for a *bus,* of all things." She looks at Jess but doesn't say anything, just sets her jaw and then glances away.

A string of memories run through Jess, and each one hits her in the gut: a young Claudia, taking her torn rice paper and wrapping a new gỏi cuốn for her; Claudia carrying her on her shoulders, promising they'll fly together one day; the two of them playing hide and seek as children.

Jess is frozen where she stands—even if she could do something, if Claudia's at full strength or if she's been taking Orion's supplements, she can't take her sister in a fight.

"Let's go, Powerstorm," Orion says testily, shaking Claudia out of her stupor.

"Right," Claudia says, and gives the rest of them a cold look, hovering with Orion. "Good luck being villains."

They fly out the broken window, and the last thing Jess hears is Orion saying, "You really need to work on your one liners, Connie."

THINGS DON'T GO BACK TO normal right away. Jess thought that it'd be easy; publish the evidence about Orion, show the whole world what's been happening under their noses. Unfortunately they can't find any traces of the video on the Net; even the buzz that started on conspiracy forums when they posted it—everything is gone the next day.

They still need to find Master Mischief, but now that Genevieve is back and Jess' parents are in the loop, the adults want to handle the situation. Jess and her friends are supposed to go back to school, focus on their studies, pretend everything is normal, but Jess doesn't think Abby will stay put when her dad is still out there. Jess wants answers too, wants the world to know what Orion's capable of.

"At least wait until you finish your final exams," Li Hua says testily. "Your grades, Mei-Mei, think about your grades!"

Jess hardly thinks it's a priority compared with everything that's going on, but she reluctantly agrees to let the adults work on it until winter break, at least.

Emma still hasn't given up on coming up with a name for their group, much to everyone else's amusement and exasperation. Jess is glad she's taking it well, though.

"Powers? Why would I want powers?" Emma says, shaking her head when Jess pulls her aside at school to talk to her about it. "Look, the way I see it, I'm the only one here who is resistant to tantalum *and* keeps a cool head when things get rough. Sure, I think powers are neat. But not for me."

"I thought you'd be upset," Jess says.

Emma hugs her. "I was just upset when I thought Bells was secretly dating someone and didn't want to tell us. And he's not, so everything is fine."

"Fine, huh?" Jess waggles her eyebrows and is pleased when Emma's ears turn pink. She doesn't really know exactly what Bells and Emma talked about when he took her home after the Orion mess to "explain everything," but she might hazard a guess.

"Yes, fine," Emma says. "Oh hey, did you see that new transfer student from Nuevo Los Angeles? He's got dimples, Jess, dimples..."

Ah. Maybe Bells didn't explain *everything*.

Abby and Bells are already sitting in their usual lunch spot when Jess and Emma join them, apparently in the middle of a serious conversation.

"Look, you don't get it, if the League has declared Chameleon as a villain, things are going to get ugly, real fast." There's a little furrow of worry in Abby's brow, and Jess wants to smooth it out. She settles for kissing Abby's cheek as they sit down, and is delighted when Abby gives her a swift kiss on the lips in return.

"What's ugly?" Emma asks, stealing Bells' fruit cup off his lunch tray.

Bells rolls his eyes. "I can handle it," he says. "Here, look." He pulls up a newsholo on his DED. It's an official report from the League that declares the *villain* Chameleon on the run and collaborating with the United Villain's Guild for "unknown plans of heinous atrocity." Bells smirks. "Heinous, that's great. You think I should add an adjective to my name? The Heinous Chameleon. Or does that sound pretentious?"

"Abby's right," Jess says, frowning. "They're dangerous, and if they've decided you're the enemy..."

Abby nods. "I've been dealing with this my whole life. And now that my mom's back, we've taken a lot of extra precautions." Genevieve and Abby have moved out of their Andover home to a hidden place out in the canyons that Emma is absolutely not allowed to call a secret lair. "You should change your name; your whole family needs new identities, you should move, transfer schools... on paper I'm still Abby Jones, and Orion isn't going to connect my information to the Monroes at all, but *you*..."

Bells looks smug. "Well, you'll be happy to know that my parents being super-paranoid over everything, even Meta-Human Training, has its benefits. I applied to the League as Barry Carmichael, and none of them know what I actually look like."

"I take back everything I said about your weird family," Emma says. She flicks through the rest of the newsholo and frowns. "Hey, how come this doesn't say anything about Jess or Abby?"

Abby shrugs. "Probably because they don't see either of us as a threat. They don't know about Jess' powers, and they think I don't have them anymore."

Jess squeezes Abby's hand.

The physical symptoms disappeared after a few days, but Abby still hasn't been able to access her powers. She thinks they're completely gone, but Jess knows Abby's talked about being able to sense things, like the potential to use her telekinesis or her technopath abilities, but she just can't, as if there's a closed door in her head.

Emma pokes Abby in the forehead. "Look, even if you can't do all that techno mumbo-jumbo, you're still the best setter in this school—no, the entire Nevada *region*. If that's not a superpower, I don't know what is."

Abby laughs. "I have definitely missed volleyball."

"Are you going to come back to the team?" Emma asks, her eyes lighting up.

"Yeah, I think so," Abby says. "We can't just sit on our asses and not live our lives while we're trying to expose a corrupt government," Abby says.

One Saturday, Abby convinces Jess to come with her to the school. Jess follows her warily until they get to the gymnasium, and Abby unlocks the storage closet and pulls out a volleyball.

Jess ties her hair back, not bothering to check how it looks. She looks around the empty gymnasium. "Are you sure about this? Aren't we like, trespassing or something?"

"Look, the school is funded by tax dollars. I think we can be here. Plus, I have the keys to the gym and if I say you can be here, you can totally be here," Abby says, grinning.

"I'm not an athletic person," Jess warns.

"This isn't about that. It's about having fun!" Abby tosses the volleyball in the air, and bounces it on her forearm. Abby's skin turns pink and shiny with the impact. Abby keeps bouncing the ball, keeping it in rhythm. She aims the ball and sends it flying toward Jess in a slow, easy arc.

Jess throws her hands up and shrieks; the ball hits her hands and falls to the ground.

Abby laughs. "That was a good start. Figuring out where the ball is and protecting yourself! It's awesome. Okay, this time, try hitting it back toward me."

"I'm not good at this, okay," Jess says. "I'm not sporty like you."

"This isn't about being sporty or not. That's not… it's not even a thing. It's just about practice and hard work. I think certain people are inclined to like it or start off liking it better than others, but ninety-nine percent of all sports—or anything, really—is a person just working really, really hard at their craft. Like… okay, you know how you are with your writing? I'm not anywhere near as good as you are. Like that time you were talking about imagery and symbolism and like, I don't even know how to do any of that. How did you get good at that?"

"Practice."

"Right! You weren't born an amazing writer. You worked at it, read a lot, got better at it over time. Same with me and volleyball. We do training and conditioning, and I can say for every kid who's supposedly a natural talent, there's another person who works their ass off and gets better than that person. You can't coast by on talent alone. It's hard work that makes all the difference."

Jess nods.

Abby tosses the volleyball in the air and gives it a careful spin. "Okay, you ready?"

Jess holds her arms together in the position that Abby taught her and stands with her feet apart.

Abby tosses the ball and then lobs it over, and this time Jess hits it back.

Abby catches it, and then jumps up and down in excitement. "Woo! You did it, you did it!"

Jess blushes. "It wasn't that amazing."

Abby tosses the ball aside and rushes toward Jess, hugs her and picks her off the floor, spins her in a circle. They tumble, laughing, to the floor. The gym smells of old sweat and the lights are too bright, but they might as well be in the most romantic place in the world. Abby's hair tangles with Jess', and then Jess, emboldened, leans forward for a kiss.

"Okay, *that* was amazing," Jess admits.

Abby laughs and laughs and laughs.

"WHAT'S THIS?" ABBY ASKS AS she takes the blue journal.

Jess twists her hands. It seemed like a good idea this morning. Abby was sharing something she enjoyed with her, and she wanted to do the same. "It's just some stories and stuff that I've written."

Abby opens the cover and looks at the handwriting on the first page. "By Jess Tran," she announces to the room. "Your handwriting is so cute here."

"Ah, that's from when I was twelve. I've had this journal for a while. I keep filling it with stuff, just random ideas. There's a longer story that I've been working on in the back. It's an adventure story.

It starts... right here." She flips to the most recent section, and Abby's hand curls around hers.

"Thank you for letting me see this," Abby says softly. "I know it's hard to show someone what you're working on."

Jess flushes. "Well, you're important to me, and I care what you think, so... yeah. Here it is."

Abby grins. "Am I gonna see, like, hearts doodled around my name anywhere?"

Jess snorts. "That's a different notebook."

Abby holds the notebook in one hand and takes Jess' hand in the other, pulling her close for a kiss. "I like your stories," she whispers. "And I knew that our characters in the one we were writing for Rhinehart—that you imagined them to be us, because I did too. I was hoping you'd pick up on it sooner."

"You knew?" Jess' eyes widen. She pulls back so abruptly she bumps into Abby's nose. "But—then you knew about my hugely awkward crush on you!"

"Yeah, but you also told M that," Abby says, raising her eyebrows. "That never occurred to you?"

"Yes, I mean, but like, I did know but I was too caught up in the whole rescue-your-parents thing I just... forgot."

"You are so cute when you're embarrassed. You're just realizing it now, aren't you?"

"Đụ!" Jess curses and buries her face in her hands. "I talked about you to your face, oh my God, how did you let me do that?"

Abby laughs. "It was kinda funny. I mean, I didn't know you very well at the time, but it was really interesting, and I did learn some interesting things about what you thought about me."

"Look, I didn't know you then, I just... I don't know. I had this crush on this idea of you as a person, but then it developed into something real once we started hanging out and then it was worse, oh gosh, the feelings..." Jess shuffles backward, nearly falling, but Abby steadies her with an arm around the waist.

"Hmm, pesky feelings." Abby kisses her on the nose, making Jess giggle, and then kisses her again on the lips.

On Monday, Ms. Rhinehart passes back their completed short stories. "Good job, everyone," she says. "I'm quite pleased with your progress, especially the collaborative effort from everyone. My favorite thing about this assignment was seeing writers with different styles pair up and how everyone learned by doing. And you might not think I'd recognize it, but I did warn you not to let one person do all the work, and I'm quite proud to say that everyone gave their best effort and did collaborate. I'm in touch with a local literary magazine, and I suggest you all submit your pieces to it."

Everyone looks at their grades, and Abby and Jess hold their folder, looking at each other.

Jess takes the first step, tossing back the protective cover.

"What is it? Don't tell me—okay tell me—okay no, all right, now I'm ready," Abby says.

"We got an A," Jess says.

"Oh," Abby says, eyes widening in awe. "Oh, that's awesome!"

They look through the document together, reading Ms. Rhinehart's comments on the story, laughing at one of the appreciated jokes, and then they get to the end.

Jess reads aloud, her smile broadening as she goes. "This ending is nice, but a bit vague. If you do a bit of polish, this would be an excellent work for publication. What happens after they defeat the evil Schuester? Do Rebecca and Michelle have a happy ending?"

Jess looks at Abby, and she thinks about the future. There's a lot in question, what with figuring out what the government plans for the heroes and the villains, and she has no idea how to make sure that this doesn't happen again, but she has Abby at her side.

"Yeah, I definitely think so," Abby says. Under the table, she squeezes Jess' hand.

"Most definitely a happy ending."

IT'S A THURSDAY AFTERNOON, AND Jess is at Abby's home again, and this time there's no pretense of studying or working on a writing assignment. The new house is full of light and the reflected red hues of the canyons that surround it.

Jess is sitting on a half-assembled couch in the space that will be the living room, laughing as plates of food float in the air.

"Mom, I said we're fine, we already had a snack—" Abby shakes her head, and the plate of cookies flies back toward Genevieve.

"Yeah, but dessert! Oh, but we're out of milk. I can go down to the store and buy some. Jess, you're staying for dinner? What would you like? Oh, this pantry is so empty, I hate it. Abby, what did you eat while I was gone? Please tell me it wasn't just Jacks' grilled cheese sandwiches." Genevieve wrings her hands, and a plate of chocolate chip cookies wafts toward Jess. "Is chocolate chip okay? I made peanut butter, too, they should be ready—oh!"

The oven dings and the door opens with a flick of Genevieve's wrist. The cookies fly out of the oven and onto another plate, which then flies toward the living room. Genevieve insisted on making cookies today instead of continuing to unpack boxes.

Abby buries her face in her hands.

Jess takes the plates, laughing. "Thank you, Mrs. Monroe. Er, Mrs. Jones? Your Mischiefness?"

Genevieve chortles, waving her hands at Jess. "Oh dear, Gena is fine." She leans on the kitchen counter, giving them an indulgent smile.

"We're going to be in my lab. Mom, don't wear yourself out with cookies. I'm serious." Abby rolls her eyes, but Jess can tell she's pleased to tease her mother like this.

Abby's new lab is already cluttered, boxes open and workstations haphazardly set up, scattered with moving holos that show Abby's older projects. It's fun to see the evolution of her MonRobot designs through the years, and holos that picture Abby and her parents.

Abby lingers at one of her and her dad, grinning at each other over a workstation. She traces the flickering edges with a wistful smile on her face.

"We'll find him. Don't worry," Jess says.

Abby gives her a grateful smile. "Thanks. C'mon, I have something to show you."

There's something on the farthest worktable under a canvas drop cloth. A few lights flicker, and it comes to life as Jess gets closer, and a familiar oblong silver case wheels out from under the fabric, meeping at Jess.

"Chả!" Jess shrieks. The robot cheeps at her and wheels about in circles around her feet. Jess gasps. "Already?"

"Yeah, of course. I know you love that thing. I made a few improvements in motor functions, but the A.I. is exactly the same, so it shouldn't—"

Chả starts vacuuming, cheeping rapidly, as if it's excited. It spins back and forth on the tiled floor of the workroom, confused, and then rolls right under one of the worktables and promptly gets stuck.

Jacks and Jills are watching from the corner, and both of them meep and hover forward. Jess is pleased to notice that Abby could have upgraded Chả to the newest design, even given it the ability to fly, but she kept the original shape and functions.

"I, ah, I can fix that," Abby says, twirling a finger in her hair. "I mean, I'm so used to building things with my powers, I probably messed up when I was—"

Jess curls an arm around her waist and draws her close, kissing her without hesitation.

Abby kisses her right back.

The robots spin about them, making celebratory-sounding noises. Jess opens her eyes and realizes that Chả is chasing Jacks and Jills, like a disobedient puppy. She laughs, picks up the robot, runs a hand along Chả's new silver casing, and laughs. "It's perfect. Thank you."

Jess' DED lights up with a new notification—a message from Emma.

"Hey, there's a new episode of *The Gentleman Detective* out," Jess says. "We usually watch it with Bells. Wanna come?"

Abby raises an eyebrow. "Weren't we going to try and figure out what to do about the corrupt League and the NAC cover up? I know that my mom said to wait, but—"

"Hmmm," Jess says. "That's not going to get done in one night, and you know we've done all we could. Pretty sure the only thing we could do at this point is wait and worry about what they're going to do next."

"That's true," Abby admits. "So we might as well have fun and be normal for a night, right?"

Jess laughs. "Well, I hardly think we'll ever be *normal,* but I heard that's overrated."

THE END... FOR NOW!

ACKNOWLEDGMENTS...

Writing this series has been a rollercoaster of emotion. I'm so thankful to my friends and family for the support they've given me.

Thank you to my parents for encouraging me and also especially my mother, who listened to all my questions about my fictional immigrants and also endured strange phone calls about where accent marks go. I forgive you for talking my ear off about how to make the meatloaf, and, as you can see, I did not include the recipe.

I am indebted to the LGBTQIA+ activists who came before me for the rights and freedoms we enjoy today and continue to strive for.

To the amazing team at Duet Books and Interlude Press, thank you for giving my little story a home. Candy, thank you for every little thing you do, behind the scenes and getting all the parts of this beautiful organization together. Annie, endless thanks to your passion and time, and being open when I said, "Um, so I don't think it can be one book? It's... going to be three?"

Thank you to CB, my wonderfully talented name twin and incredible person through and through; your artwork has blown me away every time you reveal a new cover. The first time I saw mine I cried and had to walk around to collect myself; everything about it was incredible and absolutely captured all the elements we talked about. Thank you for making it clear she's Asian on the cover, thank you for drawing Jess with such style and aplomb, thank you for everything, everything, everything.

Kate, your friendship and encouragement were the only things that pulled this story out of my head and into existence. Those first few weeks when I started were so rough; thank you so much for believing in me, for telling me to write, for keeping me level-headed, for laughing with me and being there in all the stages in which this was written.

Darling, darling Jennifer, thank you for the endless amounts of positive messages when I thought I couldn't keep going, for the steadfast encouragement and suggestions. Michelle, at the drop of a hat, you stepped up, and I cannot even begin to talk about how much it meant to me during that busy time. Bells and Emma, thank you for being wonderful friends and allowing me to name my characters after you. Zane, Hunter, and Mel, thank you for all the discussion and encouragement and letting me bombard you with questions. I guarantee you this will continue for books two and three.

Mai, Laura, Cal, Kelly Ann, Stacey, Niamh, your talent and friendship inspire me and I'm always be grateful for your energy and positivity. Freck, Michelle, Sylvia, Em, Maggie, Mel, Tay, Frek, Beth, Rachel—amazing writers, and even more amazing friends— endless thank you's for the infinite moments of laughter and joy, the support and the love.

And definite love to the writers of NaNoWrimo Los Angeles, whose writing sprint sessions made much of this novel possible.

Last, but never least, for everyone who started this journey with me and read my writing from the beginning. Thank you for being my anchor.

ABOUT THE AUTHOR...

C.B. Lee is a bisexual writer, rock climber, and pinniped enthusiast from Southern California. A first-generation Asian American, she is passionate about working in communities of color and empowering youth to be inspired to write characters and stories of their own. Lee's debut novel *Seven Tears at High Tide* was published by Duet Books in 2015 and named a finalist in the Bisexual Books Awards.

COMING IN 2017

NOT YOUR VILLAIN

C.B. LEE

Bells thought he had it made when his powers manifested early. He kept it a secret at first, using his shapeshifting abilities to live in the body he's meant to. The superhero thing came later—after all, it's an honor to be selected for the Heroes' League of Heroes.

But Bells isn't able to fight crime as Chameleon for very long before he and his friends discover the League is corrupt and the power-hungry, former-hero Captain Orion is loose with a dangerous serum that renders meta-humans powerless.

Catch the bad guy; save the day. Bells has a lot on his plate, especially considering he also has to graduate from high school and figure out how to tell his best friend Emma he's in love with her.

One **story**
can change **everything**.

@duet**books**

Twitter | Tumblr

*For a reader's guide to **Not Your Sidekick** and book club prompts, please visit duetbooks.com.*

also from duet

Seven Tears at High Tide by C.B. Lee

Kevin Luong walks to the ocean's edge with a broken heart. Remembering a legend his mother told him, he lets seven tears fall into the sea. "I just want one summer—one summer to be happy and in love." Instead, he finds himself saving a mysterious boy from the Pacific—a boy who later shows up on his doorstep professing his love. What he doesn't know is that Morgan is a selkie, drawn to answer Kevin's wish. As they grow close, Morgan is caught between the dangers of the human world and his legacy in the selkie community to which he must return at summer's end.

ISBN (print) 978-1-941530-47-4 | (eBook) 978-1-941530-48-1

The Star Host by F.T. Lukens

Ren grew up listening to his mother tell stories about the Star Hosts—mythical people possessed by the power of the stars. Captured by a nefarious Baron, Ren discovers he may be something out of his mother's stories. He befriends Asher, a member of the Phoenix Corps. Together, they must master Ren's growing power, and try to save their friends while navigating the growing attraction between them.

ISBN (print) 978-1-941530-72-6 | (eBook) 978-1-941530-73-3

The Rules of Ever After by Killian B. Brewer

The royal rules have governed the kingdoms of Clarameer for centuries, but princes Phillip and Daniel know that these rules don't apply to them. In a quest to find their own Happily Ever After, they encounter meddlesome fairies, an ambitious stepmother, disgruntled princesses and vengeful kings as they learn about life, love, friendship and family—and learn to write their own rules of ever after.

ISBN (print) 978-1-941530-35-1 | (eBook) 978-1-941530-42-9